PRAISE FOR
THE NOVELS OF CHANEL CLEETON

"A beautiful novel that's full of forbidden passions, family secrets, and a lot of courage and sacrifice." —Reese Witherspoon

"A sweeping love story and tale of courage and familial and patriotic legacy that spans generations." —*Entertainment Weekly*

"*Next Year in Havana* reminds us that while love is complicated and occasionally heartbreaking, it's always worth the risk."

—NPR

"A thrilling story about love, loss, and what we will do to go home again. Utterly unputdownable." —PopSugar

"A remarkable writer." —*The Washington Post*

"You won't be able to put this one down." —*Cosmopolitan*

AN INFINITE LOVE STORY

∞

CHANEL CLEETON

BERKLEY

NEW YORK

BERKLEY
An imprint of Penguin Random House LLC
1745 Broadway, New York, NY 10019
penguinrandomhouse.com

Copyright © 2026 by Chanel Cleeton
Readers Guide copyright © 2026 by Chanel Cleeton
Penguin Random House values and supports copyright. Copyright fuels creativity, encourages diverse voices, promotes free speech, and creates a vibrant culture. Thank you for buying an authorized edition of this book and for complying with copyright laws by not reproducing, scanning, or distributing any part of it in any form without permission. You are supporting writers and allowing Penguin Random House to continue to publish books for every reader. Please note that no part of this book may be used or reproduced in any manner for the purpose of training artificial intelligence technologies or systems.

BERKLEY and the BERKLEY & B colophon are registered trademarks of
Penguin Random House LLC.

Book design by Daniel Brount

Berkley hardcover edition: 9780593816950

Library of Congress Cataloging-in-Publication Data

Names: Cleeton, Chanel author
Title: An infinite love story / Chanel Cleeton.
Description: First Edition. | New York : Berkley, 2026.
Identifiers: LCCN 2025046760 (print) | LCCN 2025046761 (ebook) |
ISBN 9780593816936 trade paperback | ISBN 9780593816943 ebook
Subjects: LCGFT: Novels | Fiction | Science fiction | Romance fiction
Classification: LCC PS3603.L455445 I54 2026 (print) |
LCC PS3603.L455445 (ebook)
LC record available at https://lccn.loc.gov/2025046760
LC ebook record available at https://lccn.loc.gov/2025046761

First Edition: July 2026

Printed in the United States of America
1st Printing

The authorized representative in the EU for product safety and compliance is
Penguin Random House Ireland, Morrison Chambers, 32 Nassau Street,
Dublin D02 YH68, Ireland, https://eu-contact.penguin.ie.

To my husband, who wanted to watch The Right Stuff
when I was in the mood for a love story,
and who is the only answer I would ever give to the question:
"Who's the best pilot you ever saw?"

In 1968, the divorce rate in the United States was .0029%, or 2.9 divorces per 1,000 marriages. There were thirty-nine married astronauts in the Mercury, Gemini, and Apollo space programs. Twenty of those marriages ultimately ended in divorce.

This novel is a love story.

AN
INFINITE
LOVE
STORY

PROLOGUE

That night, she dreamed of space.

Of stars, and planets, of a yawning void that appeared to stretch on through eternity, its vastness astounding her. She dreamed of things she'd never seen, things she likely never would see, and yet, impossibly, they surrounded her, so close that she could nearly reach out and grab on to a star as she hurtled through oblivion.

And then—a whisper—her name, the sound of it beating in her heart like a drum.

Viv.

When she woke, her husband was gone.

ONE

In the early hours of the morning, astronaut Joe Mitchell's spacecraft lost contact with Mission Control in Houston at approximately three a.m. Two other astronauts are aboard the spacecraft that was on a mission to the Moon to complete a lunar orbit—"

Vivian Mitchell stared at the TV screen, at the news anchor dressed in a somber dark suit, immaculate white shirt, and subdued tie, as though he'd selected the outfit precisely for the severity of the occasion. Even though the broadcast was in color, there was a gray hue to the entire business.

Graham Carlson.

His tone was calm—after all, his was one of the voices the nation turned to in times of difficulty and despair, and they'd sure had plenty of those lately. But if you listened closely, you could make out the hint of grief threading through his voice as though he already knew the conclusion they were careening toward as surely as Joe's spacecraft had blasted through space, could hear the way in which his voice broke over the last name *Mitchell* as though the loss wasn't just professional to him, but a personal one, too.

If you knew Graham Carlson at all, you'd notice the way his right hand lifted as though his fingers itched to smooth down his tie as they always did when he was nervous. If seven years—a lifetime—ago you'd known him as closely as two people could know each other, you'd see the way he looked at the camera, the emotion in his eyes as though he were speaking directly to Vivian.

She'd thought about calling the newsroom in D.C. herself to see if Graham had any information about the missing spacecraft, but she wasn't sure their history would be enough to keep their conversation private. Astronaut wives had long been subjected to public fascination and consumption, and considering the army of reporters camped out on her front lawn waiting for a glimpse of her, they didn't care that this was one of the absolute worst moments of her life.

Her living room was filled with people, but if someone had asked Vivian who was there, she couldn't have answered save for a few. Some had been there with her last night when she'd begun what all the astronaut wives termed as "the death watch," for how excruciating it was sitting, waiting, praying that your husband would return to you from space, but most had left in the late evening hours. The wives who had traveled from Houston to Florida to view the launch returned to her home like clockwork after the initial knock on her door at six a.m. when Joe's boss at Cape Kennedy had come to notify Vivian that they'd lost contact with his spacecraft.

"Astronaut Joe Mitchell is a decorated fighter pilot, an American hero, and one of the elite astronauts chosen to be part of the Apollo program to go to the Moon."

"Turn that off," Polly Abbott snapped, rising from her seat on the sofa beside Vivian and striding toward the television ready to do it herself if no one obeyed her. "She doesn't need to keep hearing the same thing over and over again. If there's a change, we'll know about it first," Polly added, sending a pointed glance to Rick Adams, the astronaut NASA had sent over to act as Vivian's liaison and support.

Rick's presence had multiple functions—ostensibly, he was there to help Vivian and keep her informed as they tried to re-establish contact with Joe's spacecraft; undeniably, he was there to help NASA and keep them informed. He felt like a handler who had been assigned to Vivian to make sure she didn't discredit herself, Joe, or, most importantly, the space program.

One of the newer, younger wives jumped up to do Polly's bidding, the unofficial hierarchy that existed between their group playing out in Vivian's crowded living room. Polly was the undisputed leader of the wives given her husband's seniority at NASA, and while Vivian had all but eschewed the spouses' networking and the social interactions that came with it, having a best friend who people listened to and respected counted for a great deal in moments like these.

If any astronaut was going to be Vivian's support, it would have been Polly's husband, Frank, who'd known Vivian as long as she'd known Joe, but Frank's position as flight director leading the mission on the ground meant he was needed at the command center, and so they'd sent Rick to do the death watch with her.

The television cut off, and still Vivian stared at that blank screen as though it would somehow give her the answers she sought, would help her understand how they had gotten to this place. She kept waiting for the door to open and for Joe to stride into their living room, to wrap his arms around her and sweep her up as he pressed a kiss to her lips that set off flutters inside her.

Vivian kept waiting for someone to tell her that it was all a mistake, a communication problem that had been resolved, that they'd made contact and all was well. She kept waiting to wake from this nightmare. It was her worst fear realized, the scenario she had dreaded for years, and despite all the time she'd spent anticipating such an event, now that it was here, she couldn't make the event land, couldn't conceptualize the fact that she was staring down the reality of her husband lost in space.

She'd known when he went up that the chance of him coming back to her alive was as good as a coin toss. Now those odds seemed decidedly worse and stacked against her.

How could they lose a spacecraft?

Or did it count as being lost if it was out there and they just didn't know how to contact it or where it was?

Did Joe realize that they'd lost communication with NASA?

He must have.

Was he panicking right now thinking of how he was going to get himself and his men back to Earth? Or was he still focused on trying to salvage the mission, to get them close to the Moon? There were three astronauts aboard that spacecraft, but it was Joe's mission, Joe's responsibility.

Vivian kept waiting for someone to tell her how she was supposed to act in a situation like this, what she was supposed to say, what expression she should school on her face. There was an understanding about these sorts of things—they were astronaut wives, and before that they were fighter pilot wives, and when your husband had the sort of job where you kissed him goodbye when he went off to work knowing that he might not come back, you steeled yourself for the possibility of a crisis such as this one.

Or at least she thought she had.

Maybe there were some things no amount of worrying could prepare you for.

I'll come back to you. Always.

How many times had Joe told her that?

When he said it, despite all the odds that suggested otherwise, it had been impossible not to believe him. After all, it was Joe—one of the best and brightest the space program had to offer, and most importantly, he'd promised her he'd always come back to her, and Joe had kept almost all his promises to her.

"I'm going to get some fresh air," Vivian murmured to no one and everyone at once, not even sure if the outside was what she needed. All she knew was that she couldn't be stuck in this overcrowded room anymore, waiting for word that wasn't coming.

Surely, if there had been an explosion or something terrible like that, NASA would have evidence of such a catastrophe. The launch had been fine. Everything had gone according to plan.

Until it didn't.

How did a man disappear in space?

When you were doing things no one had ever done before, crossing barriers mankind had never encountered, it was difficult to know what was possible, to understand all the vagaries of the universe and their daring quest to navigate it. There were some questions math and science had yet to answer, some things that existed just out of their reach.

Vivian wove her way through the living room, into the kitchen, past murmured words of condolence and comfort that floated through her as though she were made of air. They'd only been in the little beach house near the Cape for three months, and she couldn't tell if that made it easier or harder to feel grounded at a time like this. There were fewer memories of Joe to haunt her, but given the nature of their lifestyle—the uncertainty that came with being an Air Force pilot's wife, and now an astronaut's wife—she'd learned to carry her memories inside her rather than packing them in boxes that shuffled from house to house or were affixed on ever-changing walls.

Joe was her home.

There were fewer wives filling her living room than would be here if she had chosen to remain in Clear Lake—or "Togethersville," as it had been nicknamed—in the Houston suburbs like the rest of the wives. Her departure had raised more than a few eyebrows, but she'd felt like she was suffocating in Clear Lake.

Besides, in her mind it had never made sense for Joe to spend his workweek at the Cape, flying his little T-38 airplane cross-country to come home on weekends. Not after the accidents, not after some of his fellow astronauts had died flying their T-38s. There was nothing keeping her tethered to Togethersville anymore. Cocoa Beach, Florida, had become home—for a moment, at least, same as all the other places they had lived.

Vivian opened the sliding glass door in the kitchen, slipping wordlessly outside onto the tiny cement patio, shutting it gently behind her lest the noise draw unwanted attention and interrupt her much-needed solace.

They used to sit out here at the end of the day, sipping cocktails Joe mixed at the little bar off the dining room and making conversation about their days.

None of the homes they'd had throughout their marriage and Joe's military career had been particularly glamorous. A military officer's pay didn't go far—and Vivian had learned to economize with a frugality that made her proud. But even she had to admit that the diminutive house on Cocoa Beach with a postage stamp for a backyard had been a bit of a disappointment.

When she'd heard "Florida" and "beach," she'd envisioned towering palm trees and crashing waves. The ocean was beautiful, to be sure; it was just that their stretch of street was too far away to properly enjoy it. The landlord had sold them on the fact that the beach cottage had a view of the water, but he'd neglected to mention that you had to be standing on the roof to see it and, thus, enjoy it. She knew this because a few weeks after they moved in, Joe and some of his astronaut buddies had ended up on the roof drinking beers and eating peeled shrimp by the pound while they set off fireworks to celebrate the Fourth of July, seemingly impervious to the fact that a storm was building in the background.

Those were the moments in her marriage when she just had to shake her head and accept that Joe and his friends were built differently, that while it was impossible for her to fathom why grown forty-something-year-old men would think it was a good idea to climb up on the roof of their rental home and shoot off pyrotechnics—*think of the security deposit*, she'd implored him—given their line of work there was little that fazed them, little that they would say "no" to, particularly if it came in the form of a dare from another astronaut.

These were the instances when Vivian vacillated between wanting to scream and falling a little bit more in love with him, because there was something so utterly charming about Joe when he was incorrigible.

And so, despite the dubiously appointed "beach view," Vivian set out making the cottage feel like a home, just as she'd done in the three other places they'd lived in the last five years.

Not that Joe minded where they resided or if he could see the beach, or mountains, or any other vista. He had the sky— and his eyes turned toward space—and nothing else really mattered.

A helicopter sounded overhead, and Vivian almost regretted that she hadn't taken NASA up on their offer to move her to a safe house for the period surrounding the launch to escape the overwhelming media attention. The other wives who had gone through this before her had warned her that it would be unlike anything she'd ever experienced, but even so, she hadn't been prepared. There were some things you just couldn't anticipate until you were thrust into the middle of them.

Thankfully, today Polly had the foresight to draw the drapes closed.

Vivian had never grown used to the notoriety that came with being an astronaut's wife, never warmed to the instant celebrity that had followed them because of Joe's job. There were reporters camped out on her lawn at this very moment, their flashbulbs trained on the beach cottage's front windows. They'd been there since the week leading up to the launch, yelling questions out at her when she got in the car to go to the grocery store or went to the salon to get her hair cut and colored. They climbed in bushes, knocked on doors, and generally made a nuisance of themselves even though much of the interest that the initial astronauts evoked had lessened throughout the Gemini missions and now for the Apollo ones. The novelty had somewhat worn off, the idea of a man going into space no longer as awe-inspiring as it had once been.

Frank and Joe had hypothesized that going to the Moon might be the thing that rallied the nation and the world, and Joe's lunar orbit was supposed to be a critical first step on that journey, particularly after the series of setbacks the space program had faced.

Vivian glanced up at the sky, at the fluffy white clouds, the placid blue, and the unknown beyond. She tried to imagine Joe out there somewhere, pictured him floating through space in the little spacecraft they'd built as part of their quest to eventually put a man on the Moon.

It was a moment she'd repeated on military bases throughout his career, when she'd heard the roar of an engine and glanced up at the sky, wondering if he was flying above her, holding her breath until he landed.

Sometimes it felt as though she were strung together by those moments, all those held breaths, luck, and bravado enough to get by on.

Until now.

"Come back to me," she whispered to the sky.

The words escaped on a broken sob.

Vivian slipped her hands into the pockets of her launch dress that she'd hastily put on this morning when it became clear that the parade of casseroles and brightly colored gelatin salads at her door wasn't going to stop. Not that she blamed them. She'd done it, too, when there was a crash or an accident.

They all had.

Every single time she'd wondered if she would be next.

Now she was.

Her fingers grazed a slip of paper in her right pocket.

Vivian rubbed the object between the pads of her thumb and forefinger, a habit she'd picked up when she was a kid and was trying to calm herself down.

The sliding glass door slid open behind her with a thud.

Vivian whirled around.

Joe's best friend and Polly's husband, Frank Abbott, walked out on the patio.

He looked like he hadn't slept since the launch yesterday.

"I'm sorry."

Vivian's heart sank. "What are they saying?"

Frank raked a hand through his hair, his fingers trembling slightly. "It's not looking good. We've lost telemetry. We aren't getting any data from the spacecraft, aren't able to track it or Joe. There's no contact, Vivian. For him to be unreachable for this long . . ."

The rest of the sentence hung between them, unspoken, as though Frank had already reached the conclusion that Joe was lost to them for good.

"What if it's just that the comms are down? That's possible, right?" Vivian asked. "Surely, things like this happen during training."

"They do, yes. It could be that there's a problem with the system, but Joe is alright—it could be a lot of things—we just don't know. That's the tricky part—without comms we're pretty much guessing at this point. It's complicated. No one has done this before. You train for it, you simulate, you run tests, but there are things out there we can't account for, variables that can change the whole thing. We're doing everything in our power to reestablish communication with the capsule, to figure out if they're still on course like they should be."

There was so much they were still learning about space travel, too many unknowns and unpredictable factors. There were things Joe couldn't tell her, parts of his job he had to keep secret given the sensitivity of the mission and the fervor with which the Soviets were pursuing their own aims in space. All the things she didn't know, all the things NASA likely didn't know, absolutely terrified her.

What kind of hubris did it take to launch a man into space

with the hope—but no pretense of certainty—that he might come back?

"Look, we're doing everything we can," Frank added.

"Yes, you said that already," Vivian murmured. "What exactly are you doing? What actionable steps are you taking?"

"I'm sorry, Vivian, but I really can't go into more detail about it. You know how this stuff is. Everyone there is doing everything they can think of to bring Joe back. I promise you. But, Vivian—" He hesitated. "It's been nine hours now, and we aren't getting any sign that his capsule is where it's supposed to be. If it was blown off course, or if some kind of accident happened, well, getting into space has never been the hardest part."

"It's getting home," she whispered, echoing the words that had filled her with dread the first time she heard Joe say them at a press conference when a reporter asked Joe what part of space flight worried him the most.

"I'll be honest with you—I think—I think you should prepare yourself for the possibility—"

Vivian shook her head, interrupting Frank before he had the chance to finish the thought, to put her greatest fears into words.

"No. That I won't do. If he were gone—" She *wouldn't* say the word. "If he were gone, I would know. I would feel it. I'm telling you—he's out there somewhere. He's going to come back. He promised me."

"I hope you're right." Frank glanced at the house behind him. "I wanted to stop by to check on you—to let you know what's going on—but I need to head back. Polly's here if you need anything. One of the secretaries' daughters is watching the girls, so whatever you need—she's here."

"Thank you. Frank—the other families—how are they doing?"

Joe was the mission commander, but he was joined by two other astronauts—Michael Drayer, the navigator, and Paul Robin, the command module systems expert. Paul was single— one of the few in the group—but Michael was married with three kids. Vivian had never been close to his wife, Bridget—in fact, if she was being completely honest, she'd never liked Bridget all that much. If there had been a poster child for the perfect astro wife, Bridget Drayer was it, and she'd never hesitated to show her disdain for how much Vivian failed to fit the mold. Of all the reasons Vivian felt inadequate as an astro wife, many of the encounters involved Bridget.

And now, absolutely none of that mattered. All she could think of was how Bridget must be feeling in this moment. Not to mention their children. And Paul's parents—

"Are they still here at the Cape or are they back in Texas?"

"Bridget's in Texas. She didn't want the kids to miss school, thought it was best to keep them in a routine while Michael was away, so she was already flying home when all of this began unraveling."

It made sense considering the spacecraft was supposed to be completing a ten-day-long mission orbiting the Moon.

"Paul's parents live in Pennsylvania, and we're in contact with them. They're worried, but Paul's father is a Navy man. He understands the drill," Frank replied, his voice weary.

"Everyone is looking for answers. Everyone wants to know where they are."

Vivian fiddled with the piece of paper in her pocket as the moment stretched on between them, as Frank stood there looking very much like a man who had something more that he wanted to say but didn't know just how to get the words out.

When Vivian was a young journalist, trying to make her mark in D.C., she'd learned the art of letting other people fill silences. The most extraordinary things tumbled out when someone was trying to erase an awkward pause, and considering her temperament had always been drawn to the conversational breaks such beats provided, she was all too happy to let others fill the void for her.

Frank knew more than he was letting on.

Vivian twisted the paper around in her fingers, trying to remember the last time she'd worn this dress before yesterday's launch and what she had left in the pocket. Quite frankly, she was surprised it had survived the wash.

A ghost of a smile played at her lips, a memory rising unbidden.

Joe was forever leaving items in his pockets, and early on in their marriage she'd realized that she needed to empty everything out before she did a load of laundry. It had been a running joke between them—the fact that he was so fixated on his job, able to solve complicated problems and focus under intense pressure, and yet, he never could remember things like emptying his pockets or putting the cap on the toothpaste.

Vivian pulled the paper from her pocket and glanced down

at it; when Joe returned from space, she'd share this little story with him, and they'd laugh about it in that way that only the two of them could.

At first she thought perhaps it was some household accounting, judging by the math on the paper. On closer inspection, the math didn't look anything like the addition and subtraction Vivian did when balancing their funds. It was filled with what appeared to be numerical calculations—and complicated ones at that—but the sliver was too narrow, cutting off any decipherable pattern or equation. She unfurled it more and flipped it over.

Here, she recognized the handwriting instantly, had seen it penned across countless birthday cards and love letters.

It was Joe's hurried scrawl, the letters spiky and exuberant.

Wait for me.

Her heart pounded.

When had Joe written this? How long had it been in the pocket of her dress, waiting for her to read it? Did Joe leave it there as an inside joke between them given their playful fights over the laundry?

Joe often left love notes for her around their house, folded airplanes on the pillow for her to discover when she awoke, a message waiting for her on the inside. He always signed his notes with his name, though this time he hadn't, his messages usually longer and more romantic than this one. And yet—

Wait for me.

Those three words felt a lot like hope she could cling to.

It was just like Joe to somehow leave her the message she needed most at the exact moment she needed it.

Vivian rubbed her fingers over the wadded-up paper again.

"Vivian—"

She glanced up.

Frank stared back at her, shifting from side to side on the balls of his feet. "I need to go—I need to get back to work. If we have any hope of reconnecting with the crew, then it's going to be all hands on deck."

"Thank you. I really appreciate all that you're doing to get them back. Don't give up hope, Frank. Please. I know they're out there. I know they're waiting to be found. They just need us to find them."

Vivian held the note out to Frank so that he could read the words Joe had written before he left, so he could understand what this meant to her, how badly she needed to see this through to the end, how desperately she needed to know that there were people out there searching for her husband and the other astronauts, that they would bring them home.

Frank took the paper from her gingerly, as though he was afraid of the emotion contained there, of the grief that shrouded her. They all were treating her that way—save for Polly—as though her misfortune were something catching, no one in this community eager to confront the realities of space travel and the danger it brought to their lives. Easier to chase invincibility instead, to believe that they could do the impossible and reach the ultimate limits of humanity's reach than to acknowledge that something as mundane as death could wreak havoc on their best-laid plans.

Frank glanced down at the words Joe had written for her, passing over them so quickly she wondered if he'd even read them at all. He flipped over the page—

He froze. "Where'd you get this?"

"It was in the pocket of my dress. Why?"

"This is my handwriting. They were some calculations I did for the space flight yesterday. I gave it to Joe right before the launch, minutes before he boarded the spacecraft."

TWO

1961

No pilots."

Vivian's roommate, Polly, gaped at her. "Honey, why not? I thought you would be *thrilled*. Do you know how hard it is to find a decent date these days, and here I found us *two*. And not just any dates—think of the uniforms, those flight suits are so dashing and—"

"You can't expect them to show up in their flight suits for a *date*."

"Well, no, maybe not for a date, but you can imagine what they look like in their flight suits," Polly countered with a twinkle in her eye.

"I'm not really one for uniforms . . ."

"Or pilots, apparently," Polly added, casting a sidelong look at Vivian as they walked into the bar together.

In just two months of sharing an apartment in Arlington,

Vivian had learned that Polly did everything with gusto. Their apartment was filled with the sound of records playing during the evenings when Polly wasn't working at the hospital, usually accompanied by the melody of the door opening and closing, heralding dates or friends who stopped by for casual gatherings that started off as groups of three or four and often swelled to parties of two dozen or more.

It should have annoyed her considering how different they were, but Vivian was pragmatic enough to acknowledge that without Polly's outgoing nature, their apartment would be a far quieter place. Polly brought the party to them and frequently pulled Vivian outside of her normal routine—much like she had this evening.

The invitation to join Polly had come at the last minute, and Vivian had barely had enough time to change her clothes from a day at the newsroom before they were jumping into a cab together. She should have asked more questions. But if she was being honest, she'd come home from another demoralizing day of fetching coffee rather than writing stories, fending off increasingly lecherous come-ons from her coworkers, convinced that trying to make it as a journalist was proving more and more elusive with each day she spent in D.C.

She just needed a story. The right story. A story that would prove to her editor that her writing had value. So far each one she'd pitched had been summarily shut down, leaving her relegated to doing the grunt work for her male coworkers whose voices often were the loudest in the newsroom.

"Just stay for an hour," Polly cajoled beside her. "If it's boring, you can go home to watch *Perry Mason*, and I'll give your excuses."

Vivian laughed. "Are you going to tell them that I ducked out to watch *Perry Mason*?"

"If that's what it takes. I promise I won't subject you to a bad evening. Although, if Joe's friend Frank is anything like him, I think you'll have a good time despite your aversion to pilots, which you really must explain to me sometime."

Vivian scanned the room, trying to pick their "dates" out of the crowd. It was a busy night in the city, and the bar was popular for the seafood it offered, the room already teeming with young professionals looking for romance, others with more professional bents in mind, clearly intent on networking.

"How did the two of you meet anyway?" Vivian asked.

Why had she never thought about going out like this? She'd already spotted at least one young member of Congress at the bar. Maybe this was where the stories were happening, a way to finally feel like she was tapped into the scene. She should come back tomorrow night and people watch at the bar.

"He came into the hospital with a sprain in his shoulder," Polly answered. "Motorcycle accident. We started talking while he was waiting to see the doctor. Joe's here from out of town. He asked if he could invite his buddy Frank, who he had plans with tonight, and I said sure, that I'd bring someone for his friend."

"And they're both pilots?"

"That's what Joe said, although his friend Frank lives here. He's stationed at the Pentagon. What do you have against pilots, anyway?"

"Nothing," Vivian lied. She shrugged. "Just not my type. I'm not exactly a risk-taker."

"Let me guess, you go for one of those quiet, academic guys?"

"Something like that."

"Alright, so you're not going to meet the love of your life tonight—but Joe's friend Frank is supposed to be a nice guy. Worst case, we got to get all dolled up and eat some amazing seafood."

Vivian could go for some shrimp right now, and the bar was known for it. Besides, there was always the promise of pajamas and *Perry Mason* waiting for her if the evening went downhill.

"There they are," Polly whispered, linking her arm through Vivian's and propelling her forward.

Two men stood at the bar. One, muscular and blond. The other, equally built and brown-haired. They were both dressed in slacks and a collared shirt, nary a wrinkle in sight, their clothes pressed with military precision, their leather shoes so shining that Vivian hazarded she would be able to see her reflection in them. And despite the differences in their hair color, the inch or two between them in height, the fact that the blond one was a bit more broad-shouldered, there was something in the way they carried themselves, as though they were standing at attention even when they were seemingly relaxed.

A group had formed around them, about a dozen or so people, their laughter reaching where Vivian and Polly stood. Whatever the blond one said—his face animated as one hand moved in the air, the other in a sling with decidedly less movement, as though he were mimicking the actions of two objects— airplanes, perhaps—interacting with each other—the crowd was rapt. Men elbowed one another and gestured with knowing grins at the blond man's antics as though they had personal familiarity and experience with the aerial display being acted out in front of them. There were a few women in the little group that had formed, and by the smile the blond one gave a pretty redhead standing near him, the men knew the attention they drew and were happy to encourage it.

Polly was going to have her hands full tonight, and the odds of Vivian sitting at home in front of the television rose exponentially. Were they going on a double date or joining the audience of a late-night variety show?

She didn't blame Polly for trying, but neither one of them could have been less Vivian's type.

Polly was right. Vivian tended to gravitate toward quiet guys, the intellectual ones more inclined to academic pursuits than athletic ones. Physical appearance did little for her, but rather the common denominator with the admittedly few men she'd dated was that they were all smart and funny. Ultimately, a good conversation carried the day, and this hardly looked like a discussion with reciprocal give-and-take, an interest in getting to know each other.

No, this was a performance, and Vivian couldn't help but think whatever woman ended up on a date with the blond one would probably feel like she was perpetually in the audience of his ongoing show.

Polly strode toward the blond one, a wide, easy smile on her face that suggested she was completely undeterred by the scene before her. It wasn't surprising considering Vivian had yet to see anything that intimidated her roommate. It was likely what made Polly such a good nurse. She came home with stories of situations Vivian couldn't fathom being placed in, but Polly navigated them all with the same calm, affable temperament. If anyone could handle a man who was a handful, it was Polly.

The blond one broke off in the middle of whatever he was saying, his airplane-hands abandoned, a cocky smile affixed on his lips, and between the sling and the reminder of just how Polly had met their dates for the evening—

This must be the infamous Major Joe Mitchell.

Objectively, she could see what had attracted Polly.

Her roommate had described Joe to a T. He was five or six inches taller than Polly and Vivian, broad-shouldered, and undeniably handsome. He resembled something out of central casting if one were looking for a heroic type.

The crowd behind him slowly dispersed, story time clearly over, as Joe fixed his attention on her roommate with the same focus he'd adopted earlier when he was captivating the audience.

Once they'd finished exchanging pleasantries, Vivian's gaze connected with Joe's, and she carefully schooled the expression on her face. Polly liked him, and out of respect for her roommate, she'd make him feel welcome even though there was something about the whole business—the crowd, the cocky smile, the glossy appearance—that felt like far too much for her to take him seriously.

Their gazes caught, and for a moment she wondered if she hadn't been quick enough to hide her opinion of him, because Joe's eyes widened slightly as though he'd registered her reaction and was a bit taken aback that she wasn't as impressed by him as everyone else seemed to be.

Polly missed the exchange entirely—or she was too eager to care—because she smiled widely and said, "Vivian, this is Joe Mitchell. *Major* Joe Mitchell. Joe, this is my roommate, Vivian."

Joe's lips quirked at the emphasis Polly placed on his rank, his attention still on Vivian as though he was gauging *her* reaction to Polly's introduction of him.

"It's a pleasure to meet you, Vivian."

He had a voice made for television or radio, and she could see how it would help draw a crowd.

Somewhere on the periphery of her vision she noticed Joe's friend and Polly chatting with each other. Joe held his hand out to Vivian, and she placed her palm in his, their fingers grazing as they shook.

"It's nice to meet you," she replied.

And then he smiled. Really smiled. Not the smile he had given the crowd earlier, that glossy, impersonal, too-slick smile, but something altogether different that had her glancing away, a nervous sort of energy radiating from the point where their hands met through her body.

The redhead near the bar shot her a curious glance.

Vivian waited for Joe to release her, but instead he maintained the contact of his hand against hers, a little line appearing between his brows as though he were puzzling something out.

Had she been making another face?

She'd always had the uncomfortable habit of wearing her emotions for all to see, another reason why she had chosen to be off camera rather than on. She could only imagine the reactions she would evoke while reciting the news if she let her true feelings be known.

Vivian tried again to make her expression as neutral as possible, but apparently she didn't achieve her desired effect, because if anything, Joe seemed as amused by her as she had been of him.

He still hadn't let go of her hand, though.

And the longer he held on to it, the less that Vivian would term her feelings as "amusement," and the more she, well, wasn't quite sure how she felt.

At this point, it was just becoming a little awkward.

Vivian slid her hand from Joe's, taking a step back.

A ghost of a smile flitted across his lips, the effect sending a little thrill down her spine.

Polly was *definitely* going to have her hands full with this one. Speaking of Polly—

Vivian glanced over at her roommate to see what she'd made of the entire business, but Polly's gaze was firmly trained on the other pilot.

"And this guy is Frank," Joe replied after a pause, breaking the moment between them as he patted his friend on the back and introduced him to Vivian.

Vivian couldn't help but notice that *Frank's* gaze kept returning to Polly looking delightfully pretty in her pink dress.

Vivian grinned.

Polly was going to have her pick of the pilots tonight.

Vivian glanced over at Joe, curious to see if he was annoyed by his friend's marked interest in the woman *he'd* arranged a date with. It felt as though she were caught up in a Rock Hudson–Doris Day film, albeit without the glamorous wardrobe. She would be cast in the role of Polly's earnest and steadfast friend who gave practical—perhaps boring, even—advice peppered with the occasional amusing quip. Solid sidekick energy.

Polly for her part looked a bit bewildered by the options she'd been presented with, as though she found herself on a variety show where she was faced with two doors, equally promising, and she wasn't sure which one she should pick. Vivian could hardly blame her roommate for the confusion. On the surface, many women probably would gravitate toward Joe over Frank for the confidence the former clearly possessed. There was a charisma about him that seemed much less obvious with Frank. And still, her roommate's gaze seemed to linger more on Frank than his flashier friend.

"Shall we get a drink?" Joe asked the group.

"Yes. Please," Vivian answered, perhaps a bit too emphatically judging by the deepening quirk of Joe's lips.

Frank still hadn't looked away from Polly, and it clearly had not gone unnoticed by her roommate, who had angled her body ever so slightly closer to the dark-haired pilot's and farther away from Joe.

Perhaps it was going to be the redhead's lucky evening.

"Why don't we get drinks for everyone? I could use some help," Joe suggested to Vivian, gesturing to his arm in the sling. He turned to Polly and Frank, neatly taking charge of their little foursome as they gave him their drink orders.

"The two of you can scope out a table," Joe replied. "There might be something in the corner there."

Joe didn't wait for an answer before extending his hand toward the bar, insinuating that Vivian should lead the way. He fell into step behind her, and as she wove through the busy nighttime crowd, she could feel the hint of his palm at her back, fingers lightly splayed between her shoulder blades, steadying her should she need it.

When they reached the bar, Joe sidled up beside her, bracing his uninjured forearm on the bar top as he caught the bartender's attention with a faint inclination of his head. There was—perhaps unsurprisingly, considering what he did for a living—an undeniable swagger about him. It must be difficult to live on the edge, to have such a dangerous job and not carry yourself with a bit of a devil-may-care attitude. At the same time, though, she couldn't fathom why anyone would choose such a career, would willingly put themselves in harm's way time and time again. She understood the desire to serve, to dedicate yourself to an important cause; she'd just much rather do so with both feet planted firmly on the ground.

"Sorry about that back there," Joe said, his shoulder shrugging toward the spot where he'd held court. A few stragglers lingered, looking a bit dejected. He grinned. "I got caught up in a flying story. Didn't realize so many people had gathered around."

"No need to apologize to me. Everyone looked like they were having a good time." She paused. "Were your hands supposed to be . . . airplanes?"

He grinned again. "I was showing them a dogfight I was in a few years back in Korea. 'Course it was a little difficult with this thing," he added, gesturing to his sling with his free arm.

"Does that happen to you often—people asking you to tell flying stories?"

"Pretty much. I've learned people have a natural fascination for jobs that aren't as common, things that they've always wanted to do, but will likely never get a chance to. The stories let them live vicariously for a few moments at least."

"You consider yourself to be somewhat of an entertainer, then?"

He laughed, the sound full and rich. "Only when I'm doing it right."

He had a grin that looked like it could gobble you up in a few bites and you wouldn't complain about it.

"How much longer do you have to wear the sling?" Vivian asked, trying to move the conversation to surer ground.

"Hopefully, not too much longer. I'm due to start test pilot school soon. Just made the move to California."

He stared at her expectantly, and just like the little scene before and his earlier comment, she got the sense that he had almost taken for granted that when he mentioned what he did for a living, he would be met with a fair bit of awe and perhaps more than one offer of a free drink. After all, he proposed the kernel of information in a manner that suggested he wanted her to ask him what test pilot school was, so that he could show off about his career again.

The journalist in her was a bit curious, but the woman in her felt, well, a bit like rolling her eyes.

Working in a television studio had a way of exhausting your patience when it came to men preening about how important they were. There were some coworkers who treated her with respect, who offered advice on things they'd picked up in the newsroom along the way, who genuinely seemed to want her to succeed. But there were enough of the other ones—the "accidental" pinches, and the nicknames like "sweet cheeks"—that made her want to scream. More days than not, she came home exhausted from working in an environment where she constantly felt like she had to try ten times harder than her male counterparts who didn't believe a woman should be in the workplace, who made comments about how she needed to be home raising children, followed by a leering joke about how they were happy to make an honest woman out of her.

It was enough to put you off any hope of romance.

Ever.

"It's an eight-month course," Joe added, answering the question she hadn't asked. "Doing all kinds of research and development, pushing the envelope to see the limits of what we can do in the air. It's competitive. Demanding."

The bartender headed over to them before she had a chance to respond, and Joe turned his attention to ordering their drinks.

Vivian glanced back at Polly and Frank, who were now sitting at a table together. She couldn't tell what they were saying from this far away, but whatever conversation they were having, they were clearly engrossed, their bodies leaning toward each other, their gazes locked.

"Have you and Polly lived together long?" Joe asked her after he'd given the bartender their orders.

Vivian jerked her gaze away from Polly and Frank. "Only a couple months."

"Did you grow up in the area?"

"No, I moved here six months ago for work. "

"Where did you grow up?"

It was a perfectly natural question to ask, and most people would have an easy answer that would invite more conversation. For her, it felt like a tiny prick, a little knife that lodged itself in her breast as it brought back the memories of a childhood where she had been perpetually unrooted, moving from place to place sometimes without more than a day's warning, forced to leave whatever friends she'd accumulated behind her. It was a difficult life to explain to people who hadn't lived it, to those who had ties to their communities and families, and memories of traditions and special occasions marked with laughter and friends.

"All over, really," she answered, affixing a breezy smile to her face. "Where are you from?"

"Virginia, actually. Great Falls. I'm here visiting family." He gave her a sheepish look. "I was out with my cousins when the accident happened. There was an icy patch in the road that I missed, and the bike—" He grimaced, and she realized that while he'd come across as easygoing about the whole thing, even a bit nonchalant, the accident was clearly a sensitive subject for him. "I'm stationed in California right now, though. Edwards Air Force Base."

"I'm not familiar with Edwards, but I lived in San Diego for a bit. Ages ago, though. I barely remember it."

Which wasn't exactly true. Of all the places she'd lived, and at twenty-three she'd easily cleared a dozen, San Diego had been one of her favorites. Her mother had been engaged to a nice man there—Charlie, maybe. Or Dickie. Something with an "e" on the end, because even though there were blocks in her memory, things she simply could not recall no matter how hard she tried, Vivian remembered the way she had said his name in her childish voice and the joy that syllable had evoked.

He'd had a kid, too—a boy. A few years older than her. And the son had been as nice as his dad, albeit slightly less enthusiastic about having a little girl joining his all-male household. They'd been kind, though, which was more than she could say about every other man her mother had dated and married, and that little house just seven blocks from the beach had felt very much like paradise.

While it lasted, at least.

"How did you end up here?" Joe asked her.

Vivian's answer was cut off by a flurry of commotion near the entrance. In another town, she'd have guessed a celebrity had walked into the room based on the fanfare. Here, in this city that thrived on power, a politician seemed more likely.

And then the crowd parted.

A man in a charcoal gray suit, white dress shirt, and black tie walked into the bar. He was tall and lean, his dark hair interspersed with steel gray at the temples.

He joined a group standing near the front and was instantly greeted with smiles, a good-natured slap on the back, like he belonged there, and everyone was excited to see him, as though he was a regular in this bar, a fact Vivian filed away for future reference.

Graham Carlson.

For a moment, Vivian could do no more than gape at her hero in the flesh.

He'd been in journalism for nearly two decades, since he was reportedly fresh out of college at some Ivy League school whose name she forgot. Harvard, maybe. Or Yale. He'd made the jump to television ten years ago and had since become the preeminent on-air talent at the television station where she worked.

In an industry that could often be filled with ego and avarice, she'd never heard anyone speak of Graham Carlson with anything other than respect and appreciation.

He wrote much of his own copy, covering the political beat and items of major national interest, and he had a reputation for being tenacious when it came to a story. He could work a source like no one in the business, a fact that had earned him a Pulitzer for his reporting years ago.

In the six months that she had worked at the television station, Vivian had passed him in the hallway twice, and despite his impeccable manners, she'd been so nervous that both times she'd barely been able to manage a "hello" in response.

"Are you alright?" Joe asked her.

Vivian jerked her gaze away from Graham Carlson, belatedly realizing Joe stood there staring at her, waiting for an answer to—

What question had he asked her?

Something about living with Polly? How she liked it, perhaps?

"I like it very much," she replied, glancing over his shoulder to where Graham was now ensconced in a group that included a sitting U.S. senator.

"Like what very much?" Joe asked.

Damn.

It wasn't a question about how she felt about living with Polly.

Vivian hesitated, no longer able to pretend that she'd been paying the slightest bit of attention to him.

How many times had she mentally discarded a man she went on a date with because someone else had caught his eye? How many times had she grown frustrated when his gaze glazed over ever so slightly as she spoke of something she was passionate about? How many times had her comments in the newsroom been completely ignored as though she hadn't spoken at all?

The irony was not lost on her.

"I'm sorry. I didn't mean to be rude. I just got distracted. It's not you. I'm sure you're fascinating company. And a lovely date." She flushed. "Not that this is a date, of course. I mean it is for you and Polly, which is wonderful, because Polly is wonderful—smart, and funny, and kind . . ."

Except maybe it wasn't a date anymore considering how closely Polly was sitting with his friend. Vivian glanced around the room, searching for the redhead to see if she was still here or if she had moved on herself.

"I'm sure there are lots of wonderful women here tonight . . ." Vivian trailed off awkwardly, wondering how much longer they were due to make polite conversation considering her fix-up had never been with him in the first place. It wasn't like she had any interest in playing dating musical chairs. Besides, she'd have given anything to move a bit closer to Graham Carlson's party, to hear what they were talking about. There was an open spot at the bar near where they stood—

Joe spared her the rest of her embarrassing speech and

pivoted, looking over his shoulder at the crowd near the front door before glancing back at her.

"Someone you know?" he asked, gesturing to the group. His tone sounded more amused than annoyed by how thoroughly she was ignoring him.

"No. Not exactly. I mean I know *of* him, of course. Who doesn't? We work at the same television studio."

"You're in television? Are you on the air?"

"Good heavens, no." The idea alone made Vivian queasy. She couldn't imagine anything more intimidating than speaking in front of that large of an audience each day, praying that you didn't make a mistake on camera. Some journalists like Graham seemed to accept the fame that came with being on-air talent with a grace she envied, but she wouldn't enjoy juggling the notoriety and attention that they faced alongside the daily grind of the job. She loved what she did, so long as she was behind the camera, writing the stories. "I work in the newsroom. Working on copy and the like."

"So, you're a reporter?"

Vivian nodded. "Well, to be fair, 'reporter' might be exaggerating things. At the moment, I'm more likely to be running errands. I'm a great procurer of coffee. My boss says I make the best pot," she added, struggling to keep her voice light lest he see how embarrassed and frustrated she was by the entire business.

"Polly didn't tell me that you're a reporter."

"I wouldn't imagine she thought it was relevant." Or that he would care what she did all that much. Vivian shrugged. "Polly asked me to come because she mentioned you were bringing a friend, and she didn't want the numbers to be uneven. And the shrimp is very good . . ."

"I'm not sure I've ever come in second to shellfish," he joked.

She grinned. "Perhaps you have, and you just didn't realize it. Besides, if anything, Frank is the one who came in second to shellfish. I'll admit I haven't been on many double dates, but I'm certain I was meant to be here for him."

"Were you?"

Vivian nodded, but then their gazes collided and there was something in the way Joe looked at her, something that settled into the pit of her stomach and filled her with a sensation she couldn't name and wasn't sure she had ever experienced before.

Joe broke eye contact between them, glancing over her shoulder. "I have a feeling Frank is no longer available."

Vivian turned around. On the other side of the room, Polly and Frank sat beside each other, their heads so close together they were almost touching.

"I think you might be right. I'm sorry."

"I'll get over it. Somehow," he replied, the smile on his face belying the seriousness in his words.

"I'm sure you will," Vivian murmured, searching for the redhead in the crowd once more.

A movement caught her attention near where Graham stood. Was that a member of the Senate Armed Services Committee that Graham was speaking with? She craned her neck, trying to get a better sense of what they were discussing. They were huddled together, their conversation clearly somewhat serious by the intense expressions on their faces.

"Are you working on a story right now?" Joe asked her, calling her attention back to him.

It took her a moment to respond, distracted by the conversation going on near them. "I am. Well, preparing to pitch it to the news director."

She didn't add that so far he'd shot down every story she'd proposed, to the point where she was now wondering if she'd made a mistake moving here at all.

During her undergraduate degree at Mount Holyoke, she'd worked at the college's radio station, and it had sparked her interest in becoming a journalist. Radio hadn't quite felt like the perfect medium for her, but working at one of the oldest college radio stations in the country had been an incredible experience. She'd left with high hopes of finding a career that would give her the same sense of fulfillment, but she'd quickly learned that there was a difference coming from an environment where she was surrounded by other women who were supportive and enthusiastic about their work, and the television station, where nearly all of the women were relegated to support roles, their only purpose to bolster the men's successes.

"What's the story?" Joe asked her.

"It's a piece on the Space Race."

He grinned. "Everyone's gone a bit space mad, haven't they?"

In the last few years, it seemed like the entire country—and much of the world—had turned their eyes to space as the final frontier to explore and conquer. When the Soviet Union launched Sputnik into space in 1957, the idea of a Soviet satellite orbiting the Earth, while at first an incredible sight to behold, eventually sparked terror in the hearts of many. NASA's subsequent announcement in late 1958 of Project Mercury, a rebuttal to growing Soviet dominance in space, had galvanized Americans to support the U.S. space program. The goal: sending seven Project Mercury astronauts to space. The sheer scope, cost, and aim of the project were staggering.

Some would say too much so.

Vivian nodded. "Exactly. That's my point. All of this money that they're spending—hundreds of millions of dollars. And for what? To send a few men to space? Just think of all the good that money could do elsewhere. How many people could be helped. I think we should be doing a better job of asking ourselves if the risk is worth the reward or if we're allowing the Soviets to tie us up in this whole business simply because our egos can't stand the possibility of the United States coming in second."

Joe gaped at her. "You—you don't think we should go to space? That we should, what, abdicate the Space Race?"

He looked so flabbergasted by her comment that he resembled one of those cartoon characters with how comically overdrawn his expression was.

And then she remembered a salient point she had conveniently forgotten.

The Mercury Seven all had one thing in common:

They were former fighter pilots.

"I'm not saying that exactly," she hedged, feeling a bit churlish for diminishing his profession, especially considering the lack of interest she'd shown him all evening. "I'm just saying perhaps we should think about it more, consider whether it's really the best use of our resources when there are so many other issues in this country that could be addressed with those funds. Quite frankly, it seems like we have enough problems on this planet before we turn our gaze to space."

Joe's expression shifted slightly, from gobsmacked to earnest.

"Are there needs that must be addressed? Of course. But that doesn't mean that we shouldn't dedicate ourselves to space. Just think of the scientific benefit, all we can learn from space. We could use that information for medical advancements, to offer solutions to problems here on Earth. There's so much about the universe that we don't know, so many questions that could be answered. Not to mention, it's a matter of national security. Did you hear Khrushchev's speech last year? Do you really want to hand space over to the Soviets? To just lose the Space Race? You're right, there is a bit of ego involved. But it's more than that. If the Soviets can put a satellite in space, how long will it be before they're putting missiles up in space, nuclear weapons? Do we really want Soviet nukes soaring over the United States?"

"Of course not. But the issue is more complex than that. It's easy to garner support when you're positioning it in such a dramatic manner that invokes fear. No one is going to say that they want a Soviet nuke pointing at them from space. And that's how they get the funding for the entire project, isn't it? That image compels Congress to open their checkbooks. But maybe no one country should control space. If there is truly such great scientific benefit to exploring space, then perhaps it should be shared for the benefit of all.

"And if the goal was getting a man to space, as you said, the

Soviets have already won," Vivian added. "Yuri Gagarin accomplished that. We're still on the ground."

Joe's expression flared at that statement, and it became very clear that like so many, he was upset the Soviets had sent a man to space last week.

"That's just one goal, though," Joe countered. "There are other things to look toward, other ambitions to have. The science of this stuff is completely unknown. We're learning as we go. Gathering information from our mistakes. We'll get there. And eventually we'll go beyond what the Soviets have accomplished. One day in the not-too-distant future, we'll put a man on the Moon. What message would that send to the Soviets if we got there first?"

"I don't profess to know much about space exploration, but the Moon seems like a lofty goal. A giant leap considering we can't even produce a capsule capable of carrying an astronaut to space."

"You're a skeptic."

He said "skeptic" like it was a very bad thing indeed, and she couldn't help but laugh at the fact that he looked flummoxed by the turn their conversation had taken.

"I suppose I am."

If she'd had an idealistic bone in her body, it had been excised a long time ago.

He shook his head. "It is a giant leap. But that's the whole point, isn't it? If you're going to take a risk, why not take a big one?"

"Spoken like a man who flies fighter jets and races motorcycles for fun. Life feels like enough of a risk as it is. For many, far, far too many, just surviving is a lofty enough goal these days."

"Exactly. You're absolutely right. It's difficult to wake up to the daily news and not feel like the world is falling apart. Maybe this is something we can do that unifies us, something that gives people a common goal to root for, a cause that unites us as Americans. I—" He broke off for a moment. "To be up there, to see Earth from space—to learn more about the universe than we've ever understood—is an incredible possibility. Is there life out there? Someone else who is trying to communicate with us? It's an opportunity to find our place in the world, maybe to understand more about how we fit into this giant tapestry of life, to understand the relationship between space and time, if time travel is truly possible, to understand why—" Joe flushed. "Sorry, I—I get a bit passionate when I'm talking about space." He laughed, the sound altogether too charming and self-deprecating. "It's easy to get carried away."

Vivian's heart thudded as she felt a bit lost in the conversation, but at the same time she felt a bit found. Then, she realized that the entire time he'd been speaking, she'd been moving closer to him, so close that they nearly touched.

She took a step back.

And then another.

"You're a romantic," she accused.

He laughed again, and really, no one should have a laugh like that.

"You say 'romantic' like it's a bad thing."

"No, it's not. It's just surprising."

What else had she gotten wrong in her assessment of him? And why did it matter?

"Why? What's more romantic than space, than flight? I've never felt more at peace, more in awe of the world around me, of life, than when I'm in the air. There's a poetry about it, a simplicity and beauty to how very small you feel when confronted with the vastness of the universe and your place inside it. It humbles you, I suppose. Or makes you feel like anything is possible. Maybe *that's* the humbling part. I can never decide."

Oh God, he was charming. And altogether too earnest. She could see how he'd commanded so much attention at the bar, why everyone had been so entertained, and why when he walked away, it had seemed like someone took the air out of their little group.

It was *definitely* time to go home and watch *Perry Mason* before this—was it attraction?—feeling toward him grew, drink be damned.

"I think I'm going to—"

Before she could finish the sentence, the bartender finally slid their drinks in front of them.

"Sorry for the wait," the bartender apologized. "It's a busy night."

"Busy" was an understatement; in the time she and Joe had been talking, the crowd had increased dramatically.

Maybe she could stay until she finished her martini. After all, it would be rude otherwise. At the very least, she should help him carry the drinks back to the table.

They wove their way through the crowd, Vivian moving

slowly to keep from spilling the three cocktails she juggled. Joe had tried to take one of them from her, but considering his injury, she'd offered to take the rest.

When they reached the table, Polly and Frank were nowhere to be found.

Vivian sat down opposite Joe, and then her gaze drifted to the makeshift dance floor near the bathrooms. Her roommate was dancing with Frank, her cheek on his jacket, her eyes closed, and the sight of them together filled Vivian with happiness for Polly and a quick but fierce sense of longing for something she'd never had.

In her previous relationships—sparse that they had been—Vivian had never looked or felt as at ease with another person as Polly did now. Dating had always seemed like an awkward dance where two people were trying to lead at the same time, stepping on each other's toes and struggling to make small talk. Even though they'd just met, there was something about the way Polly and Frank moved together that appeared so easy and natural.

"Frank's a good guy," Joe told her, his gaze not on the couple, but rather on Vivian. "We've known each other about ten years now—since we went through pilot training." He smiled. "It looks like they've hit it off."

"It does."

Vivian struggled to think of something to say, grasping for a topic to fill the silence building between them. Anything to distract herself from the way he was looking at her, an intent gleam in his gaze. Had his attentions shifted so quickly from Polly to her since her roommate was now otherwise occupied?

Did he shuffle through women with such ease that they were replaceable diversions to him? She couldn't decide what to make of him.

Joe took a sip of his drink, studying her over the rim of his glass. "Why television?"

"Pardon me?"

"I shared with you why I love to fly. I'm just curious—what was it that drew you to a job in the television industry?"

She opened her mouth to tell him that she thought it was interesting, that television was a new medium for reaching audiences, that there was so much opportunity, an open frontier. It was the standard answer she gave when asked about her career.

She began to tell him all that, and then, she just . . . didn't.

He looked so interested in her answer, and he'd described flying as poetry, and so the truth slipped out instead.

"When I was in junior high and high school, I found myself home alone a lot. And when I would feel lonely, I would turn on the television. It helped me to not feel so alone. I know the criticisms about the rise of television—the downfall of society and all that—but I've always considered television to be a source of connection for people. It's a campfire you can gather around, a window into other people's lives, a way to see how other people live and to understand what they're going through—"

Vivian broke off, more than a little embarrassed to have been so honest with him, to have shared such intimate details. It was so unlike her, and there was the strangest dichotomy in the fact that she felt simultaneously nervous and comfortable around him.

The way he looked at her—with such marked interest—Vivian tore her gaze away for a moment, taking a deep breath, anything to steady the pounding in her heart. Attraction she could understand—sure, he wasn't exactly her type, but who could explain the different vagaries that brought people together like two magnets. Attraction she could ignore. She didn't want to *like* him on top of that. She'd come dangerously close to doing so when he talked about what flying meant to him.

"I take back what I said earlier," Joe replied, his tone so quiet that she could barely hear the words he spoke over the noisy bar crowd. "You aren't a skeptic. Not at your core. You're a romantic, too."

How quickly he'd stripped away her armor. How easily she'd let him.

"With some things, perhaps," she conceded, sipping her drink to break eye contact with him when she said it, her hand on the glass not as steady as it should have been.

"Not all things?"

Vivian flushed, the knowing gleam in his eyes sending that strange feeling through her body again, as though she was hurtling toward something inevitable and terrifying.

She met his gaze. "Definitely not. Maybe I'm romantic about television because at this moment my career prospects feel more like a dream than reality," she conceded. "I thought the hardest part would be convincing a station to take a chance on me, to hire me. I worked at a radio station in college, and I hoped the experience would be helpful in building my résumé, but postgraduation has been more difficult than I imagined it would be. There aren't many women working in the newsroom, and those of us who are get treated more like glorified gofers than journalists." She sighed some of her frustration away. "Maybe the romance is in how elusive it seems—kind of like aviation and space," she acknowledged, the parallels between their respective careers both surprising and undeniable.

Joe held up his drink in a mock toast. "To the ambitions that are just out of reach."

She raised her glass in rejoinder.

"Although, in your case, I might be able to help with that." He glanced over his shoulder to the section of the bar where Graham stood. "Would you like me to introduce you?"

She followed his gaze and realized it was indeed resting on Graham. "You know Graham Carlson?"

Joe laughed. "Don't sound so surprised. Polly didn't tell you much about me, did she?" He rose from his seat, drink in hand. "Come on."

Vivian got up from the table and followed him through the crowd, the entire evening taking on a surreal quality. She wasn't sure she'd ever felt so off-balance before in her life.

"Carlson," Joe said in greeting once they reached the group, clearly unfazed by the fact that he was standing in front of a journalistic titan.

Graham whirled around, a wide smile on his face.

"Joe Mitchell. How the hell are you doing?" He took Joe's outstretched hand, pumping it enthusiastically.

"Doing well," Joe replied, and at once Vivian realized that there was something different about him. The man who had talked about his place in the universe with such thoughtfulness and care had been replaced once again by the version of him that had been holding court at the bar when they first arrived.

Which iteration was the real one, or were they both parts of him, much like she was arguably both a bit of a romantic and undeniably a skeptic?

"It's been, what—eight years since Korea?" Graham asked. "I heard they promoted you. What are you—a major now?"

Joe nodded.

Graham turned to the group behind him, which did in fact include a member of the Senate Armed Services Committee. "Gentlemen, allow me to do the honor of introducing you to one of our country's greatest living heroes—"

Greatest living heroes?

Vivian glanced over at Joe only for her gaze to connect with his.

He wasn't paying attention to the exuberant introduction that Graham was giving him; nor was he looking at the politicians and hangers-on who suddenly seemed very interested to shake his hand. Instead, he was staring at her, a small smile playing at his lips and a twinkle in his eyes as though he enjoyed her seeing this bit of notoriety.

She inclined her head ever so slightly, acknowledging the praise being heaped his way.

Arrogance normally irked her in a man, but despite the confidence—and cockiness—that radiated from Joe, there was something good-natured in his demeanor that didn't annoy her as so many other men did. He clearly knew how good he was at what he did, but she didn't get the impression that he used it to make others feel small as too many were prone to do.

Joe looked away from her, the moment between them broken.

"Have you met my friend Vivian?" Joe asked Graham, introducing her to the famed journalist. "She's in the news business as well. In fact, do you two work for the same television station?"

Joe delivered the question with casual aplomb, his words seemingly putting them on equal footing, as though she and Graham were colleagues, as opposed to the enormous gulf between them, and Vivian felt a spark of gratitude for the way he neatly inserted her into their conversation, for his kindness in making the introduction in the first place.

Vivian had realized early on that much of life came down to a measure of luck, to an alignment in the stars, to fate, to whatever or whoever you believed ordered the universe. She thanked whatever sequence of events had strung together so that Polly would meet Joe, and Vivian would end up in this bar with him on the very night that her hero was here as well.

"No, I haven't had the pleasure," Graham returned, his voice booming in the crowded bar, his demeanor so like the one that greeted millions of people when he delivered the nightly evening news. "It's lovely to meet you, Vivian."

For a moment, words failed her. She kept a scrapbook filled with her favorite news articles, the ones she read repeatedly, trying to understand what it was about the words that brought the stories to life, trying to decipher what it took to be great. These were the stories she admired, the profiles of people and issues that were transported to people's dining room tables and living rooms—the ability to move and inform. Most of the articles had been written by Graham Carlson.

When he'd moved from the newspaper to television, she'd followed him faithfully, and on the nights in college when she'd dined alone, she'd often curled up in front of his broadcasts of the evening news, dinner in hand. Even though this was her first time meeting him in person, in a way she felt like she'd known him for a long time. It was strange to think that he had been a part of her daily life, that he had delivered some of the world's most tumultuous moments to her in that even-tempered, soothing voice of his that had made her feel slightly less afraid, slightly less alone.

"What do you do at the station?" Graham asked her.

"I just started in the newsroom," she answered. "The morning news."

Although, eventually, one day she hoped to reach the evening news, to write the stories that would greet people after a hard day as they settled into their homes, as the weight of the world rested on their shoulders, and they needed some hope or understanding to hold on to.

"And how do you like it?" Graham asked her. Before she could answer his question, he leaned in conspiratorially. "I remember those early years. Horrible. But there's something about it, isn't there? A magic to the newsroom?"

She smiled. "Yes. Exactly. There's this energy in the room when a story breaks. It's infectious."

"Addictive," Graham added, a knowing gleam in his eyes.

The crowd around them shifted, and Vivian realized that while she and Graham had started talking, Joe had been drawn into a circle of politicians, the senator from Armed Services particularly interested in what he was saying.

At some point Joe had set his drink down, and now his hands gestured in the air again, sling-clad arm rising and falling, as though he were making the motions of two planes involved in an intricate dance, and by the words drifting toward her, he was telling a story of one of his flying exploits that had the men riveted.

She hadn't realized she and Graham had drifted so far away from the rest of the group, but now looking at Joe's animated discussion, she couldn't help but wonder if he had intentionally drawn the others away to give her a chance to speak with her idol.

Joe paused his story and glanced over at her.

It wasn't difficult to see what had attracted Polly in the first place. A bit harder to understand what had caused Polly to set him aside for Frank, but no matter. He couldn't have been further from Vivian's type, but there was something about Joe Mitchell that drew people to him like the pull of a magnet. A charisma that filled the space around him.

She had a feeling he was one of the good ones.

"Thank you," she mouthed to him when Graham wasn't looking.

He didn't mouth anything back, but instead he smiled at her, and that feeling came back, like a drop in her stomach.

Their gazes held for a moment, and then Graham said something about getting her another drink, gesturing to her now-empty one, and Vivian turned away, leaving Joe Mitchell behind her.

THREE

1968

Thirteen Hours Gone

V iv."

In the dream, Joe sat beside her on the bed, dressed in his flight suit, the one he'd worn before he'd started astronaut training, when they had been young and in love, and everything had been simultaneously more complicated and yet simpler.

Vivian lay in bed, Joe's back to her, staring at the slope of his shoulders, the bend in his spine as he put his flight boots on, as he prepared to leave her once more.

She slipped in and out of the dream, unsure if it was a moment she had created in her mind or a memory from one of their many goodbyes.

How many times had they done this dance? More than she could count, certainly. Her marriage was defined by these absences, by the dramatic goodbyes that often dictated the tenor of their marriage. After all, you couldn't be mad at your husband right before he went away when there was such a high chance that he wouldn't come back, or every time he went to work when just doing his job meant a likelihood of death, or when he was about to launch himself into space, going farther in the known universe than anyone ever had before, or—

"Viv."

The voice was louder now, her name—the nickname Joe called her—piercing through the haze of the dream, the déjà vu of it all, and then, urgently now—

"Vivian."

It returned to her in waves—the tension in her living room, the little pill someone had pressed in her palm telling her she looked like she needed to get some rest. Not a surprise since she hadn't slept more than an hour or two the night before while she waited for news of Joe after the initial launch. She'd lain down for a nap, the sleeping pill and exhaustion doing the rest, the kind of sleep that came over her so strongly it obliterated all else.

What had it been? Four hours? Five?

Her head pounded, the aftereffects of the medicine making her feel a bit fuzzy.

"Viv."

Vivian lurched out of bed. Her gaze rested on the squawk box on her dresser, the speaker NASA had given her so that she could hear radio communications between Joe and Mission Control when the spacecraft passed over their house in its orbit. NASA gave it to the wives when their husbands went into space, a way for them to stay connected, a story to share with the *Life* reporter they would have to speak with when the mission was done. They'd been cautioned that NASA would cut off the squawk box if something went wrong so the spouses wouldn't hear it, and it had been silent up until—

"Vivian."

It was unmistakable now—she'd recognize that sound anywhere—Joe's voice was coming from the squawk box.

He was alive.

Vivian rushed over to the box, her heart pounding as she stared at the speaker.

"Joe? Are you alright? What happened? Are you safe?"

The words escaped before she remembered what they'd told her about the squawk box. That she would be able to hear Joe, but he wouldn't be able to hear her. She willed him to say something else, to offer some explanation of what had happened, how his spacecraft had lost contact and how long before he would return to her.

Wait.

Based on what they'd told her, he wasn't supposed to be in range for another three days. She remembered it because she circled the day with a black marker on the little calendar that hung in their kitchen.

What had changed?

Why was she hearing from him now?

How was she hearing from him now?

The red phone NASA installed for her in addition to the squawk box sat on the nightstand, and she hurried over, her heart pounding as she lifted the handle and asked the operator to connect her to Frank's office at the Cape.

A man's voice echoed in her ear on the other end of the phone line.

"I need to talk to Frank Abbott, please," she said to the man who answered the call. "This is Vivian Mitchell."

She put more emphasis on her name than she normally would lest she be fobbed off to someone who was directed to "manage" her. There was an interesting dynamic between the space program and the spouses. They weren't employees the same way that their husbands were, of course, but it was understood that they were part of the package, that in some ways—at least in the image that they presented to the world, the support that they were meant to garner among their fellow Americans—the astronaut's family was almost as important as the astronauts themselves.

After all, there was a steady line of interchangeable fighter pilots and test pilots looking to go to space. The ones that had been chosen were the best of the best, but they also had the ability to convey a message of picture-perfect Americana that would make them heroes.

Their families were trotted out for media appearances and interviews, the wives meant to clothe themselves in glamorous dresses they received as gifts or on enormous discount, considering their husband's salaries hardly funded dressing like a movie star even if the expectation for them to resemble one existed. The wives were useful tools for the space program—their presence and efforts expected to generate positive press and public enthusiasm.

And conversely, while the shopping trips to Neiman Marcus and the like held a certain appeal to many of the wives, Vivian would bet her life's savings that nearly every single one of them would—if asked—say that they would much prefer their husbands have a different job, something staid and predictable like an accountant, or a dentist, or a postman, or really, nearly any other profession. Most importantly, a safe one.

"Frank's busy right now, but I can ask him to call you back," the voice on the line—one she didn't recognize— replied.

She glanced back at the squawk box, now resting silently.

"Please. I need to talk to Frank. Just for a minute."

She'd keep calling until they put her on the phone with Frank, a conclusion the man seemed to arrive at, because he sighed, sounding very much like he was sick of dealing with astronauts' wives.

"Let me see if I can find him."

Vivian propped the phone between her ear and her shoulder while she waited, using her free hands to pick up the phone receiver and carry it over to the dresser where the squawk box rested.

She stared at the device expectantly. Waited for it to emit another sound. Joe must know how worried she was, and she'd bet he kept saying her name to reassure her, because he understood how desperately she needed to know he was alright.

"Vivian."

This time, her name didn't come from the squawk box, but from the phone's receiver.

Finally.

If anyone would know what was going on, it would be Frank.

"Frank? Where is he? What happened? Is he alright?"

Silence filled the line.

"Frank?"

"Vivian, I'm sorry. We still don't know anything. I promise you that as soon as I hear something, I'll let you know. I need to go—"

"What are you talking about? Joe just spoke on the radio. You heard him, right? Surely, you're communicating with him. Did he tell you what happened? Is he safe? Are the comms back up?"

"Vivian. We haven't had any communication from the spacecraft."

That wasn't possible.

She stared at the squawk box, dread sinking in her stomach like a meteor. But no—she'd heard him clear as day. It had unmistakably been Joe saying her name.

Only Joe called her Viv in that tone of his that often had the capacity to make her forget about why she had been annoyed with him.

"I heard Joe on the radio. It came through on the squawk box that they brought over a couple of days ago. He said my name. A few times."

Definitely four. Or had it been five? Was one of them her dream, or had he said her name and had she incorporated the sound into her dream? How long had she slept through the sound of Joe speaking through the squawk box?

What if he had asked her for help? What if he had said something important and she'd missed it because she was asleep, dead to the world thanks to the pill she'd taken. Surely, they were recording this in Mission Control. Someone else had to be listening besides her.

"Vivian. I promise you—we're monitoring all communications coming from the spacecraft and there haven't been any. If Joe was speaking on the radio, we would hear it in Mission Control. There's just been silence. Occasionally, a faint static sound, but Vivian—we've been listening. We wouldn't have missed something like that."

"Well, you must have, because I'm telling you—he said my name as clearly as though he was sitting here right now. I know my husband's voice. At first, I thought I was dreaming, but then I woke up and I heard it, I heard *him*, coming from the box."

She could hear the rising note of panic with each word she spoke, and she tried hard to push it down, to remain as calm as possible. She'd learned throughout Joe's career that whether she was a military wife or an astronaut wife, they would often treat her as though she existed on the verge of hysteria, the level of calm and detachment that they demanded of her unnatural.

"Maybe you were still dreaming. It's been a rough few days. Did you see Doc Wyler? Did he give you something to help you sleep, maybe to calm your nerves? Those pills can pack a wallop—"

"I wasn't sleeping. I mean, I was, at first, but I woke up. The sound of Joe saying my name woke me up. I got out of bed, walked over to the dresser, and heard that thing"—she pointed at the squawk box, her hand shaking in midair—"say my name. It was Joe. Joe said my name. He called me Viv. No one else calls me Viv."

"We'll check the tapes," Frank replied. She'd been placated by enough men throughout her life to know that if he was going to check the tapes, it was only out of a sense of obligation and a desire to calm her down and not because he believed her or thought they were going to find anything there.

"Listen, Vivian—I need to go in a second, but while we're on the phone, there's the matter of a statement that we need to think of."

"A statement?"

"Some people—that's to say there are some who think we should get ahead of this by having you say some words. We're talking to the other families about the same thing. Nothing you'd write or anything. Just a prepared statement we would have you deliver in front of the press. We could maybe have you take a question or two that we could plant with one of the reporters we work with a lot. Someone you're comfortable with. Perhaps someone from *Life*."

Was he serious?

"I don't want to give a statement right now, Frank. I want you to find my husband."

"I understand that, and like I told you, we're trying, but there's the public to think about. The space program is important. The public admires Joe. They feel like they know him. They care about him—about you."

Vivian sort of doubted that the public cared much about her beyond the fact that she was Joe's wife, but she wasn't going to belabor the point.

"It would be helpful if you reminded the American people of how much Joe believed in this mission, of how committed you are as a family to the mission of going to the Moon. We think it would give people something to rally around. If you put on a brave face—we don't want them to get the wrong idea, to think that space flight is too dangerous," Frank continued. "We're so close to the Moon, Vivian. Joe wouldn't want anything to jeopardize that."

For a moment, she could do little more than stare at the phone—her husband was missing, *Frank's* best friend was missing, and Frank's priority was the space program.

"We'll draft something," Frank said, not waiting for her response. "I'll be in touch, Vivian."

He hung up before she had a chance to say anything at all.

Vivian set the phone back on its cradle. Was Frank right? Had she been so eager to hear from Joe that she had imagined the whole thing? Had she been dreaming? After all, it didn't make sense that Joe would be in range at this precise moment in time. The squawk box only worked at a certain point in Joe's voyage—they'd been over all this before. And still—she knew what she had heard. She'd heard her husband's voice as clearly as though he were standing here.

A knock sounded at the door.

"Vivian? Are you up? Can I come in?"

Vivian walked over to the door and opened it.

Polly stared at her over the threshold, closing the door behind her as she entered the room.

"You didn't change yet?" Polly asked.

Vivian glanced down at her outfit, belatedly realizing that she was wearing her launch dress from yesterday. She and Polly had bought it on a shopping trip together when they'd first learned Joe was going to pilot this mission.

A new dress will make you feel better, Polly had suggested as she dragged Vivian from store to store while dread filled her stomach.

"I—I meant to. It just slipped my mind."

Vivian placed her hand in her pocket, her fingers closing over the note that Joe had written her, the piece of paper Frank gave Joe before he boarded the spacecraft. She pulled the note out and read the words there again.

Wait for me.

When had Joe written this? Frank must have been mistaken—hardly surprising considering he was so focused on the launch—because there was no way this could have been the paper Joe took into the capsule. Had he slipped the paper into her pocket earlier in the day when she wasn't paying attention? But how? It didn't make sense—she hadn't even seen him in person the day of the flight.

"What's that?" Polly asked.

"It's a note Joe gave me. Before he left."

Polly shook her head, a faint smile on her lips. "Joe always did put the other men to shame. How are you doing after the nap, honey? Can you eat a late lunch? I must tell you, you have your choice of casseroles out there, although I'd advise against trying Cecilia Murphy's." Polly rolled her eyes. "Like we all don't know she can't cook."

Despite the horrors surrounding her, Vivian bit back a grin. Polly's rivalry with Cecilia was legendary in the astro circles.

"I don't think so. I'm not hungry."

"I know, but it would be good for you to keep your strength up." Polly hesitated. "I have to warn you, there are a lot of people in your living room."

"Define a lot of people?"

"Seven. No one wanted you to be alone right now." Polly made a face. "And Rick's still here, of course."

"To manage me for NASA."

"To be with you during this difficult time," Polly replied, her deadpan tone saying what she thought of the matter more than her words did. Frank may have been a company man where the space program was concerned, but Polly had never been afraid to voice her opinions, even if she did so carrying a casserole dish.

"Polly—I think I heard Joe's voice on the squawk box."

No, she wasn't going to do this now, wasn't going to let Frank's dismissiveness make her doubt herself. She'd learned that being a fighter pilot's wife and now an astro wife meant that there were times when no matter how much she was surrounded by people, she would be utterly alone, with only herself to rely upon. She'd learned that sometimes—too often—it felt like she was going up against the very institutions her husband belonged to. She needed to be strong, to advocate for herself, her family, her husband.

"No, I know I heard Joe's voice. He said my name. A few times."

Polly's entire demeanor transformed, and Vivian realized

just how tightly her friend had been holding on to her emotions. "Vivian, that's amazing. Mission Control was able to reestablish communication with the spacecraft?"

Vivian hesitated. "That's the thing—I just spoke with Frank. He said he hadn't heard anything."

"How is that possible? If you heard it on the squawk box, how could they have missed it? Don't they record these things? Maybe the communication problem is on their end, something in Mission Control."

"I don't know. Perhaps. I got the impression, though, that Frank thinks I imagined it or was dreaming."

"Oh, Vivian." Polly stepped forward and wrapped her arms around her. "I'm sure you didn't imagine it. Hopefully, he's out there and there's just a problem with the radio or something. You know how tricky these systems are. How much the guys complain about things going wrong when they're prepping for a launch. They'll get it figured out. They have to."

Joe had talked to her about how much pressure they were all under at work. Vivian had seen how Joe carried himself in the weeks and days leading up to the mission, although every time she'd asked him if everything was alright, he'd said that it was.

Had there been something else bothering him? A problem with the spacecraft he hadn't wanted her to know about?

"Frank wants me to give a statement," Vivian added. "To give the nation hope and to make the space program look good."

Anger flashed in Polly's gaze. "I wish I could say that I'm surprised, that your worry and grief are bigger than the space program, but, well, that's not true, is it?"

"'The mission comes first,'" they both echoed in unison,

their voices soft, but the words rote now for how much they had been drilled into them, how many times those words—spoken or not—had been given to them in moments of deep worry and pain, drowning out the hope that perhaps once—just this once—it wouldn't be the mission that won.

The mission came before wives, children, elderly parents, ill relatives, family weddings, holidays, vacations, first steps, and last breaths. It came before the dreams of every other member of the family. It came before moments that could never, ever be replaced, memories that could never be replicated.

They were often told it was what they had signed up for, which was a complete and total load of bullshit as far as Vivian was concerned. There was no road map for this life, and no timeline for it, either. It was constant and unending, more than one spouse buckling under the weight of it.

They also all knew that Vivian was spectacularly bad at it.

She glanced back at the squawk box, anger filling her as she remembered how quickly Frank had rushed her off the phone, how he'd dismissed the evidence she'd presented him with, years of being ignored and devalued, of watching the other spouses be forced to perform under immense pressure, tragedy, and heartache, culminating together in this moment of striking clarity. Of being forced to do the same herself.

"I don't want to give a statement. Talk to the press. Any of it. It feels like—" Something squeezed tightly in the vicinity of Vivian's heart. "It feels like they're laying the groundwork to accept that the spacecraft isn't recoverable, that they're already looking to the next mission, and they're more interested in safeguarding that than bringing Joe and the others home."

Polly glanced at the closed doorway behind them and then back at Vivian. She lowered her voice. "Then don't say the statement they want you to deliver. You're a journalist. You don't need someone to tell you how to feel, how to express yourself. And you don't need to be worried about carrying the space program's message for them. You go out there and you speak from your heart. You tell the public what you want them to know about Joe. What do you want to say?"

"I'm not—I'm not good at this stuff. I'm not good on camera, or with interviews. You know that."

"Then you're going to have to be," Polly replied. "For Joe. And for yourself. If you're going to address the world, we'd better get you ready."

Polly strode over to Vivian's closet, flipping through the clothes hanging there before she settled on a dress that they'd bought on the same trip when they'd purchased her launch outfit. This one was a sedate navy.

At the time, neither one of them had spoken it aloud—there were some things you just didn't discuss, whether it was a test flight, or a combat mission, or a trip to the Moon—but they'd both understood what they were doing, had both known that the navy dress would be saved for an occasion such as this one, a moment in time when Vivian might be forced to face the world and address the terrifying part of her husband's job.

She'd hoped she would never have an occasion to wear it.

Vivian glanced back at the squawk box.

She would give anything to hear her name once more.

Silence greeted her instead.

Where was Joe?

FOUR

1961

Are you covering the launch?"

Vivian glanced up. Graham Carlson stood over her desk in the newsroom, a cup of coffee in hand.

She shook her head in response to his question, her voice momentarily failing her.

"For you," Graham said, holding the coffee out to her. "I wasn't sure what you'd like, but I took a guess and went with black with a splash of milk, no sugar."

Had she fallen asleep? Was she dreaming? That felt like the only explanation to account for Graham Carlson bringing her coffee.

He smiled. "You look like you could use it," he added, not unkindly. "Long night?"

She wasn't dreaming.

Vivian straightened in her seat, fighting the urge to run her fingers through her hair. No wonder he thought she needed coffee—she most definitely had fallen asleep at her desk, hardly surprising considering she'd spent the last twenty-four hours working on a story.

"Thank you," Vivian murmured, her cheeks heating as she took the coffee mug from him. She looked around the newsroom. It wasn't the first time they'd spoken since Joe had introduced them at the bar a few weeks ago; Graham had been kind enough to give her a couple of opportunities to work on some of his stories. Still, she couldn't help but wonder: Was anyone watching their interaction and wondering why one of the station's most prominent on-air talents was bringing a lowly assistant coffee?

For the most part, their coworkers seemed preoccupied with preparing for today's space launch. This morning, Alan Shepard—one of the Mercury Seven, America's first group of astronauts—was set to become the first American in space. They'd attempted to send Shepard to space three days earlier, but bad weather had forced them to scrub the launch, a collective sigh of disappointment echoing around the world—well, besides the Soviets, who no doubt relished each setback in the Americans' space ambitions.

Vivian had hoped she would get a chance to work in the newsroom considering it was *the* story that had the entire nation—and the world—riveted, but instead she'd found herself assigned to a murder at an apartment complex in Arlington. It had her working for a full day straight, only catching a few hours of sleep on one of the couches they crashed on in the newsroom, the sleep deficit catching up to her so much that she was now falling asleep at her desk.

She took a sip of the coffee, the jolt of caffeine a much-needed boost to her system. "It was a long night."

"The murder in Arlington?" Graham guessed, as though he had his finger on the various stories that pulsed through the newsroom.

Vivian nodded, taking another long sip of the coffee, suitably impressed that he'd managed to accurately guess her preference.

"I'm leaving the station soon," he announced, his voice quiet, but still casual.

Surprise filled her. "I didn't know."

"Most people don't. Jerry's going to announce it to everyone soon," he said, referring to the station's president.

"I won't say anything to anyone. Are you moving out of town, then?"

"I appreciate it." He smiled. "I'll still be in D.C., just going to a different network."

He named one of their biggest rivals; it would certainly be a blow for the newsroom to lose him to a competitor.

A voice interrupted them. "Vivian—"

They both turned their heads as Kerry Krieger, one of the few female reporters who worked at the newsroom, walked toward them. She looked as tired as Vivian felt, the twenty-four hours that they'd spent working the murder together obviously taking its toll.

Kerry gave Graham a clipped nod in greeting, before turning her attention toward Vivian.

"You did great work today. The questions you wrote for me to ask the woman who discovered the body—they were good.

It's a delicate balance getting the facts and emotion out to our viewers, and you did a nice job with both."

"Thank you," Vivian replied, fighting—and succeeding—from keeping the giddiness that filled her at the uncharacteristic praise from one of the station's most veteran reporters.

Kerry didn't have the same level of celebrity as Graham, but she didn't give the indication that she wanted it, either. She kept her head down, her no-nonsense attitude drawing Vivian's notice and admiration. Kerry seemingly cared about the work more than the accolades it brought, and the fact that she thought Vivian had done a good job on the first story they worked on together meant everything.

Kerry didn't wait for Vivian to say anything else before she was striding off, presumably in search of her next story.

One day I'm going to be like that, Vivian vowed to herself. *One day.*

"Would you like to get coffee sometime?"

Graham's question tore her attention away from Kerry's retreating back. He'd leaned in a bit closer to her since Kerry had walked away, the tone of his voice a bit lower than it had been when he told Vivian he was leaving the station.

Was he—

Was Graham Carlson asking her out for coffee as . . . a date?

It was unlikely. Impossible. And yet, by the look he was sending her—the interest there—combined with the fact that he was famously single, the consummate bachelor, well, it did indeed seem like he was asking her out. Except she had never heard any whisper of him being involved with someone at work, and—

"After I leave the station," Graham clarified. He looked around for a moment, and then pulled back as though he realized the impression he might be giving the rest of the newsroom. "I wouldn't want to do anything to cause gossip. I know how things can spread." He inclined his head toward the direction Kerry had gone. "It sounds like you're doing great work. I don't want us going for coffee together to give people the wrong impression. I know how hard it can be to be taken seriously in this industry, and I imagine for a young woman even more so."

Several things hit her all at once—

The way he said "young woman" cemented the fact that he was decades older than her—two decades, if she had to guess. He was charismatic, the energy surrounding him so vibrant that the age difference didn't jump out at her first, but it was also impossible to ignore. And despite the respect and admiration she felt for him, the way she'd looked up to him for so long—perhaps because of it—Vivian had never once considered him in a romantic light, as someone she would think of *dating*. He was practically a national treasure, an institution. It would be like dating the Washington Monument.

But he stood there, his expression hopeful, expectant, and in a moment, her perception of him shifted, from the public persona to the man, and as far as men went, he was intelligent, polite, considerate, handsome. They had a great deal in common considering their shared passion for journalism, and as far as reasons to agree to go on a date with someone, well—she could think of worse ones.

The date would have to wait until after he'd left the station, of course. The last thing Vivian wanted to do was to give the impression to someone like Kerry Krieger that she was trying to date her way into her career. So she surprised him, and perhaps even herself, when she replied quietly—

"I'd like that."

"WE'RE HAVING A SPACE PARTY," POLLY ANNOUNCED AS Vivian walked into the apartment. A bottle of champagne dangled from Polly's hands.

Vivian glanced over at the clock in the hallway, confusion filling her. It certainly had been an unusual morning what with Graham Carlson asking her on a date and now—

"It's—it's eight in the morning."

Polly smiled. "I know it's early for champagne, and I considered diluting it with orange juice, but then I thought 'where's the fun in that?' If you can't have champagne in the morning when the first American man launches himself into space, then when can you?"

Polly had certainly dressed with a space theme in mind. Her silver mod dress and matching go-go boots looked straight out of a sci-fi flick. On her head, she'd fashioned a matching silver headband with little foil protrusions no doubt meant to resemble stars.

Vivian grinned despite the exhaustion wearing her down. If anyone could carry off such an ensemble, it was Polly. She had the uncanny ability to take outfits that would seem utterly ridiculous on anyone else and make them look like she was walking off the pages of *Vogue*.

"A space party?" Vivian asked, setting her purse down on

the little entry table she'd rescued after someone set it out on the curb. With a bit of love and care, she'd been able to turn it into a piece that looked good in their apartment and brightened up the space.

"We have space-themed food as well."

"Space-themed food?"

"Nothing too fancy," Polly replied. "I cut little tea sandwiches into the shape of rockets." She frowned. "I'll admit, they didn't come out as well as I'd hoped. I've been working on them since seven."

Polly must have seen the exhaustion on Vivian's face, because she quickly added—

"I'm sorry. I know this is last-minute. I wasn't planning on hosting, but then people started asking me what I was doing and if I wanted to watch the launch, and, well, it seemed like a fun idea for a bunch of us to watch it here.

"I should have talked to you about it, and I did try calling the station, but they said you were out on a story. I wasn't sure if you would be back in time. I thought we could have the apartment back to normal before you even noticed." Polly grinned. "But now that you're home, you'll join us, right? Please. It'll be so much more fun if you're here."

"I'm not dressed for a party," Vivian protested, the little round mirror in their entryway confirming that she did indeed look exhausted, her skin pale, dark circles forming under her eyes. Whatever makeup she had put on when she went to work had worn off. Normally, she wouldn't care too much, but coupled with the fact that her mind felt hazy from lack of sleep, a party hardly seemed like the best idea.

"Nonsense. You look beautiful like you always do." Polly's gaze narrowed speculatively. "I'll help you fix your hair. And I have the perfect dress for you. I couldn't decide if I should wear it or this one. Besides, Frank is coming. You always like him. He's bringing his friend Joe, too."

Later, in the privacy of her room, Vivian would dissect why that fact was salient, and why it had her asking—

"Is the dress also space-themed?"

"It's the color of the surface of the Moon," Polly replied with a wink.

Vivian hesitated, her heart pounding. "Well, in that case, how can I refuse?"

Polly grinned. "I was hoping you would say that. Let's get you ready."

POLLY FLIPPED ON CBS NEWS AND THE GROUP CROWDED around the little television in their living room, the stand another item Vivian had rescued and refurbished until the wood gleamed. She'd never considered herself particularly crafty or handy, but after a childhood spent drifting from apartment to apartment, never staying anywhere long enough to put down roots, there was something immensely satisfying about building a home that was all her own.

Most of the guests were strangers to Vivian, friends of Polly's from the hospital and the athletic club she liked to frequent. It didn't bother Vivian, though. Maybe it was the same trait that had propelled her toward journalism, but she liked being in a room surrounded by people she didn't know. You were under no obligation to perform that way, could simply fade into the background and drift from group to group with casual ease. You got the measure of people by watching them in settings like these, seeing how they interacted with others, in the way they carried themselves. There was something comforting in learning what made them tick.

Once again, Vivian's gaze drifted toward the wall, where Joe stood in conversation with Frank.

Polly and Frank had been inseparable since the night they met, and Frank had become a frequent visitor to the apartment. Vivian liked him a great deal. He was straightforward, honest, and clearly enamored of her roommate.

Today he'd brought Joe along as well. Joe's sling was gone, and it looked like whatever injuries he'd sustained from his motorcycle accident had mostly healed. Vivian barely had a chance to exchange more than a quick hello with Joe before he was swept up in another group.

Walter Cronkite's voice filled the room as he reported on the launch from Cape Canaveral, and Vivian's attention shifted from Joe to the legendary news anchor.

You could hear the gravitas in Cronkite's tone, but today there was something else there—an excitement that mirrored that of everyone in the room. For all the influential stories he'd covered in his illustrious career, it was clear that Cronkite understood the magnitude and importance of the moment before him. No one watching or listening to the launch could doubt that history was being made, and for all of Vivian's skepticism about the enormous cost of the space program, the enthusiasm was infectious. How much were their lives about to change because of this space exploration?

"Everything looks good," Frank murmured more to himself than anyone else in the room as they went through the final checks, ten minutes to liftoff. His body moved from side to side, his gaze riveted on the television.

Polly stood beside him, her arm wrapped around his elbow, holding him steady, as though keeping him from leaping into the television and inserting himself in the scene occurring before them by sheer force of will.

Vivian's gaze drifted from Polly and Frank, to Joe. He'd moved from where he'd been standing in conversation with the couple to a spot in the corner where he was now largely alone.

As active as his friend was, Joe was still, his focus wholly on the scene playing before him. Vivian wasn't sure she'd ever seen anyone look as alone as he did in that moment, and it was silly, of course—she barely knew the man—but she took a step forward, had to catch herself from walking over to him.

There was something that tugged at her—perhaps it was the contrast between the man she had seen holding court at the bar a few weeks ago, the man who had seemed so confident, so at-home in his skin, the man who seemed to crave social interaction, and the man who looked so very alone now, as though there were a wall erected around him that kept everyone else at bay.

"T-minus six minutes and counting," the reporter announced.

A few gasps and exclamations erupted through the group, a dozen people swelling to the sensation of many more, thanks to the energy emanating like a ripple that carried its way through the room.

Polly gripped Frank's arm more tightly.

Vivian glanced back at the television, focusing on the Redstone rocket that would propel Alan Shepard on his suborbital flight. It looked so small on television; it was hard to imagine someone willingly putting their body in such an object and hurtling through space. The claustrophobia alone would terrify her. But she supposed if you'd spent your career as a fighter pilot or a test pilot, as all the astronauts had, then you were used to such things whether it was air or space.

Her gaze traveled to Joe once more.

Their conversation came back to her, the way he had spoken about flying, about the space program. And now—he looked at that rocket carrying an astronaut into space with something akin to the deepest longing, and she knew with a certainty that resided in her bones that if she asked him at this very moment what he wanted more than anything in this world, his answer would be to be strapped into that rocket, heading for space.

"Liftoff."

There were cheers all around her, the relief of a crowd who had spent the last three weeks and scrubbed launches wondering if they were going to ever be able to catch up to the Soviets after Yuri Gagarin had beat them to it. She hadn't realized how badly the nation had needed this until now.

Once again, her gaze drifted to Joe. He stood there quietly, somehow removed from the proceedings, his mouth slightly agape as he watched the rocket soar through the sky. He rocked back on his heels for a moment as though he were experiencing the thrust himself, and then he turned his head.

The longing in his eyes—

Their gazes connected, and that feeling tumbled through her again—the one she couldn't describe and wasn't sure she wanted to try—and Vivian felt as though she'd been knocked back on her heels as well.

The moment stretched on, past the kind of polite gaze that could be expected at a gathering such as this one until Vivian couldn't take it anymore, and she glanced away, her attention returning to the broadcast, her heart pounding madly, her skin surely flushed.

She'd thought about him more than she cared to admit in the weeks since they'd met, snippets of their conversation in the bar sneaking up on her in the most unpredictable moments. The fact that she'd spent more time dissecting their conversation than they'd actually spoken wasn't something she was particularly proud of. She couldn't explain it. Any of it. He couldn't have been further from her type. And the sinking, dropping feeling in her stomach that she got when she was around him—the one that reminded her of riding a roller coaster on a trip to Coney Island—was singularly unpleasant.

And yet, here she was, wearing Polly's Moon-colored dress, her hair freshly coiffed, makeup on her face, palms slightly damp, her nerves pinging around the room so much that she finally took a glass of champagne solely for the fact that it gave her something to occupy her hands with.

"Can you imagine what it must be like?" one of the guests asked. "That has to be the most amazing feeling."

"He's on top of the world right now," another guest quipped, laughter rippling through their little group.

When Vivian was in college, the world was introduced to the "Mercury Seven," the seven astronauts who were to take Americans to space. The astronauts had seemed so confident—cocky, even—when they spoke of the mission, when they addressed the dangers associated with it.

At the same time, their wives were launched onto the world stage, becoming instant celebrities, and Vivian had wondered what sort of woman would choose a life like that, how they would possibly navigate both the danger of their husband's job and the fact that they were supposed to do so while caring for their families and appearing as though it were all effortless on magazine covers and during press conferences.

What was it like for Alan's wife, Louise, left behind on the ground? How could she stand there knowing the inherent danger that awaited him and wondering if her husband was about to perish while the whole world watched?

The entire room seemingly held its collective breath for the fifteen-minute space flight, nerves frayed as Shepard navigated reentry, and ultimately, splashdown.

For the woman who loved him, fifteen minutes must feel like an eternity.

And then it was over—and everyone was toasting with champagne even though it wasn't yet ten o'clock in the morning.

Polly embraced Vivian, clinking their champagne flutes together with an ebullient "cheers."

"Thank you," Polly whispered in Vivian's ear. "I know how

tired you are from work, but thanks for going along with this. It was fun, right?"

"It was fun. I'm glad you suggested it." Vivian hesitated, more than a little embarrassed. "Have you seen Joe?"

Polly's brow arched. "Is that how it is?"

Vivian flushed. "I just wanted to thank him for introducing me to Graham Carlson. I didn't get a chance the night we met, and there wasn't an opportunity when he arrived today to do more than say 'hello,' but I wanted to express my gratitude."

"Hmm. Well, I think he went out on the balcony." Polly grinned. "And you have my full support should you be so inclined to not just express your gratitude for the work introduction. He's a nice man. Frank couldn't speak more highly of him."

Vivian wove her way through the crowded living room, where most people were still watching the television and the coverage of the Freedom 7 launch. She walked past them and headed toward the small balcony off their apartment.

Joe stood outside, his back to her as he took in the city skyline before him.

As far as views went, it wasn't the most beautiful one, but it was theirs, and Vivian often found herself going out there when she needed to think or take a moment to herself.

Joe appeared to be deep in thought because he startled when she opened the door.

"Sorry, I didn't mean to interrupt you," Vivian replied as she closed the door behind herself, feeling guilty for having intruded on his private moment.

"It's no trouble." A self-conscious smile flashed across Joe's mouth. "I'm out here feeling sorry for myself, if you must know.

I think I'd prefer the company to my wallowing." He glanced back up at the sky. "It's amazing to think of all that's out there above us, isn't it? I studied engineering, so I'm supposed to look at this space business with a scientific, practical eye, but damn, it's hard to do so when you think of all the possibilities, of the vastness of the universe. The absolute heartbreaking beauty of it all."

"There you go being romantic again," she joked, although the words escaped on little more than a whisper that was nearly lost to the wind, because he was close to irresistible when he talked like that.

She needed to thank him quickly and then she needed to go back inside.

Before she had a chance to collect herself enough to speak, Joe broke the silence between them once more.

"When we met at the bar, I told you I was going to test pilot school."

Vivian didn't understand the significance of what he was saying, the nuances between a test pilot and the fighter pilot unclear to her, but she could see that whatever those differences were, they were incredibly important to him, and he wanted her to know it.

"When I graduated from West Point and commissioned in the Air Force, I knew I wanted to fly. Hell, I've known I wanted to fly since I was a little boy and my uncle took me to a fair. I was six years old, and there was this man doing stunt flying in his little biplane, and it was the coolest thing I'd ever seen. The pilot was nice, and he took me up with him, and I never wanted to come down.

"From that moment on, there was nothing else I wanted to do. I used to run around the fields of my aunt and uncle's farm with my arms out in the air pretending I was an airplane, used to sit on hay bales and imagine I was piloting my own."

This really had been a terrible idea.

Because as he said it, she could envision it—a little boy whose exuberant smile matched the fairly devastating one on his face now. And it was that enthusiasm, that passion, that tugged at her once more.

"If I'm being honest, it's why I joined the military—so I could fly. I love flying, have been lucky enough to do it now for over a decade," Joe added. "But when they announced that they would be sending astronauts into space a few years ago—that was it. I was hooked."

He wanted to be an astronaut.

Of course.

Now she understood why he had looked at Alan Shepard's launch the way he had, the longing in his gaze.

A thought rose in her unbidden—

That it must be an extraordinary thing to be loved by a man who felt things so deeply, so passionately, that he devoted his life to a vocation with such singularity.

Or was his love for flying, for his dreams of space, so great that there was room for little else?

She really should thank him for the introduction and be done with it.

And still, she stayed, ensnared.

"There are a few requirements to becoming an astronaut. You have to be under forty—I'm thirty-three."

He was a full decade older than her.

Vivian wasn't surprised, necessarily. The thing about your first job out of college was that you frequently found yourself to be the youngest person in the room. She'd gotten used to that part. More alarming was the fact that many of her friends from college were already engaged or married, and she definitely didn't feel ready to be married now—or possibly ever.

"You can't be taller than five feet, eleven inches." Joe grinned. "I'm pushing that one a little bit, but I'm good to go."

God, his grin was infectious.

It transformed his whole face, his entire demeanor, and the recipient of it—well, she was pretty sure she felt it all the way to her toes.

"You have to be in excellent physical condition . . ."

Thankfully, he didn't say anything, but then again, he didn't need to. No one would look at him and question that one.

She could feel her cheeks burning.

Joe didn't take his eyes off her, and the heat in his gaze told her everything she needed to know—he enjoyed her reaction, knew she wasn't immune to the figure he cut.

Joe took a step forward, as though seizing on the opportunity, just as Vivian took an answering step back, putting more distance between them.

Confusion flickered in his gaze, but he remained where he was, giving Vivian the space she needed.

"You must have a bachelor's degree or its equivalent," Joe added. "Luckily, they were nice enough to give me my engineering degree at West Point despite my best efforts to get into trouble."

That he was smart—and self-deprecating—only made everything worse.

Vivian gripped her champagne flute more tightly, needing something to occupy her hands, to keep from reaching out—

"You need fifteen hundred hours of flying time," Joe continued, reciting the list of NASA's requirements for the astronaut program with the familiarity of someone who had gone over it many, many times. "That one was easy, all things considered."

"Where have you been stationed?" Vivian asked, wanting to know more about him, about his life, even about his career, because she now understood that the two could not be separated, that being a pilot wasn't just what he did, but who he was. And perhaps he did have an ego about his job, but there was more to him than just his swagger, and it was those parts of him—the depths he showed her the more they spoke, the emotions he wore so plainly on his face—that made her want to know more, cockiness be damned.

"I started flying T-6s at Columbus Air Force Base in Mississippi. I got lucky and tracked to fighters, which was always the plan, but considering how competitive it was, I worried a time or two that I would end up flying something else."

He said the part about worrying whether he would get fighters with the same self-deprecation he'd adopted throughout their conversation, but there was a false note to his words, the sentiment not quite aligning with the determination in his gaze when he spoke about his career. Vivian would have bet anything that as soon as Joe decided he wanted to become a fighter pilot, he moved mountains to do so, and given the intensity that radiated off him, she didn't really believe that he'd ever considered failure to be a possibility.

"I found myself doing what I'd always wanted to do, what I loved. I bounced around several bases, flew a few different airframes, spent some time flying in Korea. Before my assignment to Edwards, I was at Luke Air Force Base in Phoenix flying the F-100."

How much longer would he be here? His injuries seemed mostly healed. Surely, he would be returning to his home on the other side of the country soon.

They'd likely never see each other again.

"And of course, the last requirement is that an astronaut must be a graduate of test pilot school." Joe gestured toward his injured arm. "I was out here on leave visiting family right before my class started. Thanks to my recklessness, well, I missed the class because the doctors still haven't cleared me to fly."

He delivered the "thanks to my recklessness" line as though he was parroting something that had been said to him. The military probably didn't take too kindly to their pilots injuring themselves racing motorcycles, although she had to imagine that in his line of work, Joe wasn't the first or last fighter pilot to take such risks.

"Did you get in trouble for the accident?"

Joe grimaced. "Let's just say it wasn't the best thing for my career. They're talking about sending me to a fighter squadron in Europe since they don't want to keep me sitting around waiting for another opening in a test pilot class, and my dreams of going to space, well, I don't think it's meant to be. I always knew an astronaut slot wasn't a guarantee, and as much as that was the end goal, I'll admit test pilot school was compelling in its own right."

"What was it that inspired you to want to be a test pilot?"

Strange how badly she wanted to know.

"I confess, I don't really understand the distinction," Vivian added.

"The flying we do now, the limits that we test—it came from the pilots—military and civilian—who were risking everything to push the boundaries of human flight by testing new technology and possibilities. Men like Chuck Yeager who were daring enough to break the sound barrier, who were willing to risk their lives to test new aircraft and systems, evaluate their—and our—capabilities. I want to be part of that legacy. I want to push the limits of what I can do."

She waited for him to elaborate, but she got the sense that he was holding back, as though there were elements of being a test pilot that he *couldn't* talk about because of the secrecy that surrounded such experimental work.

"In a career that is probably more dangerous than ninety-nine percent of the jobs out there, you were looking for something even *more* dangerous," she returned.

He laughed. "It sounds a little ill-advised when you put it like that. But basically, yes."

"Have you ever thought of having a safer, more boring job?"

"Like what, an actuary? You're killing me here."

She felt more than a little sorry for whoever he finally settled down with. He was undoubtedly a heartbreaker, and Vivian couldn't imagine what it would be like to be with a man who was always chasing danger. Exhausting, terrifying. Not to mention the added complication of there being elements of his job he wouldn't be able to share with others.

"I'm sorry. I could see—watching you during the launch—I could tell that something was bothering you."

"I debated not coming today," Joe admitted. "I didn't think I would be good company. I had grand plans to watch it at my cousins' house, but then Frank told me there was a chance you would be here. I came over a few times with him to see Polly, but you were never home," he added, almost as an afterthought.

He'd wanted to see her? It was surprising, and yet, if she was being honest, part of why she had thought about him so often through the last few weeks was that she had somehow known that she would see him again. And not just because of his connection to Frank and Frank's relationship with Polly, but because it felt like they'd started a conversation that night at the bar that they were somehow meant to finish.

"I—I didn't know. Polly didn't say anything."

"I know. I didn't ask about you—I should have."

What did that mean?

Was it possible that two men were expressing their interest in her in the same morning? It felt too bizarre to contemplate, considering it had never happened before, and she hadn't exactly been inundated with dates in college. And yet, she couldn't ignore what he'd just said—

I didn't ask about you—I should have.

Vivian wanted to press him on it, to know why he didn't ask about her, but he spoke again before she could get her thoughts in order.

"I was curious how things were going with you at work. How is the television business?" Joe asked.

"It's going well. I never thanked you that night—what you did introducing me to Graham. I really appreciated it. It's hard to break into this business. Harder still when you're a woman, and you're young, and no one wants to hire you for anything other than fetching coffee no matter the degree you attained."

"It was my pleasure. Did it help?"

"It did. I've done some background research for a few stories Graham has reported on. I think seeing that someone of his stature trusts me has given other reporters the impetus to offer me more opportunities around the newsroom."

"Good for him. He's a good man."

"Yes, he is."

It felt strange mentioning Graham to Joe, considering the coffee date they'd agreed to earlier in the newsroom—an interaction she still couldn't believe—especially in light of what Joe had just told her.

I didn't ask about you—I should have.

Silence fell between them, and then—

"I confess, when I watch the news now, I wonder which stories you've worked on," Joe added after a moment, the grin tugging at the corners of his mouth sending a thrill through her.

Vivian smiled even as she fought the fierce instinct to blush. "I appreciate the vote of confidence. I worked on a story with this reporter last night—Kerry Krieger—she's amazing. At the end of it, she told me I had done good work, and it felt like maybe the dream isn't so out of reach. Like I might have a shot at this. I want to have a career that makes a difference."

"You will. You're easy to talk to." Joe looked slightly abashed by the admission. "I'm not saying that as a line or something. I know how it sounds. But you are—you have a way of making people feel comfortable confiding in you. I know you just made me feel better right now."

"I didn't do anything, really."

"You listened. The frustration I'm feeling—all of it—I haven't even told Frank. I haven't told anyone. It was nice to be able to tell you."

"When will you know about Europe—if you're being sent there?"

Joe was silent for a beat, tearing his gaze away from her and looking out over the skyline once more. "Soon. My orders should be cut any day now. It's all but a done deal."

"Where in Europe?"

"Italy. Aviano Air Base. It's a couple hours north of Venice."

"That sounds lovely. I've always wanted to go to Venice. I checked out this photography book from the library when I was a kid and the pictures of the canals—it was like nothing I'd ever seen. I always told myself I would go there someday. How long will you be stationed there?"

"Two, three years, maybe. It's hard to predict. You tend to go where the military sends you for however long they want you to be there." Joe was silent for a beat. "I probably have a week or two before I leave, and I was wondering if you'd like to get a drink sometime. Have a proper date."

His gaze met hers once more, and he studied her with that same earnestness he'd displayed when he looked at the rocket soaring into space.

He was moving to Italy for years.

Her job was here. Her life was here.

And most importantly, well—

"My father served in the war." Vivian said it quietly, like it was a secret, which in essence it was because it was a part of her life she never talked about, but she wanted to tell him, needed him to understand. "The Second World War. He was in Europe. He didn't come home. He was a pilot."

Just like the sight of Alan Shepard launching into space had him rocking back on his heels, Joe absorbed her announcement with the same reaction.

"He flew fighters," Vivian added, that familiar tightness filling her chest. "I was six years old when he died."

She barely remembered him, and that was one of the cruelest parts of all. Vivian had flashes here and there, moments from her childhood that she wasn't sure were real memories or products of her imagination, inventions designed to fill in so many blanks. Sometimes she thought that those blanks existed because there were things she didn't want to remember, incidents that were simply too painful. She remembered the idea of him, what he had represented to her, but she couldn't recall the details that felt important.

Joe didn't say anything aloud, but there was something steady in his gaze that gave her the confidence to continue.

"His death was the single worst thing that has ever happened to me. He was—" She searched for the right words to describe what her father had meant to her, the effect that his presence had on her, on their home. "He was my best friend, my family, my home. My mother—" Vivian swallowed. "My mother was complicated. I never quite knew where I stood with her. She could be happy one moment and it felt like everything was wonderful, and then something would set her off, something no one even realized, and all that happiness would turn into a cloud that made me want to go into the closet in my bedroom and hide until the storm passed.

"My happiest moments were when my father was home with us. He would take me out of the house when she would get upset. It was like he knew that I just needed to get away. She was happier when he was home, too."

"And after your father died, were things still difficult with your mother?"

It was the worry in his voice that undid her. The way he asked the question as though he really cared about her answer, as if he needed to hear that there was a happy ending to her story.

"She didn't—I don't think she enjoyed spending time with me when I was younger. I was always too loud, too clingy, too needy. It was easier as I grew older, as I learned to become the version that she wanted me to be. She liked me better when I didn't need things from her, when I didn't expect things from her. And I learned not to rely on her. Not to rely on anyone."

Perhaps it was too much to tell him so early on, certainly more than she'd ever told anyone, really. And yet—there was something between them. She'd never felt anything like it before, but it was here and she recognized it, knew he did, too, by the way he looked at her, and so it felt important to put a pin in this, to explain that despite whatever connection she felt between them, she wouldn't be going on a date with him.

A line formed between his brows. "Was there no one else—"

"No. We lost touch with my father's parents after he died. I'm not sure why, to be honest. I always got the impression that they weren't particularly fond of my mother and the way she lived her life. After his funeral, I never saw them again. And her parents? They died when she was young. I never knew them.

"She was an only child, so it was just the two of us. We'd moved around while my father was in the military, and then after he died, we moved around even more. She remarried, and divorced, and remarried again, and divorced, and remarried again—and I suppose I just got used to being on my own. It was easier that way."

Vivian smiled despite the sad tone their conversation had taken. "I am a tremendously boring person at heart. I don't get lonely. I don't yearn for the company of others. Give me a book or some paints and I can happily spend the entire weekend ensconced on my own."

"Or a good television show," he added, clearly remembering what she had told him the night they met about what had drawn her to a career in television.

"Yes. Exactly."

A moment of understanding passed between them, the intensity of it surprising her. She studied him for a beat, as though she could figure out what quality he possessed that made her share so much, so quickly.

"I'm sorry." Vivian flushed. "I shouldn't have told you all that. You were probably just looking for a polite 'yes' or 'no' to your question, and instead you got my entire life story," she joked, embarrassment settling inside her.

"Don't apologize. I would very much like to hear the rest of your life story sometime. To know you better. I don't—" Now it was his turn to look frustrated, to break off and turn away from her. "Like I said earlier. It's easy to talk to you. You don't— I feel differently with you than I do with other people. It's the strangest thing."

Vivian nodded, because she felt the same inexplicable way, too, and then she realized he couldn't see it because he was looking out at the city and not at her.

"Is your mother gone, too, now?" Joe asked her, his gaze off in the distance, trained on some point that she couldn't see.

"No, she's still alive. It just feels like that relationship, that part of my life belongs to someone else. I started working as early as I possibly could, and I saved up enough money so that I could leave when I was eighteen to go to college. We haven't really kept in touch. Last I heard she was living in Atlantic City."

"You're on your own."

"Yes."

Joe was silent for a moment, his back still to her. "My parents and my sister died when I was little. A car accident. I was in the car with them. It was a miracle that I survived—I was thrown from the car. A driver in a passing vehicle saw me on the roadside and got help."

"I'm so sorry." She reached out, unable to resist laying her hand on his arm to give comfort.

The muscles of his forearm tensed beneath her touch, and she pulled her hand back like she'd reached for a hot stove, curling her fingers into a little fist by her side.

Vivian swallowed. "How old were you?"

He turned to face her. "Six years old. My aunt and uncle—my mother's brother—took me in and raised me."

Ah.

Was that it? Did the sense of recognition she felt when she was around him come from the fact that they both lost so much at such a young age? It made more sense than any other explanation she could come up with. After all, growing up, she'd always struggled to see her experience reflected in that of her friends and their families. When she'd gone off to college, it had been difficult to explain to her roommates that she was going to spend her school breaks working rather than traveling home to visit family. That she would have a far happier holiday on her own than she ever would with her mother.

"Do you see, then? Why us having a drink together—or something more—would never work? Why I can't?" Vivian asked him, hoping he understood why she had told him about her father and the rest of it, why there was no point in this going any further.

"Yes. I think I do." Joe shook his head as though he had found himself the butt of a grand joke the universe had decided to play on him. "In a way, I understand. I like my life the way it is. I love flying planes. I enjoy moving around the world. I love having the freedom to pick up and go where I need to go without worrying too much about anything other than how I'm going to get from point A to point B. And when I'm up in the air, when I'm flying, what makes me such a good pilot, what makes me a great pilot—"

There was no arrogance in the way he delivered the line, a

lofty achievement considering she doubted very few men could call themselves great and get away with it.

"—is that I'm not afraid of dying. There's nothing on the ground keeping me tethered, no one waiting for me, no one for me to come back to. I'm not looking for anything else. I don't want anything else."

He delivered the words with a quiet ferocity that suggested he wasn't just trying to convince her, but maybe himself as well.

Perhaps she should have taken offense at how definitively he said he wasn't looking for someone in his life, since he'd just asked her on a date, but she understood completely.

Neither one of them was interested in romantic entanglements, was looking to find love or even a relationship.

And still—he'd asked her out on a date.

Vivian glanced up at the sky above them, the words she searched for floating up until they hovered just above her grasp.

"There's no hope, then?" Joe asked after a silence that stretched on and on. "For us, I mean. No grand love affair around the corner," he joked, even if the humor didn't quite meet his eyes.

"I suppose not," she replied, struggling to match his playful tone, because the way he said "grand love affair," even though his tone was light, teasing, made her more than a little regretful that she was missing out on something grand indeed.

FIVE

1968
One Day Gone

Mrs. Mitchell, do you believe your husband is alive?"

Vivian glanced up, a flashbulb exploding in her face, the brightness momentarily obscuring her vision.

"Look over here, Mrs. Mitchell," a photographer shouted at her.

Her head swiveled more out of reflex than anything else.

Another flashbulb.

"Frank," Vivian murmured, reaching out to grab hold of his arm, searching for something to steady her in this melee.

Frank had assured her that he had spoken with the press in advance, that the questions would be friendly, that she had nothing to worry about. Judging by the frenzy of reporters and photographers camped out on her front lawn, Frank had severely misjudged the situation before them.

"Can we have a picture, please, Mrs. Mitchell?" another photographer asked, his tone a bit gentler than the first. "A smile to reassure everyone."

"Do you think your husband is alive, Mrs. Mitchell?" the first reporter shouted again, his tone more insistent now.

She understood they were just doing their jobs—how many times had she found herself covering a story that represented the most difficult moments a person could face? Countless. And yet, now that she was on the other end of the camera, she hoped she had exercised more care in those moments than was being afforded to her now.

"Do you believe that this was an accident?" another reporter shouted. "Was there perhaps some operator error involved? After the last safety incident—"

"Back off," Frank growled, putting his hand out to fend off the reporters circling around them. "Give her some space."

Vivian ducked her head, reaching into the little clutch purse Polly had thrust into her hands, searching for her sunglasses, her fingers shaking as she tried to slip them on her face to shield her from the flashing bulbs and prying eyes.

If Joe were here, he would be furious.

From the beginning, there had been a tension between the amount of access that the press wanted to have to the astronauts' wives and the women's willingness to be constantly put on display. When the space agency held the cards and an astronaut's family life could affect his ability to go up in space, could threaten his livelihood and ability to support his family, the spouse often felt pressured to play along. A few times, though, the astronauts themselves had gotten involved, standing up for their wives or banding together to ensure some protection for their families from the intrusive eyes of the press.

"What was your husband's mindset before going into space?" someone else called out to her.

Frank stiffened beside Vivian, and then he moved forward, placing his hand on her arm as though signaling her not to answer the question.

"Was he nervous at all?" another reporter shouted. "Did he get good rest the night before the flight?"

"Were things happy at home?"

Vivian's head whipped up, and she felt grateful for the dark sunglasses shielding her expression.

"Could your husband or one of the other crew members have made a mistake?"

There it was.

Anger filled her, piercing through the haze. She should have known they would start pointing fingers this early, that they would introduce operator error as quickly as they could. After all, it had happened before when there had been other mishaps and accidents.

How quickly they turned from praising the astronauts for their heroism, bravery, and ingenuity to blaming them when something went wrong.

And then—because it was inevitable, of course, now they were looking at her, at their marriage.

When Joe first joined the space program, Vivian had been made aware in no uncertain terms by the powers that be that her role was to maintain a household that was a haven for her husband. She was to wake far earlier than Joe in the mornings, preparing a full, hearty breakfast that gave him the energy he needed to go out and conquer space. When he returned home from a hard day of work, he was to be greeted by a wife whose hair was perfectly coiffed, clothes pressed and elegant, makeup flawless. Vivian was to ask him about his day but understand that due to the sensitive nature of his job, there were certain topics that were off-limits, and she was never, ever to pry or hold it against him when he refused to tell her certain things.

Above all else, the astronauts were not to be bothered by the minutiae of daily life. Unhappy spouses were meant to keep their frustrations to themselves, to paste a smile on their faces and offer a supportive ear for their astronaut husbands. Because at the end of the day, as a wife you were constantly reminded that your husband could die at any moment in his job. Going to space was a dangerous endeavor—even the training missions. Flying around the country in the T-38 they piloted between the Cape, headquarters in Houston, and the various contractors' offices brought its own set of dangers. They'd already lost astronauts in both training and in cross-country flights. No wife wanted to be the reason her husband was distracted and made a deadly mistake, that their children lost a father.

And yet—

It was an impossible load they were asked to carry. An impossible standard no woman could achieve in the face of all she was forced to contend with as an astronaut wife.

"My husband—" Vivian took a deep breath, those two words evoking a great deal more emotion than she had bargained for.

Tears pricked her eyes.

She would not cry.

She would not lose her composure in front of them.

She would not give them this private piece of herself.

When President Kennedy was assassinated in 1963, Vivian had been glued to the television screen like the rest of the world, had first learned of his death when she was in the newsroom and the story that he had been shot during the parade first broke.

The image that stayed with her from that time wasn't of the parade or the panic that had befallen the crowd that day, the collective grief that had swept the nation and the world. It was of Jackie Kennedy standing by Lyndon B. Johnson while he was sworn in as president hours after her husband was shot while riding next to her in what should have been a happy occasion, her husband's blood staining her pink suit.

When Vivian faced difficult times in her life, when she thought that she was being confronted with something she simply could not bear, she was reminded of that moment, and of the unimaginable grace and strength Jackie showed in the face of such a devastating loss.

Vivian channeled that courage now.

"My husband Joe is a great astronaut. He is an even better husband, an even greater man. Paul and Michael are great men. My husband was honored to command this mission with them." Vivian removed her sunglasses, giving the press what they wanted, allowing them to take the photograph that would grace newspapers and magazines around the world. Allowing them to propel Joe's plight to the front of the public's mind despite the urge inside her to flee.

"I don't know why we lost contact with the spacecraft." She glanced over at Frank, who by now had realized that she was deviating from the agreed-upon script and had paled considerably. "I'll leave it to the experts to decipher why there are problems with the telemetry. I have every faith that they'll be able to restore communication with the spacecraft. After all, if we're going to send men to the Moon, maintaining communications with the astronauts undertaking this important mission must be their top priority. They sent these men to space. They have an obligation to get them home."

A tremor threatened her voice, but she pushed it out, her tone firm, resolute. She glanced over at Frank once more. His mouth had slackened, and a glimmer of panic entered his gaze as though he'd realized the error in giving her such a public platform.

"I ask every American, everyone around the world, to pray for my husband's safe return, to pray for Michael and Paul and their families, who are surely worried sick, and to pray for the brave men and women who are working so hard to bring them home," Vivian continued, hoping that the emotional appeal would tug at the world's heartstrings and keep the astronauts' plight at the forefront of everyone's minds. "I am heartened by the commitment and promise NASA has shown to doing everything in their power to bring Joe, Michael, and Paul home to us and by the knowledge that they will not give up until the crew is returned safely. Thank you all."

"Mrs. Mitchell—"

"Mrs. Mitchell, look over here."

"*Do* you think the agency is committed to bringing your husband and the others home?"

"Are you worried that they've been gone so long that the likelihood that they were able to survive what happened to their spacecraft diminishes with each hour?"

Frank took hold of her arm, pulling her away from the reporters, and their questions, and likely whatever else she had to say that was not among the prepared lines the agency's media office had given her.

Vivian had read the words they wanted her to repeat in the comfort of her bedroom, Polly beside her. There had been more mentions of going to the Moon than of Joe, the mission before the man.

One of the reporters came a little too close, his arm connecting with hers, and Vivian stepped away, the frenzy building around her filling her with a sense of unease.

Frank pivoted from her, telling a photographer to his right to step back, and a voice whispered in her ear—

"I have some information about the capsule. There were problems well before the launch."

Vivian whirled around, her heart pounding. A man pressed a piece of paper into her hand before she was swept up in the crowd and she lost sight of him completely.

SIX

1961

How was your date?" Polly asked as Vivian walked into the apartment they shared in Arlington.

"It was—" Vivian searched for the right word to describe how it had felt. Too many possibilities came to mind, so she settled on, "Good. It was good."

If someone had told her a few months ago that she would go on a date with Graham Carlson, she never would have believed them.

"He's very handsome," Polly mused, sitting up on the couch. "I'll admit I've never been one for older men, but he's distinguished. The gray at the temples—there's something debonair about them."

"He's nice," Vivian replied neutrally, not sure she could reduce her journalistic hero to salt-and-pepper temples. "Very smart."

"Did you kiss him?" Polly asked, a grin on her face.

Vivian flushed. "He kissed me on the cheek at the end of the evening."

"That's it?"

"It was nice. He smelled good," she added. Judging by the expectant look on Polly's face, her friend was hoping for more details than what Vivian had just given her.

"Do you like him?" Polly asked, sounding a bit disappointed that the evening hadn't been juicier.

"Of course I like him. I respect him and admire him a great deal." Vivian hesitated. "He asked me to dinner next week and I said yes."

Polly's eyebrow rose. "You don't sound very excited for a girl who just got a second date with one of Washington's most eligible bachelors."

Was Graham one of Washington's most eligible bachelors? On paper, perhaps, by virtue of his career and stature, but Vivian truly didn't get a sense that he was a playboy. There was nothing overly smooth or insincere about him. He seemed like a decent man who was committed to his job and had little time in his life for much else, a sentiment that Vivian could appreciate and understand. After all, she enjoyed his companionship, but she wasn't looking for any distractions right now. She'd moved to D.C. for her career, *not* because of any romantic interests.

"I am excited. It's just—" Vivian sank down to the couch beside Polly. "I guess I'm not like you. I see how you are with Frank, and it's so lovely. It's like I'm in a Doris Day film," she teased. "I've just never felt that way about anyone. I don't think I'm built for such emotions. Graham is kind and interesting, and I still can't quite believe that he is interested in me. I am happy. Truly. My happiness is a quieter sort, I suppose."

"I'm sorry," Polly replied. "I shouldn't have pushed. It's none of my business. I just want you to find someone who is as wonderful as you are. I suppose being in love inspires you to want the same for people you care about."

They'd become close in the time that they'd lived together, and Vivian now considered Polly to be one of her dearest friends. The further she got from college, the more it seemed like those friendships that she had considered to be close had faded without the proximity of life in the dorms, the shared experience of working at the radio station or studying for their classes. In a sense, they had all gone in separate directions, their lives flung around the country, and Vivian felt as though she was starting all over again, and this time it was much harder to make friends, particularly when she worked in such a male-dominated environment at the station.

Vivian had partnered with Kerry Krieger on a few more stories, and while Kerry was unfailingly polite, she gave no indication that she was interested in making friends at work, her personal and professional lives clearly separate.

And so, despite the differences in their personalities, Vivian and Polly had become close, their little apartment bringing them together as they bonded over their careers, some of the challenges Polly faced with being taken seriously and treated with respect in her job at the hospital so relatable to Vivian.

"There's a stack of mail on the table," Polly announced. "I sorted through it already; what's left is yours."

Vivian rose from the couch, walking toward the little two-seater table with a sense of dread. Her job at the television station barely covered her living expenses, and too often, the mail heralded bills. Wouldn't it have been refreshing if just for once she flipped through the stack and found that a previously unknown, long-lost relative had left her a fortune?

"You got a postcard," Polly called out as Vivian approached the table.

Who would be sending her a postcard? Her mother, perhaps? Unlikely, considering Vivian hadn't heard from her since graduation, but Vivian had sent her a birthday card, which would have had her return address on it, so perhaps.

"From Italy," Polly clarified, and this time there was no mistaking the note of glee in her voice.

Italy?

Italy.

"Oh really?" Vivian asked, struggling to keep her voice calm.

"*Italy*," Polly repeated. "Frank talked to him the other day, you know. Joe called his desk at the Pentagon about some work thing. He's been in Italy for about two months now. He seems to like it. Frank said that before they hung up the phone. Joe asked him about you—how you were doing—asked him if you were seeing someone."

I didn't ask about you—I should have.

Her lungs constricted, a tightness building in her chest.

"What did— What did Frank tell him?"

She wasn't sure what she wanted the answer to be.

"That you were doing well. Frank told him we all went to the movies the other night."

They had. Vivian had expected to feel like a third wheel tagging along on a movie date with Polly and Frank, but it had been surprisingly fun.

"Did Frank—" Why did she feel so uncomfortable asking the question? Why did Polly's answer matter so much?

Later, she would interrogate it for sure.

"Did Frank mention that I went out on a date with Graham?"

"I didn't tell him." Polly smiled, a knowing gleam in her eyes. "I figure we ladies have to stick together. Besides, you and Joe are little more than acquaintances, right? I couldn't imagine why he needs to know about your dating history."

IN THE PRIVACY OF HER BEDROOM, THE DOOR FIRMLY closed behind her, Vivian stared at the postcard.

A Venetian canal looked back at her.

She reached out, her fingers tracing the image. It was all too easy to imagine herself sitting in the little boat as the gondolier moved them along.

Them.

Because of course, in the fantasy, Joe was sitting next to her on the bench.

Ridiculous.

Not to mention how absurd it was that her heartbeat picked up, a tremor sliding through her fingers as she flipped the postcard over.

Vivian—

Saw this and thought of you. Italy is beautiful. I keep thinking of what you said, how you've always wanted to see it one day. I find myself making a list in my mind of all the places I'd show you if you were here. Hope you're well.

And then, two words scrawled at the bottom that sent a thrill through her.

Write me.

SEVEN

1961

Vivian slid her key into the apartment mailbox she shared with Polly, anticipation filling her as she turned it with a twist of her wrist, the little door pulling open to reveal—

Nothing.

Absolutely nothing.

Not a bill, not a letter from a college friend, not a postcard from—

Well.

She shouldn't be so disappointed that he hadn't written. It had only been a week since his last postcard, and he had mentioned that he was busy with training. And still—she had been thinking of that trip to the mailbox all day. While she was working on the afternoon news story for Kerry Krieger, her thoughts had drifted to this moment, wondering if Joe had written again. It was unlikely, considering she had just sent her own response to him a few days ago, but over the last few months she'd learned that Joe's letters came at unpredictable times with no discernable rhythm. It was as though he thought of her during random moments in his day, and decided to send her a note to let her know.

Vivian closed the mailbox and walked up the stairs and down the hallway to her apartment, trying to convince herself that it was perhaps for the best that he hadn't written as she unlocked the front door and shut it behind her. Maybe he'd moved on from their correspondence as he reached the conclusion that it wasn't going anywhere, or he'd met someone—

"I'm getting married," Polly shrieked, thrusting her hand in front of Vivian as she stood in the front hall, a sparkling diamond sitting atop Polly's left ring finger.

Vivian didn't have a chance to respond before Polly embraced her.

Tears filled Vivian's eyes.

She'd never considered herself to be much of a romantic, but watching her roommate fall in love with Frank was enough to sway even the biggest skeptics.

Frank was still stationed at the Pentagon, and he spent so much time at their apartment that Vivian jokingly called him their third roommate. Sometimes when he spoke about his time in the military or told stories about his flying, Joe would feature in them, and it felt like Vivian was getting glimpses into his life. In all of Frank's stories, Joe was always the one accepting a dare or taking a risk, and he always seemed larger than life to the point where she couldn't decide if the version of him she'd seen those two times they'd met was the real Joe, if perhaps he'd let her see a side of him that few did.

"I'm so happy for you," Vivian whispered in Polly's ear. "So happy for both of you. You deserve every happiness in the world."

Polly pulled back, absolutely beaming from ear to ear. "Thank you. Will you be one of my bridesmaids? You've been so supportive from the beginning of our relationship—it would mean so much to have you standing up there with us."

"I would be honored," Vivian replied, tears filling her eyes.

Polly grinned. "I was hoping you'd say that. Listen, we're having a small engagement party in a couple weeks. Just a little get-together for friends at the bar where we met. You'll come, won't you?"

"Of course." Lately, it felt as though all she did was work, and it wasn't like breaking news operated on a schedule you could anticipate, but there were some things that were more important than her job, and Polly's friendship was one of them. "I wouldn't miss it for anything."

"Graham is invited, too. We'd love to have both of you there."

It still took getting used to, the idea of being part of a "both of you." She kept telling herself that it was just that it was so new—they'd only been dating for four months, only known each other for a few months longer than that.

In the moments when Vivian questioned her own feelings on the matter, she focused on the things she knew to be certain: she had admired him for nearly her entire adult life; he was a good man, a man who treated her with respect, which seemed like a rarity these days, a kind man, a smart man. He hadn't even taken her out on a date until a week after he'd left the station, and in the beginning they'd kept their relationship private to avoid any suggestion that she'd received any favoritism at work. It was hard enough to be taken seriously as a woman in this industry, and the last thing she wanted was for the career she was working so hard to build to be undermined.

And he loved her—or so he'd told her a month ago.

She tried to tell herself that it didn't matter that she hadn't been able to tell Graham she loved him back. Or that each time she walked to her mailbox and found it empty, disappointment filled her.

"Graham will be in New York for work then," Vivian replied. "I know he'll be sorry to miss it."

"We'll miss him," Polly replied. She waved her hand in the air, the diamond catching the light. "I need to go call my parents and tell them the good news," she squealed.

Polly took off in the direction of their little living room, and Vivian couldn't resist asking—

"Who will be at the party?"

She tried to keep her tone casual, but she must have failed miserably because Polly turned around, meeting her gaze, answering the question Vivian hadn't been able to fully ask.

"Joe's coming to town. He'll be there."

VIVIAN GLANCED AT THE ENTRANCE TO THE BAR FOR what must have been the twentieth time all evening, her fingers nervously stroking the champagne glass a waiter had passed her.

The party had started thirty minutes ago, but Joe hadn't arrived yet, and the more she waited, the more the anticipation built inside her, until she felt like she would combust.

Laughter filled the room, followed by a smattering of applause, and Vivian tore her gaze away from the entrance to the makeshift dance floor where Frank—normally quiet, staid Frank—spun Polly around in the air.

When she thought of the life Polly would embark on with Frank—the uncertainty and danger that they would be forced to confront because of his job—she marveled at her friend's willingness to take on such a choice. And at the same time, watching them together, Vivian had to believe that if anyone stood a chance of making it work, it was these two.

Did it matter that she didn't look at Graham that way? That their relationship was different, quieter, more muted? They wouldn't have the same challenges to face that Polly and Frank did. In fact, one of the things that had attracted her to Graham was how easy things were with him. She didn't get that dizzy feeling in her stomach when she was with him, didn't feel off-balance and antsy. In the beginning, she'd been nervous enough considering how much she had looked up to him, but Graham had a way of putting you at ease—likely what made him such a good reporter. Their relationship was comfortable in a way that suited Vivian just fine. Let Polly have fireworks. After the childhood she'd had, Vivian wanted companionship and ease, a home to call her own, a place to put down roots. She wanted a man who didn't demand too much of her, a man who would understand that she needed her life to run parallel to his rather than intertwined.

She glanced at the entrance once more.

No sign of Joe.

"Toast, toast, toast—" a voice cheered from across the room.

One of Frank's Air Force buddies lifted a glass in hand, and the others moved in, surrounding the engaged couple. His pilot friends were a rowdy group, their good-natured energy injecting quite a bit of life into the party. Seeing them in action reminded her of Joe, and she could easily see how he fit into the bunch—

Her gaze drifted to the entrance and her breath hitched.

He was here.

His hair had grown a bit in the months since they'd last seen each other, although it was still cut short with military precision. He'd acquired a tan in Italy, and it was easy enough to imagine him in the settings of those postcards he'd sent her—on a beach or skiing the slopes.

He looked good.

The night they met, she'd registered that he was objectively handsome in a predictable sort of way, like a movie star, but now that she saw him after the postcards he'd written her, the conversations they'd had, now he seemed handsome in an intrinsic way—the sum of all the things that made him interesting taking her breath away for a beat.

Joe scanned the room, moving past the entourage surrounding Polly and Frank until his gaze settled on her.

Vivian gripped her champagne flute more tightly, waiting to see if he would approach her, torn between hoping that he did and wondering if it was better if he didn't, and despite all the time she'd spent thinking about what she would say when she saw him again, her mind went completely blank.

Neither one of them moved.

Joe stared at her as though he was registering every detail about her, and Vivian tried to smile and found that her composure failed her, the anticipation that had been growing inside of her in the two weeks since she'd found out she would see him again building to a crescendo.

Joe took a step forward, a step toward Vivian—

"Joe!"

Vivian whirled around in time to see Frank stride toward his friend, calling out to him.

For a moment, it seemed like Joe hadn't even heard Frank because he made no move to turn toward his friend, but then he broke the connection between them as he greeted Frank, offering him his congratulations before the two men strode over to Polly.

Vivian stood there, watching their retreating backs, and then she turned, heading over to where a few of the other bridesmaids—Polly's friends from nursing school—congregated together, discussing the bridal shower they wanted to throw, and the dresses Polly was considering they wear for the ceremony.

Vivian tried as best she could to follow their conversation, to interject her own responses when someone asked for her opinion, when they tried to draw her into the circle more and more. She tried to keep her attention focused on the women around her, even as it kept drifting to the other side of the room where Joe stood talking to Polly and Frank.

Would he come to say hello to her? Or should she go to him?

Twenty minutes later, a hand grazed her elbow.

Vivian took a deep breath, steadying herself, and then she pivoted.

Joe stood before her. He smiled, his gaze steady on hers. "Fancy seeing you here again."

As far as lines went, his was rather awful, and then she realized—

He was nervous.

Uncharacteristically nervous.

Joe drew her away from the group of bridesmaids, until it was just the two of them in a corner of the bar.

It felt good to see him again.

Too good.

Even though none of her reasons for saying no when he'd asked her out had changed, she had thought of him often since then. Their correspondence had unlocked something inside Vivian so that she felt comfortable with him in a way she'd never imagined possible. This was only their third time seeing each other in real life, but because of the postcards and letters they shared, it felt as though she knew him intimately, and she realized that somewhere along the way a friendship had sprung up between them.

"Are you back from Italy for good?" Vivian asked, voicing the follow-up question she hadn't had the guts to ask Polly when she'd mentioned that Joe would be at the party.

"No, I'm just on leave. I sent you a postcard telling you I was coming back, although I guess in this case I beat the mail."

With each postcard that had arrived since the first one he sent her—eight in total now—Vivian wondered why he wrote them. She'd spent countless minutes—hours, if she was being honest—studying them as though they contained some clue that would help her understand what Joe was thinking when he wrote them, when he slipped them in the mailbox.

On the backs, he scribbled little messages, the sight of his handwriting now sending a thrill through her when she got the mail. Joe spoke of nothing serious, rather told her about his days, hikes he had taken in the Alps, meals he'd eaten, travel he'd undertaken to other nearby European countries. And at the end of them, he always asked her how she was doing, how her work was going, and so she wrote him back, feeling more than a little self-conscious each time she did so, unsure if she was sharing too much or if he even cared about her responses.

And still, the postcards came, his handwriting growing smaller with each one as he fit more and more news onto that little card, as he referenced things in her letters that let her know he'd been reading the words she wrote. It was like they were engaged in a monthslong conversation. Her responses were undeniably more verbose than his, but he had a way of seemingly saying a great deal with few words. There were plenty of things he didn't say—things she wondered about far too frequently. Like whether he had someone accompanying him on these jaunts throughout Europe, or if he thought of Vivian as often as she thought of him, or if—

"How have you been?" Joe asked her.

Was it her imagination or was there a hint of something contained there—more than a casual question, but a probing interest in what her answer would be because he had a suspicion? Did Frank tell him she was seeing Graham?

Polly hadn't said anything, but last week Frank and Graham

had crossed paths in their apartment, and while Frank hadn't said a word about it to Vivian, she couldn't help but wonder if he'd said anything to Joe.

She'd thought about mentioning Graham in her letters, had started to a time or two, but it had never fit into the correspondence she and Joe shared. She'd never found an organic spot between the details he gave her about his life in Italy, the dreams and aspirations she put down on the page. And if she was being honest, she hadn't known how he would respond if she injected Graham into the conversation; it felt as though her boyfriend was an interloper to their friendship. She'd considered telling Joe, but each time she had started to mention it, something had held her back.

If Joe knew she was seeing someone, would he stop writing to her?

Silly of course to worry about such a thing considering their letters were strictly platonic, and still—she had.

"I've been well," Vivian replied.

Surely, this was the moment she should say something to him, and yet, he hadn't mentioned his love life to her. Neither one of them owed anything to each other, even though, somehow, impossibly, it felt as though they did.

"And work?" he asked, his tone somewhat distant, overly polite.

"Work is going well, too."

Kerry had taken her under her wing, and they had begun working on even more stories together. As far as mentors went, she was as good of one as Vivian could have hoped for.

"Graham Carlson is a very lucky man," Joe finally said after a silence that stretched on for far too long and had her wrapping her arms around her torso. "I heard the two of you are—ahh—together."

That look was on his face once more, the one he wore when he looked up at Alan Shepard launching into the sky.

Why did she suddenly feel like she wanted to cry?

Vivian swallowed, her voice rough as she pushed the words out. "Thank you."

She waited for Joe to say something about the fact that she didn't mention it in her letters, to ask her why, but he wouldn't meet her gaze, and suddenly, she wasn't ready for what she would see reflected at her when he did.

"Did Frank tell you?" Vivian asked, focusing on what seemed to be the least emotionally complicated question she could ask.

"He did. We had lunch together earlier today. I asked about you and, well—"

I didn't ask about you—I should have.

Now that she glanced at him, he turned away so that all she could see was his profile, his gaze shielded from her.

"It must be nice being with someone in a similar career field to yours. Someone who understands the highs and lows of your job."

"It makes things easier, I suppose." Vivian paused, not sure what else to say, more than a little desperate for him to look at her.

Finally, Vivian couldn't take it anymore and she placed her hand on his arm, somewhere between wanting to give comfort—an unspoken apology, perhaps—and needing to get his attention.

Joe stilled, his gaze finally drifting down to the point where she touched him, her hand lightly resting over his suit jacket.

Suddenly, the proximity between them seemed like a very bad idea, indeed.

Vivian jerked her hand away, wishing very much that she'd never reached out and touched him.

"Are you happy?" he finally asked her.

Vivian nodded.

She was happy.

Wasn't she?

"Good. I'm glad." He moved forward like he was going to step toward her, lean into her, but he stopped himself. "It was good to see you again," he said instead.

Joe moved away from her, and it hit her that this was the second time she had stood in this very bar watching Joe Mitchell walk away from her, except this time she couldn't help but wonder if she'd just made a very big mistake.

LATER THAT NIGHT, VIVIAN PICKED UP THE PHONE IN their apartment, and when the operator came onto the line, Vivian gave her the number she wished to be connected to, her heart pounding as she waited for the call to go through.

Was she making a mistake?

As soon as his voice came on the line, she knew what she needed to do. Knew what was right.

Vivian took a deep breath. "We need to talk."

EIGHT

1968

Two Days Gone

The morning after the press conference, Vivian read over the letter the man had slipped her once more, trying to understand what she was reading; the scientific information was a piece of the puzzle, but she was still missing the rest of it.

The letter looked to be an internal corporate memorandum from someone who had worked on the capsule's navigation system as a contractor to another person in the company. The technical aspects were a bit too complicated for her to understand, and she figured you needed an engineering degree to parse some of it, but the intent was clear. There were concerns that the space program was moving too far, too fast, and that in the desire to beat the Soviets, corners might be being cut that could compromise the astronauts' safety.

A knock sounded at the door, followed by Polly's voice on the other side.

"Are you awake?" Polly asked.

"Yes. Come in."

The door swung open.

"What do the newspapers say?" Vivian asked Polly as she walked into the bedroom carrying a stack of periodicals.

Her bedroom had become her only sanctuary in a house that felt as though it was perpetually filled with people. She'd considered asking them to leave—or better yet, asking Polly to ask them to leave—but she couldn't quite summon the courage to do so. There was an inevitability to her eventually falling apart; no matter how hard she fought to keep it all together, if Joe didn't come home soon, she was going to break.

Vivian just couldn't decide if it would be easier or harder if there were people around when it happened. Her personality tended toward solitary pursuits, but everyone kept telling her that the company of others would make this easier, and what did she know of how one would respond when their husband was lost in space? She'd never been in this position, and no amount of fearing and dreading the possibility of it could have prepared her for the reality.

"You're on the front page," Polly replied, shutting the door behind her and walking over to the bed where Vivian lay tucked under the covers. "Everyone is talking about your speech, about Joe."

Vivian glanced at the headline above a picture of her stricken face.

BRING THEM HOME!

"Is Frank furious?" Vivian asked.

"Don't worry about Frank. He's a big boy and he can deal with the fallout himself. After all, he wanted this job, didn't he? Wanted the power, and the responsibility, and all the official duties that come with it. Frank's fine."

Polly delivered the last word with an uncharacteristic edge, as though "fine" had teeth.

Polly set the newspapers down on the edge of the comforter so that Vivian could see them, and then she climbed into bed next to her.

Vivian glanced through the headlines of the other papers—

WHERE ARE THEY?

One of the papers had placed a photograph of Joe in his uniform—his official photograph—next to the one of her in front of the house yesterday. Vivian reached out, tracing his image with her fingers.

He looked so vibrant, so happy, like the world was waiting for him to conquer it.

"How are you doing?" Polly asked her. "Which I know is a terrible question, because of course, the answer is 'not well,' but I don't know what else to say. Maybe better to say, 'What do you need from me?' Right now? How can I help you?"

"Just being here right now is enough. Thank you."

"Of course." Polly glanced over at the squawk box. "Have you heard him again?"

Of all the reasons she loved Polly—and there were many—gratitude filled Vivian at the fact that she didn't question *if* Vivian had heard Joe, but accepted it.

"No. Nothing."

It was the main reason why she was reluctant to leave the bedroom—the squawk box—and what felt like her only connection to Joe now—was here. She was afraid that if she did leave, she'd never hear her husband's voice again.

"Maybe the spacecraft just isn't in the right position," Polly replied. "You know how sensitive these things can be."

"Maybe. I just don't understand why they didn't hear him at Mission Control but I did." Vivian took a deep breath. "I keep wondering if I imagined it like Frank seemed to think I did. If it was my worry making my mind play tricks on me. And at the same time, I'm not sure I'm ready to accept that possibility. Because at least if I heard his voice, then I know he's alive and he's out there somewhere, trying to come home.

"Do you know how things are going in Houston?" Vivian asked. "With the other families?"

"Frank asked me to check in. Bridget seems calm, all things considered. The wives in Togethersville are rotating in groups of three to make sure she's never alone. Paul's parents are a wreck."

"I wondered if I should call Bridget, but then again, we've never been close. I wasn't sure if she would welcome it or not."

Polly hesitated. "I would wait. She—when I spoke with her—"

"What?"

"There have been some rumblings in some of the news reports. I didn't want to tell you, didn't want to upset you, but I suppose it isn't surprising given the questions the reporters asked at the press conference. There are more folks who are saying this was the result of operator error."

"They're blaming Joe," Vivian guessed.

Of course they would blame Joe.

Joe was the mission commander. Ultimately, the spacecraft was his responsibility. He'd told her as much when they first talked about the mission. He'd explained to her that he felt an obligation to ensure that the mission was safe, that everything went smoothly, that Michael and Paul returned home to their families. Not to mention, she'd seen the same finger-pointing play out in his career as a pilot. Whoever oversaw the controls, or was the flight lead in charge of the formation, held the lives of their colleagues in their hands.

Was that why the mysterious man had slipped a note to her?

"People are rushing to judgment, looking for answers in the absence of an actual investigation being done," Polly replied. "Bridget asked Frank if Joe had made a mistake. It made him angry, I could tell, but at the same time, she's grieving. It's a complicated situation."

"How could there even be an investigation when it's too soon to know what—if anything—even went wrong? It seems like the priority should be getting them home safely.

"Joe is a good astronaut. He is careful. He is serious about what he does."

"I know that, Vivian. We all do." Polly took her hand and held on. "Emotions are just running high right now. I think a lot of people are afraid that a mishap broader than operator error will be chalked up to a problem with the program and will jeopardize a future mission to the Moon."

"I don't care about the Moon right now. Don't care about anything but them coming home safely. And at the same time—I don't want Joe's reputation to be diminished in all of this. It seems unfair that while his life is in danger, while he's missing, there are people actively accusing him of causing this. Is there any evidence that Joe was responsible for something going wrong with the spacecraft? I mean, how do they even know that anything went wrong? They keep saying that they don't know where it is or what happened."

"I don't know. If Frank does, he hasn't said anything to me. Frank—Frank doesn't say much to me these days."

"Is everything alright?" Vivian asked Polly.

They hadn't seen each other in a couple of months. Polly had traveled from her home in the Houston suburbs, in Togethersville with the other wives, to be with Vivian in the days preceding the launch with the intention of staying until Joe returned home. Since she'd arrived, before the launch even took place, Vivian had noticed that Polly wasn't quite herself, but then again Vivian had been so distracted by Joe going to space, so worried about her own problems, that she hadn't thought much about it.

Now she wished she'd asked her friend if something was wrong in the beginning.

"Of course. Everything is fine," Polly replied, not meeting Vivian's gaze. "Frank has just been so consumed by the launch. He hasn't had time for much else."

"Come on. It's me. How long have things been like this?"

Polly sighed. "I don't know. A year, maybe?"

"A year?"

Longer than the focus surrounding the launch, then.

"Maybe more." Polly glanced down at the comforter, her fingers tracing the floral pattern. "I didn't want to tell you. You've been dealing with so much—it felt insignificant in comparison."

"It's not insignificant. I'm sorry. So sorry you've been going through this. I wish I could have been there for you. Even if you just needed someone to listen."

"I know. And I think part of why I didn't tell you was that I knew that if I told you, you would be there for whatever I needed, would want to help me fix it. But I wasn't ready to face what I needed to do. Wasn't ready to face this." Polly was silent for a moment. "We're getting divorced," she finally added.

She said it so softly, so quietly, and yet so *loudly*, and for a moment, Vivian considered the possibility that she'd misheard her. But it was the expression in Polly's eyes—an expression that Vivian had never seen in all their years of friendship—that told her differently.

"Polly."

"I didn't want to tell you," Polly added. "Before—I knew you were nervous about the mission, and I didn't want to add to your concerns. And then after—how could I tell you when you're dealing with all of this?"

"We're astro wives. I think we've gotten used to juggling multiple crises at once." Vivian put her arm around her friend's shoulder. "You're my best friend," Vivian replied. "You're my family. I'm going to be here for you no matter what. What do you need? Do you want to talk about it?"

Polly laughed, the sound devoid of humor. "God, no." She hesitated. "I don't know. I haven't really talked about it with anyone. For a while after I told Frank I wanted a divorce and he ultimately agreed, it didn't have to be real. For months it was like this secret that I held inside. Finally, I told my parents that I was leaving Frank. They haven't spoken to me since. My mother said I was breaking my father's heart, that I was selfish and foolish, and that I should think of the girls. No one in the family has ever gotten divorced, and she was horrified I was breaking that streak."

"I'm sorry."

Polly shrugged. "I'm not surprised. I was dreading telling them. My parents have been married since they were eighteen. My father sleeps on the couch more nights than he sleeps with my mother, but they would never consider divorcing. What was I expecting?"

Of all the couples to end their marriage, Vivian never would have predicted Polly and Frank. They were the model so many astronauts and their wives aspired to. They were the ones who hosted holiday gatherings, inviting others to join in. Their house was the unofficial home base for the astronaut families, and even though Polly had come to the position somewhat reluc-tantly, she was the wife they all looked to for guidance. Polly was unquestionably Frank's partner, and while Vivian had her doubts about the Space Race and whether they should be in it at all, Polly believed in going to the Moon, was proud of the work the astronauts did, even if she shared the same complaints and concerns about the lifestyle that others either voiced aloud or felt privately.

Divorce, though, was still very much a taboo in their circle. After all, the competition for the astronauts to get a spot on a space mission was as cutthroat as it could get. No one worked this hard or came this far to be left on the ground or relegated to a less important or prestigious mission. But NASA wasn't just looking for great astronauts—they were looking for good public relations, and that meant happy, intact families. The wives were meant to be an ideal no woman could possibly achieve—in fact, one of the Mercury Seven wives, Rene Carpenter, had created a caricature of such a woman and given her the apropos moniker of "Primly Stable."

No astronaut could afford to admit that there were cracks in their home life if they wanted a shot at going to the Moon.

There were rumblings that there were unhappy astro marriages, wives who were unraveling, who had turned to a bottle or pills that Doc Wyler prescribed, husbands who spent more time with their girlfriends than at home with their families. Vivian often wondered what would happen when the cracks came to light in the public eye, if the wives were finally able to speak out loud about the things they'd only hinted at up to this point.

They'd yet to have a divorce in the space program. Once they did, how many other marriages would follow? Now that it was going to be Polly and Frank, well—who was next? How many spouses would be emboldened by Polly's choice since she was the first one to acknowledge that this wasn't working?

There were more than a few wives whose husbands were

quite frankly awful, and Vivian would be the first to congratulate them when they finally said they'd had enough of being cheated on and treated horribly by men who were supposed to love and honor them.

There was an unspoken code that what went on at the Cape, stayed at the Cape. While most of the wives lived with their children in Houston, some of the astronauts effectively lived secret lives, going out every night with girlfriends—which the wives had nicknamed "Cape Cookies"—on their arms. It was an open secret, but one that many of the astronauts protected for their fellow brothers in space. And it wasn't just the astronauts who turned a blind eye to their compatriots' infidelities— the wives seemingly did as well, a fact that Vivian had never understood or expected. They ignored the telltale, even blatant, signs that their husbands were cheating, and if a wife knew that another astronaut was stepping out on his wife and family, well—let's just say no one acknowledged what was happening.

"Did he—" Vivian didn't want to finish that question, didn't want to introduce the dreaded Cape Cookie into the conversation, but they both knew how much of a reality it was when you were married to a man who everyone in the world wanted a piece of, a man who inspired a level of hero worship.

She'd never heard any whispers about Frank, but that didn't mean he didn't have someone on the side. Vivian liked to think that she knew him well, knew the sort of man he was, wanted to believe that Joe would have told her if something was going on, that he would have stood up for Polly and the girls, but she'd been an astro wife for too long and had seen too much to be anything but pragmatic about such things.

"No, there wasn't anyone else. I asked Frank that once when I was frustrated, and I don't think he could have faked the surprise on his face at the question. He genuinely looked like the possibility of cheating hadn't even occurred to him. I don't think Frank would have had the time anyway considering how consumed he is with the mission. Besides, Frank?" Polly gave a tired little laugh. "He'd have given himself away after the first time he cheated. Frank's terrible at keeping a secret."

That was true. The other guys had always given him a hard time about that, joking that if the Soviets wanted to learn anything about the space program, Frank was their man. Considering how seriously Frank took his job, the indictment had annoyed him tremendously, which only made the other astronauts tease him more.

"It almost would be easier if it was another woman," Polly added. "How do you compete with the Moon?"

It was a common lament among the spouses. Before it was the Moon, it was space, and before space it was breaking the sound barrier, and before that flying a jet plane in the sky, and before that flying any plane, and before that—

It was difficult being married to someone who was always chasing the next thrill, the next leap forward.

It was tough being the one left behind at home to worry and wait, harder still when their lifestyle didn't offer many opportunities for careers of their own since the astro wives with children were essentially single mothers while the men were at the Cape during the week, gone more than they were home, the rearing of children and keeping of homes set against the backdrop of their erratic and dramatic lifestyles often involving a Herculean effort.

And that was just life as a space wife.

It was heaven compared to what their previous lives as military wives had been. Between the constant threat of deployment to a war zone, the frequent moves every couple of years, the ever-present absences that came with the various training and duty obligations, the imminent risk of death, and the fact that it wasn't unusual to have a year go by where you only saw your husband for two or three months out of twelve, it could wear on even the most supportive spouse.

Not to mention, at one time or another many of the spouses had worked to financially support their husbands' aspirations, from holding down jobs so the men could study to heavily contributing to the meager salary that their husbands' military careers provided. And still, when it came down to it, they were relegated to a back-seat role, their contributions minimized and dismissed in the face of their husbands' positions as astronauts.

Betty Friedan would have had a field day with the dynamics at play in the space program.

It was utterly demoralizing that women were viewed solely in their roles as support for their husbands; it was hardly surprising that the same space program had made no efforts to include women in their astronaut program in the near decade since its inception.

"I haven't told the girls yet," Polly continued. "I think they know something is going on, at least Grace does. Frank and I have been fighting more lately. I've tried to avoid doing it in front of them, but it's hard. It's not like our house is that big, so they overhear everything. We've taken to trying to schedule our fights to the evening when the girls are already asleep. How sad is that? A couple weeks ago Grace woke up and her eyes were red, and it hit me that I think she heard me and her dad fighting and cried herself to sleep. What kind of a mother am I?"

The last part emerged on a sob, Polly's shoulders shaking.

"You're a great mom," Vivian replied honestly, wishing she could say something that would help her friend believe it. "And the girls love you. You've been their constant through this wild, unpredictable ride."

"I know. And that's the part I feel the worst about. The girls are used to Frank being gone, to worrying about him, to the moves, and changing schools, and all the things they shouldn't have to think about at their age. But they've always seen me as the one they can count on. I've been the steady one, the one who put a smile on my face when Frank told us he was getting sent away on another mission, who told the girls everything was going to be alright. And now it feels like I'm letting them down, because I'm the one telling them that everything in their lives is about to change even if they don't want it to. They're going to expect me to fix it like I've fixed everything else for them, but there's no taking them out for ice cream to make this better."

"I wouldn't completely discount the power of ice cream. It's small, yes. But it's your way of showing them that you care, that you understand their pain. You get to be human, Polly. You don't have to be perfect all the time. You get to say when it's too much, when you can't do this anymore. It's always about them, and yes, we married them, and we love them, but sometimes when we need it, it gets to be about us, too.

"I didn't learn that when I was a little girl. I thought that I had to look pretty and be sweet, and not upset my mother, and it took me forever—too long really—to feel like that wasn't the case. Hell, sometimes I think I'm still figuring that out even at my age. Look at what you're teaching your girls; at the example you're giving them. You're showing them that it's alright to say when something isn't working, when you've had too much, when you've wrung every bit out of yourself and there's nothing left. I can't think of a better lesson to teach them."

Polly wiped at the tears on her cheeks. "Thank you. For always knowing exactly what I need to hear and saying it right when I need to hear it."

"Whatever you and the girls need, I'm here for you. Always."

Polly hugged her. "Thank you. We're going to get through this. Somehow." She pulled away and lifted one of the newspapers. "And we're going to figure out how to get Joe and the others home. What you're doing—bringing attention to this mission—he would be so proud of you."

Vivian hoped so.

Vivian handed Polly the memorandum she'd been reading before Polly walked into the room.

"A man gave this to me at the press conference yesterday."

She waited while Polly read the memo.

Polly's eyes widened as her gaze connected with Vivian's. "Was something wrong with the spacecraft? Were they aware of it and did they send them up anyway?"

"I don't know."

"What do you want to do?" Polly asked. "What's the endgame in all of this?"

"To bring Joe home. For him to be safe."

She couldn't think past that now, couldn't think past the tightness in her chest that arose every single time she imagined her husband not coming home.

"And what if you can't?" Polly said it softly, and she was probably the only person who could ask that question without giving offense, because Vivian knew that she would be by her side no matter what.

"Honestly? If something went wrong up there, if there was a problem with the spacecraft like that reporter intimated, then I want to tear it all down. All of it." Vivian took a deep breath. "Joe would hate it, of course. Would hate if he was the reason we gave up on going to the Moon. That's what I keep telling myself, at least. He believed in this mission, this dream."

"I don't know," Polly replied. "You know Joe better than anyone. And he loves you more than anyone. He knows who he fell in love with. And he knows who he married. I don't think you can do wrong by doing what you think is right."

"Thank you."

"You should ask Frank about the memo," Polly encouraged. "See what he knows about it. I can't promise he'll tell you the truth. And if it comes down to doing the right thing by Joe or protecting the space program, I don't know what he'd do. But you should still bring it to him. He owes you the truth. They all do." Polly was silent for a beat. "This wasn't how any of this was supposed to turn out, you know? At the beginning, it seemed like there was so much ahead of us. Our futures were so bright—" She broke off, as though she'd just realized who she was talking to, that Vivian was all too well-versed in "this wasn't how any of this was supposed to turn out." Polly reached out and squeezed her hand. "For what it's worth, I wouldn't blame you for a second if you brought it all tumbling down. Hell, I'd be standing there next to you."

"If you had it all to do over, would you have said 'no' that night I asked you if you wanted to go on that double date?" Polly asked.

Vivian laughed even as she wanted to cry. "Maybe? Definitely? Definitely not? I don't even know anymore. I'm still not sure what made me say 'yes.' I had big plans to watch *Perry Mason.*"

Polly flashed her a watery smile. "See what you would have missed out on?"

Everything.

She would have missed out on everything.

It was strange to think how many small moments, how many innocuous choices had led her to this point in her life. She remembered standing in front of the bulletin board at the YWCA and seeing the little note card with Polly's advertisement for a roommate posted there with a pushpin. She'd almost walked away from the board without writing down the phone number, because truthfully, Vivian hadn't wanted a roommate— had been perfectly fine with living alone. But something had tugged at her—the low rent and the good location, perhaps— and she'd jotted down the phone number on the back of a newspaper.

Vivian glanced down at the newspapers Polly had strewn on

the bed, and flipped through them, until she got to the last one, and beneath it a stack of mail.

"I picked it up from your box," Polly said. "I figured it was the last thing you needed to worry about, and I didn't want those vultures out there going through it."

"Thank you."

When was the last time she had remembered to pick up the mail? A day or two before the launch, perhaps. It simultaneously felt as though the past few days had happened in the blink of an eye and the span of a year.

Vivian froze.

A postcard stared back at her.

A gondola floating in the Grand Canal graced the image.

Venice.

Vivian's fingers trembled as she picked up the postcard and turned it over.

There was no stamp. No address. No handwriting.

It was completely blank.

"Are you alright? What's wrong?" Polly asked.

Vivian handed the postcard to Polly wordlessly, unable to formulate a response to her friend's questions.

Surprise flashed across Polly's face as she recognized what it was—and the significance of it as well.

"That's—that's just like the postcards Joe used to send you when we lived in Arlington." Polly did the same thing Vivian had, turning it over and studying it. "That's so strange—there's no postmark or stamp or anything. How did it even get in here?"

"I have no idea. Are you sure it was in the stack of mail that was in the postbox?" Vivian asked.

"I think so. Could Joe have left it in there before he left?"

"I suppose so, but it doesn't make any sense. If he did leave it in there for me, why wouldn't he have written something on it?"

Not to mention, whenever he'd sent her a postcard before—and there were many, all bound with a ribbon in a drawer in her dresser—it had always been from a place where he was, not somewhere he'd been stationed seven years ago. And certainly not a blank one.

The note in her dress, the voice over the squawk box, and now this postcard—they felt like signs, like Joe was trying to communicate with her somehow.

She just wished she knew what she was supposed to do to help get him home.

"What if he's still alive?" Vivian blurted out. "What if he's out there somewhere and he needs me, and he's trying to get me to listen to him? What if I'm the only person who can rescue him?"

She could see the hesitation on her friend's face plain as day, the concern etched there.

"Vivian—that sounds—"

"I know. I know everyone thinks it's my grief talking, but I'm telling you it's not that. There's this feeling that I have. Like he's trying to speak to me."

"But how? How is that even possible?"

"I don't know. I don't—Joe always said that there was so much we didn't know about space. So much we didn't understand. Maybe there's some way he can communicate from there, as unlikely and impossible as that may seem."

It sounded like something out of one of the science fiction novels Joe loved to read, but what if there was some kernel of truth in those books? Joe himself had told her that all those stories were rooted in a combination of science and imagination.

"Please don't take this the wrong way—you know I love you and there's nothing I want more than for Joe to come home to you and for everything to be alright. But—"

"How do you explain the message that Joe left in the pocket of my skirt?" Vivian asked. "The one that Joe wrote *Wait for me* on. Frank said that the calculations on the back of the paper were *his*. He recognized them and said that he gave them to Joe right before he boarded the ship. How could it have ended up in my pocket?"

"I don't know," Polly admitted. "Maybe you're right. I just don't want you to have hope only for it to be extinguished."

"And if it is? Why not have hope at this point? After all, the alternative is that my husband is dead. If I'm either going to be devastated now or grieve him later, then I'd rather hold out on hope for as long as I can. Besides, it isn't just hope—it's the feeling I have inside of me that I can't shake. Like I'm missing something or there's something he's trying to tell me. Sometimes it feels like he's shouting at me."

Wait for me.

NINE

1962

Vivian stood next to the camera crew at Rice University, waiting for President Kennedy to speak. The station's on-air talent was setting up the shot, standing by for the camera-man to start rolling so he could record an introduction for the audience that would later be played with the prime-time coverage of the speech.

It was the first time they'd sent her to cover a story out of state; lately most of the pieces she worked on—often with Kerry Krieger—were political stories, typically confined to the D.C. Metro area. But she'd done a few stories on the space program, and President Kennedy's speech was being pitched as the ultimate rallying cry for America's ambitions in space. Kerry should have been in Texas with Vivian, but at the last moment she'd come down with an unfortunate case of food poisoning.

Vivian still had her doubts about the whole program, still

believed the money could be better spent elsewhere, still questioned why all of the astronauts were exclusively white men, but she couldn't deny that there was an energy here today beyond even that which normally surrounded President Kennedy, that America seemed poised to follow him to the Moon and wherever else he dared to take them.

Ever since his inauguration speech, even before that, really, to his time on the campaign trail, President Kennedy had demonstrated an ability to rally the country behind his dreams and ambitions. There was something infectious about his belief in the possibility of America to be better than it currently was, in the way he called the nation to do their part to realize that potential.

It didn't hurt that the president had a way with words, a speaking manner and presence that captivated the audience, and that he offered hope and change to a fractured and hurting nation with eloquence and understanding.

Vivian fanned herself with the papers in her hand, the heat of the day getting to her. Around her, people mopped their brows with handkerchiefs, used hats and fans to seek some relief from the sweltering Texas day. The weather seemed more suited to the dead of summer than September, but considering this was her first trip to Houston, she hadn't been sure what to expect.

Vivian hung back as they began rolling, the station's correspondent, Brian Forrester, reading the copy that she'd written on the long flight from D.C. to Houston yesterday. She'd been embarrassed to admit it in front of her more seasoned colleagues, but it had been her first time on an airplane, and the flight had awed her. The food was delicious, the service impeccable, and even though the idea of flying through the sky had somewhat terrified her, when she'd looked out at the clouds below them, she'd felt a sense of amazement and wonder that reminded her of how Joe had described flying. She'd been surprised by how badly she'd wanted to tell him about the experience, to share with him the fact that on some small level she'd seen the beauty he had spoken of.

She hadn't heard from him since that night she saw him at Polly and Frank's engagement party months ago, and like she'd suspected when he had asked her if she was happy with Graham, as soon as she'd told him "yes," he stopped writing to her. She'd received the last postcard Joe had dropped in the mail a week after the party, the wave of regret when she realized it was likely the final one she'd receive from him taking her by surprise.

She missed him. Missed the friendship that had developed between them in their correspondence.

"The crowd here is eager to see President Kennedy . . ." Brian continued in his measured voice, a gleam in his eyes as he spoke to the camera. They'd worked together twice before, and she liked him well enough. He was respectful and reliable, and while some would have complained about being paired with a more inexperienced reporter, he'd treated her well on their trip.

Vivian was growing used to the fact that she was often the only woman in the newsroom writing copy, Kerry's experience and seniority setting her apart somewhat. Going from working at a radio station where she was surrounded by women took some adjusting, particularly on trips like these, when Vivian was alone in the company of men, but she had learned which of her colleagues treated her with respect and which of them she should avoid. She'd also learned to work harder than her male colleagues, the bar for proving herself incredibly high considering the preconceived notions that so many in the newsroom seemed to have about women's roles in the workplace—or lack thereof.

Pride filled Vivian as she listened to Brian deliver the copy she'd written. She thought back to all the cups of coffee she'd made—and likely would still make—the times when she'd felt like giving up because the chance of being taken seriously in the newsroom had felt like an impossibility. And yet here it was—she was making a meaningful impact on this story, helping to share the news with the American people.

It hit her now what television had given her: All her life she had felt like she didn't have a voice, like her place in the world was defined by how she accommodated others, by the fact that she was a woman and society had certain expectations of what role she was meant to fulfill, but this—it felt like television gave her the opportunity to be seen in this world, for her voice to be heard.

It felt good.

Really good.

Brian finished up the intro, and then they moved to their designated places, waiting for the president to take the stage.

Vivian pulled out the little notebook she'd taken to carrying with her, ready to jot down whatever notes and quotes she could glean from the president's speech.

A flurry of excitement seemingly rippled through the crowd,

and Vivian received her first sight of President Kennedy in the flesh.

He was a distinguished man, handsome and hale, with a charisma about him as he smiled and shook hands with the crowd around him. That same inspiring air that came across when she watched him on television was even more present in real life. That was the extraordinary thing about television as a vehicle for communicating information to people—most of America would never get to see President Kennedy in person, but thanks to the work they did, to the advancements in broadcasting, people could sit in their living rooms and watch his speech and they could experience the sensation of what it had been like to attend in person.

The ability of a camera to transport someone to another time and place undeniably felt a bit like magic.

The president began to speak, and like the rest of the audience, Vivian was caught up in the cadence of his voice, in the timeline he developed with his words. Perhaps one of the president's greatest gifts was that he was a storyteller, and in his speech, he took the audience on a trip through time.

President Kennedy spoke of mankind's accomplishments, of all the ways scientific advancements had enriched society, of the importance of knowledge in fostering understanding. He laid out the span of scientific achievements starting with man learning to cloak and shelter himself to the belief that space seemed inevitably like the next scientific frontier for them to explore.

President Kennedy spoke of job creation, of a growing scientific community, of the positive impact space exploration would have on medical and climate programs. He sold space to the nation with grace and aplomb, his cadence building in a way that seemingly had the audience riding the crests of his speech.

It was to be a unifying endeavor for the nation, and while President Kennedy didn't directly reference his efforts in his speech, he had recently begun an attempt to diversify the space program, even though many—herself included—would say they still had far to go.

It wasn't until last year that Ed Dwight, a graduate of the elite test pilot school and a captain in the Air Force, became the first Black astronaut candidate to go through the training program at the Aerospace Research Pilot School at Edwards Air Force Base. And even though the Soviets had sent a female cosmonaut, Valentina Tereshkova, to space months earlier, there were no women in NASA's astronaut training program.

Space felt not like some uncharted frontier filled with possibility but another place where barriers existed for many.

But despite her reservations, and the undeniable fact that she had been ready to meet the speech with skepticism, President Kennedy was apparently prepared to speak to his critics as well. He directly addressed those who thought that space was too lofty a goal, that it wasn't worth the hardship and sacrifice that the program would require.

But who would be the ones bearing the most sacrifice?

It seemed like it was the astronauts and their families who would be risking the most. Vivian had seen the press conferences, read and heard the interviews where the astronauts said that it was worth it, that they were dedicated to this next American dream, but she wondered if they understood exactly what they were signing up for, if any of the nation—or the president himself—truly understood the road ahead of them. How could they when they were all essentially making it up as they went along?

Vivian glanced around her, the crowd breaking out into applause as President Kennedy spoke of America's history of growth and taking risks, how the nature of the nation depended on progress. He managed to achieve the delicate balance between portraying space exploration as a hopeful adventure that would benefit society writ large while simultaneously painting a terrifying image of what the world could look like if a hostile or nefarious power conquered space. It was a rhetorical skill done so artfully that Vivian had to admire the president's speechwriter for their prowess.

And more than anything, perhaps, what she admired about President Kennedy was his willingness to acknowledge the things that had gone wrong in the space program, to accept accountability. She appreciated that he recognized the enormity of the $5.4 billion annual space budget—an amount so vast she couldn't wrap her mind around it—and admired the skill with which he got out in front of the criticisms that had been levied his way regarding the staggering sum that the nation was spending on this dream to go to the Moon and send man to space.

Her gaze drifted around the audience—at the men and women sitting behind the president, at those in the less well-appointed seats who had come here today to be part of history being made.

America would go to the Moon.

What the president proposed—he was speaking of technologies they'd yet to develop, speaking of a journey filled with complexity and danger—seemed too audacious. That the United States was going to build a rocket the length of the football field standing before them was an incredible thought, and even though she had watched Alan Shepard's launch on television, it was hard to visualize what the scope of such a rocket would be in real life, and how very small a human being would seem standing in its shadow.

President Kennedy called it the most dangerous adventure man had ever taken, and she thought of Joe and his dreams of space, his desire to become an astronaut, and as much as she felt bad for him and how his hope of being an astronaut had been dashed, a part of her was relieved he wouldn't be in harm's way, even as she felt guilty for putting the thought out into the universe when she knew how badly he'd wanted it.

The president finished his speech, and the crowd rose to their feet with gusto, despite the overwhelming heat of the day, which Kennedy had more than aptly compared to being on the surface of the sun.

She wasn't surprised that President Kennedy received a standing ovation, and she imagined whatever obstacles he faced in Congress would pale in comparison to the support the president had from the American people.

The excitement in the air was infectious as President Kennedy left the stage. It wasn't the first time he had announced his ambitions to take Americans to the Moon, but there had been something about this speech that felt portentous, as though they were on the precipice of some great change that would open possibilities beyond anything they'd ever imagined. The world around them was changing more quickly than Vivian could wrap her mind around, and after standing there watching history be made, she couldn't help but feel like some of that change might sweep through her life, too.

Vivian stood to the side, watching as Brian and the cameraman, Chuck, shot some more footage with reactions to the president's speech.

They wrapped up, and Vivian hung back for a beat after Brian and Chuck left, not quite ready to move on from this incredible moment in time and the feeling that she had just been part of an event that would reverberate throughout generations.

Someone tapped her on her shoulder, and she turned around just as a familiar voice said—

"Vivian."

Joe stood before her, wearing a navy military uniform, a hat atop his close-cropped blond hair, colorful ribbons and medals on the breast of his jacket.

Vivian blinked, not quite reconciling what she was seeing in front of her, completely caught off guard by the fact that he was *here*.

In the United States.

In Texas.

Right in front of her.

And then her mind caught up with the sight before her, and the full impact of Joe in his military uniform hit her. She hadn't been lying when she told Polly that a man in uniform wasn't the sort of thing that would normally elicit a reaction, but there was something about Joe in his uniform, or maybe more importantly something about Joe, period, that had her feeling more than a little off-kilter.

"What are you doing here?" Vivian blurted out, glancing around them at the mostly dispersing crowd, and then back at Joe. "I thought you were in Italy."

It had been nine months since they last saw each other at Polly and Frank's engagement party. Polly and Frank both mentioned him in passing, and neither one of them had said anything about him returning to the United States.

After the engagement party, Vivian had anticipated seeing him at Polly and Frank's wedding, but Joe's request for leave from his military assignment in Italy had been denied, and so another one of Frank's pilot buddies stood up at the altar next to Frank, and Vivian accepted that she probably would never see Joe again.

"I'm still stationed in Italy. For now, at least."

Vivian absentmindedly ran a hand through her hair, belatedly realizing that the hot day had likely done a number on her. How did he look so fresh standing in this interminable heat in his heavy uniform?

"I'm here for work," Joe replied. His voice lowered slightly, his words for her alone. "I came for some meetings at NASA."

He said it solemnly, quietly, as though he were sharing something intensely private with her, as though he wanted her to know this about him, and she understood the significance of what he was saying, how he dreamed of going to space. She knew how much this meant to him, and strangely, where a few minutes ago she'd listened to the audacity of President Kennedy's speech and felt relief that Joe wasn't going to the Moon, now she felt a burst of hope for him, the strength of the emotion catching her off guard.

"Are you going to get a chance to join the space program?" Vivian whispered.

"I don't know, but after hearing a speech like that, I hope so. They're changing the requirements for becoming an astronaut. You no longer need to be a test pilot."

"Oh, Joe, that's wonderful." She moved without thinking, instinct taking over as she wrapped her arms around him and gave him a hug. "I'm so happy for you. You're going to be a wonderful astronaut. And to think that you might go to the Moon—"

Joe caught her mid-embrace, sweeping her up in his arms, holding her close.

"I'm so happy for you," Vivian murmured, her lips inches away from his ear.

"Thank you."

She could feel his breath on her skin when he said the words, in the curve of her neck, and then they both realized how close they were, and Joe released her, taking a step back, and then another, putting space between them.

"It was a wonderful speech, wasn't it? Even for a skeptic like me." Vivian smiled despite the nerves fluttering inside her. "He seemed to have written that speech with you in mind. So now it's not just space, but the Moon that you're chasing?"

"Maybe I'm chasing all of it."

She flushed at the way he met and held her gaze as he said it, at the undercurrent and undeniable intent contained there.

She still hadn't recovered from the shock of seeing him,

hadn't been prepared for him to show up where she was like this.

Vivian shook her head, unable to believe this was happening.

Joe cocked his head to the side, studying her. "What is it?"

"I can't believe you're here. When I think of you, I always imagine you in Italy, in one of the scenes in your postcards. It's going to take a girl a minute to catch up."

"How often do you think of me?"

Maybe Kennedy's boldness had rubbed off on her, because she surprised herself—and perhaps Joe—by answering him.

"Often enough."

Too often.

"I think about you, too. Often."

He said it like a confession.

Be bold.

It was what President Kennedy had implored them to do when he proposed this audacious thing.

And now, they were all going to the Moon.

It was hard not to be inspired by an invocation to be bold, particularly when you didn't have a natural propensity to such action.

"Would you like to get a coffee . . . or something?" Vivian asked him, her heart pounding.

"'Or something.'" He swallowed. "I'd like that very much."

Joe gestured toward the spot where she'd been standing by the TV crew earlier. "Are you finished with work? I didn't want to interrupt you while you were filming, but it looked like you'd wrapped up, so I thought it was a good time to come over."

If the letters they'd exchanged hadn't increased her attraction to him, and the uniform hadn't done it, either, then Vivian would say that it was the knowledge that he had waited while she finished working, had understood the spectacle it would have caused for him to interrupt their taping, and had respected the fact that she was trying to make a good impression on her colleagues. She'd said as much in her messages to him, but it meant even more to know that he had listened to her and taken her feelings into consideration.

"I'm finished," Vivian confirmed, and Joe fell into step beside her as they walked away from the stage.

"I've thought of you a lot since we last saw each other," he said, causing her to stumble, the honesty in his voice catching her off guard. Perhaps President Kennedy's advice to be bold had resonated with him as well, because she couldn't escape the feeling that he had decided to be different with her today, that everything was different today, all pretense stripped between them. "I've missed your letters. Missed your friendship."

Vivian favored his honesty with some of her own.

"I wondered how you were doing. How you were enjoying your time in Europe. All of it. I missed hearing from you. Missed your postcards."

She didn't want to tell him the rest of it, didn't want to admit that she had worried about him when she had no right to, no claim on his affections, no official place in his life. It felt like a strange thing to admit even as it was very much the truth.

So, she told him a different truth instead—

"I'm not with Graham. Not anymore."

Joe stopped short, so quickly that she nearly stumbled into

him, and he took her hand, catching her, keeping her from falling as his arm wrapped around her waist.

"Since when?"

She'd wondered if Polly or Frank had mentioned it to him,
but his reaction gave her all the answer she needed.

Vivian swallowed. "Since the night of Polly and Frank's engagement party. I called Graham after I got home. I told him
that I didn't feel the same way about him that he felt about me,
that it wasn't fair to him to continue the relationship when I
knew I wouldn't be able to give him what he wanted or needed.

"Seeing Polly and Frank together—he deserves to have
someone who loves him like that."

"Was there anything else that night that made you realize
that Graham wasn't the one for you?" Joe asked her.

There was so much hope in his eyes, something akin to
longing—that Alan-Shepard-launching-into-space look again—
and they'd danced around what existed between them for so
long, this connection that they had, and Vivian couldn't deny it
anymore. She didn't *want* to deny it.

Be bold.

"When I saw you again—" Vivian swallowed, nerves bub-
bling up inside her. Maybe it was better that she hadn't known
she would see him here, that she hadn't prepared for this. It
didn't give her a chance to try to reason her way out of what she
said next.

"When I saw you again, I knew that there was something
different in the way I felt when I was around you."

"Viv."

Oh my.

He'd never called her that before, but now she knew she wanted to hear her name—just like that—falling from his lips.

She had to ask. "Is there anyone—"

Joe shook his head. "No. No. Just you."

Vivian looked up into his eyes, and she saw the question there, knew what he was asking, knew what her answer would be.

Little moments, strung together, that suddenly felt momentous.

A double date. A space launch. An invocation to be bold.

Vivian nodded, the words stuck in her throat as anticipation built, as she waited for him to finally kiss her.

As soon as his lips touched hers, she knew this had been a very bad idea indeed.

As soon as his lips touched hers, she knew she didn't want anyone else to kiss her.

As soon as his lips touched hers, everything else disappeared and they were no longer on the fringes of the Rice University football stadium, but in their own little world where anything was possible.

At least for today.

TEN

1968

Three Days Gone

I'm sorry, Vivian. I know you're upset, but I still don't have any new information for you."

"How is that possible, Frank? How do you lose a spacecraft worth hundreds of millions of dollars and three crew members and not know where it is?" Vivian asked, sitting across from Frank in his office at the Cape.

"Do you think we haven't been getting that question from every possible interest involved and then some? You don't think the press is all over this and asking the same questions? Everyone and their mother is giving me a hard time because of the potential that we won't even be able to recover any data from the spacecraft," Frank snapped, looking like he hadn't slept in days. His desk was a mess, the surface covered in manila file folders and loose papers. Three different coffee cups sat there along with what appeared to be a half-eaten donut.

"I'm sorry. I shouldn't have lost my patience like that. I just—" Frank slumped down in his chair, looking entirely defeated, and despite the frustration welling up inside her, Vivian felt a pang of sympathy for him. Her husband was lost, yes, but so was Frank's best friend, a man he had known for nearly two decades. Not to mention, this had been Joe's mission in space, but it had been Frank's mission on the ground, and clearly tensions were running high at the agency.

"Vivian, I know you're looking for answers and I know you're angry, but I'm telling you the truth—we don't know anything. There's not some big secret that the agency is trying to keep from you. There's just—nothing."

How was that possible? She'd hoped that they had an idea of where the crew was and just weren't sharing the information, that this was another situation like so many in Joe's career where there were things they wouldn't tell her, things she couldn't know. But sitting across from Frank, seeing the frustration in his face firsthand—

She believed him.

"What does that mean? It's a spacecraft. There were three men aboard. How is it just gone? How is that possible? How do you not have some mechanism for tracking this? How can they just disappear?"

It felt like something out of one of those science fiction novels Joe loved to read, where people slipped in and out of time and space, here one moment, gone the next. At this point, she'd accept even an outlandish explanation over the agony of no explanation at all.

"It's the same question we keep asking ourselves," Frank replied. "But that's where we are. There's no record of it out there. Not where it should be and not anywhere close to its path. We are getting absolutely no information from the spacecraft. It's not transmitting *anything*. We were receiving information and then we just lost it.

"There's no debris anywhere that indicates perhaps it tried to return and had problems on reentry. And we don't even have evidence that something went wrong. The launch went well. There were no warning indicators. No systems failures. Nothing. I know you want answers, but I don't have any to give you."

Frank hesitated. "You should prepare yourself. The consensus here is starting to be that something happened to them out there and they're not coming back. No one benefits from this dragging on, from it dominating the headlines and sparking fear and uncertainty in the American public. And, Vivian, the science just doesn't support the likelihood that we're going to be able to bring them back after three days of no contact. It hasn't been done. We don't think it can be. For us to have lost contact with them for three days—something catastrophic must have happened. Something unrecoverable."

"Like what? Aliens taking over their spacecraft?" she exploded.

Maybe she didn't prefer the outlandish after all.

"No. Not aliens. But something in the environment in space that was inhospitable to the spacecraft. A collision of some sort, perhaps."

"Wouldn't you see debris, then?"

"Maybe. You would think, yes, but it's possible the space-craft ended up off course. Maybe we wouldn't know where to look for it."

Joe had explained the risks of his job to her before, and Vivian understood that they were on the vanguard of space exploration, and when you were doing something for the first time, there was an element of unpredictability. That didn't make it less infuriating, though.

"There are those in the agency who think it would be best if we got ahead of this, if we accepted that there were problems with the launch, and if we allowed the nation to grieve so that we could all move forward," Frank replied, his voice heart-breakingly gentle.

The word "grieve" felt like a knife to her stomach.

She refused to accept that death was the only possible solution. For all they knew, Joe and the rest of the crew were in space trying their hardest to return. There was no way Vivian was just going to leave him to fight his way home alone.

"'Something happened to them out there'? That's the official explanation?"

"It's space, Vivian. There's so much we don't know. So much we haven't explored, so much we don't understand." Frank took a deep breath. "Joe understood that. He accepted it. We all do. It's what comes with the territory. We knew this mission was dangerous. *He* knew this mission was dangerous. He knew there was a strong chance that he might not come home."

A stone sank in her stomach as she listened to Frank describe Joe in the past tense, as though he was already gone.

"Did you all accept the risk? Because last I heard the astronauts were being told that the risk of something going wrong was, what, .001%?"

"No one believed that percentage, Vivian. You know that. It was a coin toss."

"Then what's the point of giving it?" she snapped. "Is the entire mission just throwing numbers out in the air?" She pulled the memorandum the man had given her out of her purse and slid the paper across Frank's desk. "Did you know anything about this?"

Frank scanned the memorandum, a line forming between his brows. His head shot up, his gaze boring into hers. "Where did you get this?"

"A man slipped it to me at the press conference. Did you know about this? That there were problems with the spacecraft?"

"This memo specifically? No. But look—" Frank sighed. "I'm sure Joe told you. At times, there have been tensions between the people building the spacecraft and, well, those of us piloting it."

"Tensions" was putting it mildly, as far as Vivian was concerned. She'd heard Frank and Joe cursing up a storm as they complained about the dynamics between the astronauts flying the spacecraft and the scientists working on it. The scientists for their part seemed bothered by all the attention the astronauts received, and they clearly had little patience for the inflated fighter-pilot-turned-astronaut swagger that dominated the space program.

In the beginning, the scientists had viewed the astronauts'

roles as merely ancillary, seen them as little more than after-thoughts compared to the machines that were supposed to be operating the spacecraft—the systems that the scientists and engineers were working on, making them the heroes of space-flight, not the men who gave press conferences and received audiences with the president and ticker tape parades.

The astronauts had unsurprisingly taken umbrage to the fact that they were relegated to little more than mere passengers on this adventurous voyage, especially considering many of them had given up prestigious military careers where they were "the best of the best" to join the space program.

And so, a compromise had been struck as each faction navigated its role and cooperation in spaceflight. Still—the only thing that could get Joe going more than the doctors that poked and prodded them like lab rats was the scientists and engineers who were building the spacecraft—never "capsule," as the scientists wanted to call it. Ironic, really, considering Joe himself had an engineering degree.

"The scientists believe in their systems and their backups, maybe to a fault," Frank said. "They have all this unshakable faith in the computers to fly these things. Not everyone does. For pilots, well, you know—it's not just about the machine, it's about the person flying the machine."

"Joe is a good pilot, Frank. He's a good astronaut."

"Joe was the best damned pilot I've ever flown with. And he was a great astronaut."

There it was again—the past tense. She saw it in his eyes, heard it in his voice—he'd already accepted that Joe was gone.

Neither one of them spoke, because neither one of them

could bear to fill the silence with what went unsaid between them.

Death was part of this life. They all knew someone who had perished in flight or in training for space. For the pilots and their spouses, the deaths were met with spoken assurances that it wouldn't happen to them or their spouses, because they were good pilots. Great pilots. The assurances weren't meant to demean the departed, and they weren't taken as such; rather, they were offered as a source of comfort, of bravado, of why despite the undeniable odds to the contrary, the fact that it was so damned hard to get a life insurance policy on a fighter pilot or an astronaut, their loved one would make it home. It was a lie they all told themselves to make the unbearable bearable.

It was a consolation Vivian had whispered to herself, relied upon, heard come out of Joe's lips time and time again throughout his career.

Death wouldn't come knocking at their door because Joe was a good pilot. A great one. Great enough to outrun death.

Except that deep down, living among the thoughts and fears they rarely if ever wanted to face, they all knew that one day that might not be enough.

That sometimes your luck simply ran out, no matter how good of a pilot or astronaut you were.

"Could something have gone wrong with the navigation system?" Vivian asked.

"Yes. Maybe. In theory, the computer controls the capsule, but things go wrong. People like to act like the machines are infallible, but the truth is that they're only as good as the inputs that they're given or the people who build them."

"Did you know that there were concerns about the navigation system?"

"No."

"Would others have known?"

"I don't know, Vivian. Honestly. I swear to you that if I did, I would tell you."

She wanted to believe him. Badly. Wanted to believe that the man who stood next to Joe at the altar when she married him would care more about his friend than the Space Race.

"Would you?"

He frowned. "What's that supposed to mean?"

"I don't know, Frank, it just feels like you're squarely in the agency's camp. I mean you came to me asking if I would give a statement to show support for going to the Moon while my husband is missing."

He raked his hand through his hair. "He's my best friend, Vivian. He may be your husband, but he's my best friend. I'm the mission director on the ground. I'm the one who told him the mission was good to go. You don't think it's eating me up inside to know that something might have happened to him on my watch?"

"I'm sorry, Frank. I—"

She didn't know what words to offer him, how to explain the feelings that warred within her. She'd always wished she had a different temperament for this sort of thing, watched as the other wives seemed to believe in the mission with such a fervency that she almost thought if their husbands were sacrificed to it, they would accept the loss as part of the territory. Maybe it was the fact that she'd already lost her father to war; she wasn't ready to give up her husband to space.

"I'm so worried about him," she settled on finally, the words somehow both exactly the ones she was searching for and terribly inadequate. "I need to feel like I'm doing something, like he's going to come home, because the alternative is unthinkable."

"I know."

Vivian could tell from the way he said it, by the manner in which his shoulders sagged a bit, that a part of him had already given up, and even as it frustrated her to confront the fact that he might think it was over, because he was Joe's best friend, more like family to both of them, she worried about him.

"How are you doing, Frank?"

It was the question Joe would have asked if he were here and saw his friend looking like this.

"About as well as you would expect." Frank studied her for a moment, and whatever he saw in her gaze must have confirmed it for him. "I guess you heard that Polly left."

"I did. I'm sorry. For all of you."

"Me too. I don't know what happened. I don't know what I did that made her stop loving me. I've tried racking my brain to figure it out. She told me a month before the launch. Said she would come out here for you, would keep up the appearance of everything being normal because we both agreed it was the last thing you and Joe needed to be worried about. Even after I agreed to the divorce to make her happy, I kept hoping she would change her mind, that this was some sort of mood she was in that would go away."

Vivian leveled him with a look. "Come on, Frank. You can't chalk this up to a mood and then ask why she's upset."

The thing about Frank was that at his core, he wasn't a bad

guy. She'd seen enough of the ones who had little care or consideration for their spouses and children, who treated them as though they were hardly more than accessories designed to complement their space ambitions. Frank had a terrible habit of saying the wrong thing, but she'd always known him to be someone who cared deeply about his family, about doing the right thing. He just fared better with machines than people. And considering she'd never been all that great with people, either, she had a bit of a soft spot for him even when he said things that infuriated her.

She realized that the crux of her frustration with Frank stemmed from the fact that he was likely torn between his loyalty and affection for Joe, and his unshakable belief in the Space Race and the need for the Americans to decisively best the Soviets once and for all. Frank had spent the entirety of his adult life believing in his service—that the mission he dedicated himself to was an honorable one, that his actions kept those he loved and his countrymen safe. Even though she didn't view the world through the same lens he did, she could understand how Frank felt like prioritizing the mission to the Moon was a manner of serving his family. She could understand his bewilderment, even as her heart went out to poor Polly, who had shouldered the weight of her family for so long and was perfectly entitled to say she was done and wipe her hands of the entire business.

"I don't think she stopped loving you, Frank. She's tired. We're all tired. This life—it asks a lot. I don't know anyone who doesn't break at times."

"You and Joe never seemed like that. Like it was breaking

you." He flushed. "Sorry—I didn't mean to bring up something sensitive during—"

"No. It's alright. It's good to talk about him. To think about him." Vivian took a deep breath, steadying herself. "We fight plenty, Frank."

Surprise flashed across his face. "I just don't understand what happened. With Polly, I mean. We didn't used to fight. Now it seems like it's all we do."

He looked so miserable, so clueless, that she couldn't help but feel a little bad for him, for how he looked like a man whose world had been turned on its axis and wasn't sure how to proceed. Thanks to the military and then NASA, Frank was used to following the path that was set before him, to existing in a clearly defined structure with an established hierarchy that governed the way he saw himself in the world and in his interaction with others. There wasn't a code of conduct that governed civilian relationships, and she would have bet anything that if someone handed Frank a codified handbook for how to deal with his wife, he would have gladly accepted and followed it.

"She carries a lot—Polly does," Vivian tried again.

"I *know*," Frank replied.

She recognized the expression on his face because she'd seen it enough on her husband's. She understood the frustration that Frank felt, considering she'd seen Joe be torn between his loyalty to the space program and the mission, and his loyalty to her and their marriage. It wasn't an easy situation for either of them.

Vivian hesitated, not sure how much she should get involved in her friends' marriage, but at the same time, she'd known both since before they were Polly-and-Frank, and she cared deeply about them.

"Polly makes everything look easy. Perfect. Like she stepped off the pages of *Life* magazine. But I think she works harder than anyone else to make things look easy. And when things don't go the way she thinks they should, she's the first person to blame herself."

"She's my wife. You don't think I know that?"

"Maybe you know it, but Polly doesn't know that you know it. She doesn't hear it enough. She feels like a lot of the things she does go unnoticed." Vivian sighed. "It's hard enough being an astronaut's wife. This life—it doesn't leave much room for us. The work you're doing is important—the whole world celebrates your efforts and accomplishments. But the work we do keeping everything running, the work Polly does at home and with the girls, that's important, too. Even if it's hard to compete with matters of national security and, you know, the universe."

"What do I do? How do I get my family back? You know Polly better than anyone. What would you do if you were me? How do I show her how grateful I am?"

"Show her that she matters. That you see her. I know this is the absolute worst time with everything that's going on, and believe me, Polly understands. But Polly needs to feel like she and the girls are a priority to you."

Vivian rose, taking the memorandum she'd handed Frank and slipping it back into her purse.

He made a move like he was going to stop her, and then he just shook his head as though he realized the futility in putting up a fuss.

She was moving to leave his office when he called out her name.

"I know you want to believe Joe is coming home. We all want that. But if he doesn't, if something happened to him out there, then he would want you to be happy. You're the love of his life. He was different when he was with you. More comfortable, more at peace. More than anything he would want you to be alright, Vivian."

She didn't reply, didn't think she could bear to, because it unmistakably felt like Frank was warning her to prepare for a conclusion he considered to be inevitable, and she refused to accept.

"What if he's out there somewhere? What if I did hear him on the squawk box? What if he needs help?"

"Vivian. What you're talking about—the science of this stuff. It's complicated. There's so much out there that we don't know, so much that we're learning."

She was beginning to think this was the only refrain they had to offer her, and she refused to accept it.

"Sending a man into space was complicated once, but you figured that out, didn't you? Don't tell me getting him back safely is beyond your reach now."

"We don't even know if he's out there *to* get back safely," Frank replied. He paled. "I'm sorry. I shouldn't have—"

"It's fine, Frank. Don't think it has escaped my notice that you all seem to think he's gone. I'm just asking you not to give up. Please."

ELEVEN

After President Kennedy's speech at Rice, Joe took her to a little restaurant near the university. They ordered drinks, their table garnering more than a few glances considering the dashing image Joe cut in his uniform.

Vivian grinned, a laugh escaping.

"What?" Joe asked her. "What's so funny?"

"I was just remembering the night we met. Polly was trying to"—Vivian searched for the right words—"entice me to the prospect of a double date, and one of the things she mentioned was how handsome a man in uniform could be. At the time, I told her I wasn't much for a military uniform. It's a little humbling to admit how wrong I was."

His eyes flashed with emotion, that Alan-Shepard-launching-into-space look again. "Viv."

"I like when you say my name like that," she replied, her voice low, a thrill sliding down her spine. "No one else calls me Viv."

Joe reached across the table, taking her hand, linking their fingers together, and her heart thundered in her chest.

She glanced down at the place where they were joined, their hands resting on the old wooden table.

The waitress brought their drinks, giving Vivian a moment to collect herself, to marvel at the fact that she was sitting here across from Joe, holding his hand, that he had kissed her, that she wanted him to kiss her again.

"The Moon, huh?" she finally asked when they were alone once more.

He laughed. "Hopefully."

"Does Frank know?"

"Frank is aiming for a shot himself," Joe replied. "We thought it would be the perfect continuation of our careers—the fact that we learned to fly together and then might head to space together."

Polly hadn't mentioned this new development, but it seemed like there was a level of secrecy around recruiting the new astronauts, and she didn't blame her friend for not saying anything. Polly and Frank had moved on to an assignment in Florida, and while she and Polly exchanged letters frequently, Vivian missed her terribly.

"I hope you both get it."

Joe inclined his head toward her, a question in his gaze. "You've never been much of a fan of the Space Race."

Vivian laughed. "Someone once told me that there was nothing more romantic than space. Maybe I'm coming around to it."

Joe leaned forward, kissing her so swiftly that it sent flutters racing through her, and she realized he understood what she was really saying, perhaps more than she did—

Maybe I'm coming around to more than just the Space Race.

They broke away long enough for the waitress to take their lunch order.

"I still can't believe we're here together," Vivian said. "It seems—"

"Like it was meant to be?" he finished for her.

She laughed. "You forget—I'm the skeptic, remember? I'm not sure I believe in 'meant to be.'"

"I thought we agreed that you were a romantic, too. Just in your own way." Joe studied her across the table. "You don't think the universe is trying to tell us something by sending us both to Houston, Texas, at the same time?"

She would have said "no" before today, but even she had to admit that she had felt something on that field at Rice University—an inevitability to the way she found herself gravitating toward him time and time again.

And still—

She couldn't resist giving him a little bit of a hard time, because on some level she kind of thought he liked this back-and-forth they had between them.

Vivian arched a brow at him. "The universe?"

He laughed. "I think I love your skepticism most of all."

Love.

He said it casually, jokingly, and she knew he didn't mean the word seriously, not *love, love,* but still, it felt like a premonition of things to come, and she knew as she had from the beginning—certainly from the first conversation they'd had the night they met at the bar—that there would be nothing casual with him. That if she was going to go down this path, she was going to have to be all-in. The challenges presented by his lifestyle, the emotions ricocheting through her, all demanded it.

It would be a terrifying, exhilarating, wonderful thing to be loved by this man.

"Yes, the universe. Like maybe we were both meant to be here because we were meant to see each other again," Joe replied. "When I arrived at the field, I don't know—" Joe shook his head. "It felt like I was about to experience something important. I didn't know what it was going to be—I figured it was the energy of the president's speech and the promise of going to the Moon, but then I saw you and it was like something clicked—

"I've thought about you a lot since Polly and Frank's engagement party. Wondered when—if—I would see you again. I told myself that it was enough that you said you were happy, that I didn't want to complicate that, but I guess I kept hoping like I did after test pilot school didn't pan out that maybe something would change, and I'd have a shot with you."

Joe took a deep breath, his expression solemn as though her answer was deeply important to him.

"Do I have a shot with you?"

And even though it was wholly uncharacteristic for her, Vivian didn't think before she answered him—

"Yes."

"VISIT ME IN ITALY."

Vivian stirred, rolling over in bed to face Joe.

"What time is it?" she asked him, pulling the sheet over her body as she sat up beside him.

"Just past six in the morning."

Right. It made sense that he would be a morning person given the military career. Vivian loathed waking up early, which made working on the morning news a rough endeavor. But at least on her days off, she made a point to sleep in as much as she could to make up for it.

"My flight leaves this afternoon," Joe added, his voice quiet.

They hadn't talked about when they were both leaving, as though they hadn't wanted to face the inevitable reality that they only had one night together before they had to return to their respective lives. Vivian's own flight had her returning to D.C. in a few hours.

"Did you—"

"—ask you to come visit me in Italy?" Joe finished for her. She nodded.

"I did. To be fair, though, I thought you were still asleep, so I was sort of testing it out. Seeing if it sounded as ludicrous as I worried that it did."

"It didn't sound ludicrous—"

Except that it sort of did. She'd never been outside of the United States. They had spent the sum of one evening together; they'd gone to bed together, but they hadn't discussed what came next—were they a couple or something less defined?

A trip to Italy would be a way to figure it out, would provide clarity on their relationship. And it would be *fun*. An adventure. And she hadn't had an adventure in, what, a very long time—if ever? So much of her life was so carefully laid out before her, plans neatly drawn, that she almost never took detours.

If there was anyone she was ready to change things up for, though, it was him.

Especially after last night.

She was beginning to appreciate just where all his confidence came from.

And more than anything, Vivian couldn't deny the connection she felt with Joe, how when he'd fallen asleep with his arm wrapped around her, their fingers linked, she'd known with a certainty that settled deep in her bones that this was something she wasn't ready to walk away from.

Decision made, she turned to face him, the smile on her face wide, beaming.

She was happy.

Unbelievably happy.

"I would love to come to visit you in Italy."

TWELVE

"What are they telling you?" Vivian asked Bridget Drayer, the phone receiver cradled between her neck and shoulder as she glanced out the kitchen window to the backyard, where Polly's daughters ran through the sprinkler in their bathing suits, whooping and cheering, their energetic play a stark contrast to the nagging worry in Vivian's stomach.

There were no updates.

Nothing.

After her meeting yesterday with Frank in his office, she'd come to Polly and Frank's rental near the beach this afternoon, needing a reprieve from the people crowding into her little house, needing a sanctuary where she could call Michael's wife in privacy.

She'd thought about reaching out to Paul's parents as well,

but in the end had decided against it. There was a difference in living this experience as a spouse, having a front-row seat to the space program and all its dangers, and she didn't want to worry his parents any more than they likely were.

Despite their differences and the fact that they had never quite gelled, Bridget more than anyone would understand what Vivian was going through. And she was desperate to know if Bridget had the same feeling she did, the same intuition that perhaps NASA was wrong and the three of them were out there trying to get home, waiting to be rescued.

"They're not telling me much," Bridget replied. "You?"

Vivian sighed. "Just that they don't know anything."

"That's what they're saying to me as well," Bridget confirmed. "Seems hard to believe, doesn't it? That they could just lose a spacecraft out there like that?"

"It does."

"I suppose they don't have anything to gain by keeping it a secret, though. And secrets always come out sometime."

It was the way she said "secrets" that broke Vivian's heart, the way Bridget slurred the letters together. In all the years they'd known each other, Vivian had never seen Bridget have more than a few sips of wine at dinner, and while Vivian was the furthest thing from a teetotaler—and if any situation called for coping however you were able to, it was this one—the fact that Bridget was acting so out of character, the way a thin thread of criticism toward the space program and the agency filtered through Bridget's words, emphasized the precariousness in the situation.

Bridget, like Frank, sounded like someone who had given up hope.

And suddenly, Vivian felt very, very alone.

"He cheated on me."

Surprise filled Vivian, not just at the non sequitur, but at the vulnerability contained in that admission. It wasn't the cheating part—Michael hadn't exactly done a good job of hiding it—but more the fact that Bridget was admitting it to her. Of all the wives, they were about as opposite as you could be, and neither one had ever warmed to or confided in the other.

"Did you think I didn't know?" Bridget asked, correctly interpreting Vivian's silence for discomfort.

"I—I wasn't sure."

"I knew. Always. In the beginning, he was better at hiding it, but eventually—he couldn't even be bothered to try. The more attention they all got, the more it seemed like he thought it was part of the life—like the women came with the press conferences and magazine articles, as though they just went together. After all, what's the point of being a celebrity if you can't enjoy the perks?"

Vivian had never liked Michael. All the guys were arrogant in their own way, but a lot of them were ultimately good guys.

She hadn't known him well, but based on the impression she had, Vivian wouldn't have put Michael in that category.

"I'm sorry," Vivian replied. "You don't deserve that. No one deserves that."

"What would you know about it? Everyone knows Perfect Joe didn't so much as look at another woman."

"We have our problems," Vivian replied quietly.

Bridget laughed sharply, the sound sending a sinking feeling to Vivian's stomach. She'd never realized it before, but there had always been something about Bridget that made her un-comfortable. While everyone else praised Bridget's three well-behaved children, and her elegant home, which she'd decorated on a military wife's shoestring budget, and her gourmet casse-roles, and the aplomb with which she handled whatever the space program threw their way, Vivian hadn't been able to shake the feeling that whenever she spoke to Bridget, she wasn't really speaking to Bridget. There had been something false behind her smiles, an insincerity that had reminded Vivian of when she was a little girl trying to read her mother's moods, utterly confused by the fact that what her mother said never quite matched up with what she did, leaving Vivian in a constant state of alert to make sure she'd chosen the appropriate response.

"Why didn't you live in Togethersville?" Bridget asked. "You never went to A.W.C. meetings, either," she added, refer-ring to the "Astronauts Wives Club."

Of all the questions she expected Bridget to ask her, she hadn't seen that one coming.

"I—I don't know. I suppose I've always been more comfort-able on my own. And Togethersville—it didn't feel like the right fit. It didn't make sense to me to be away from Joe during the week while he was at the Cape, to only see him on weekends. I vastly preferred having that time together. And I—I couldn't be in Houston anymore. I couldn't take it . . . Not after . . ."

Silence greeted her on the other end of the line, Bridget likely remembering who she was talking to, remembering that while she'd envied Joe's fidelity, there were other parts of Vivi-an's life that no woman wanted to bear.

Vivian knew how it sounded, how it likely made her appear

to the other wives. Polly had shielded her from much of it, Polly's loyalty impregnable and daunting to anyone who dared utter a negative word about her best friend, but she could only imagine what they had said about her behind her back when Polly wasn't there to silence them with a look and the full weight of Frank's prestigious job at NASA. The other wives took the approach that if you needed them, they were there, but Vivian often worried that the message she sent by not joining in on their monthly gatherings was that she *didn't* need them, that she'd rather be alone than part of their group, when the truth was more complicated.

But more than anything, Vivian didn't want to discuss the real reason she couldn't stay in Togethersville anymore, didn't want to offer up the most vulnerable part of herself.

"Consider yourself lucky, then," Bridget replied. "That was probably what kept him from having a Cape Cookie on the side."

Maybe. Who knew? Early on, Vivian had spent a sleepless night or two wondering if like so many of his fellow astronauts, Joe was off drinking and carousing with other women. He'd never given her any reason to doubt him—to the contrary, there was a part of her that believed in his fidelity with a certainty that resided deep in her bones—but it was impossible to ignore that so many of his coworkers seemed to view their marital vows as something to be ignored. She'd tried to maintain a healthy balance between having faith in her marriage and not overly relying on a sense of exceptionalism, as though they'd somehow managed to escape the curse of infidelity and strain that plagued so many astro marriages. And still, she looked to the couples who had been happily married for decades, the ones where the wives and husbands operated as though they were one unit, navigating the challenges the space program threw their way with a commitment to each other that Vivian envied.

"Do you think they're doing enough to get them home?" Vivian asked, steering the conversation back to her original reason for the call.

"'Get them home'?"

"Of course. That should be the priority, shouldn't it? We don't know what happened to them, don't know if they're out there, needing our help," Vivian argued.

If Bridget and Paul's family gave up and accepted that the astronauts weren't coming home, how long would it be before NASA gave up as well?

"Vivian."

She turned at the sound of her name, the phone's cord wrapping around her waist with the motion.

Polly and Frank stood in the kitchen of their rental house, side by side, their hands linked.

It was strange that they were holding hands considering they'd just told her that they were going to get a divorce, and then she looked up from their linked hands to their faces—

"Bridget—I have to go."

Vivian struggled to set the phone receiver back on the cradle, her hands trembling.

She didn't look away from Frank's face.

Somewhere in the periphery of her vision, she sensed Polly walking away from Frank, toward her, felt Polly's arms wrap around her.

Frank's expression said it all, his eyes misty with unshed tears.

She'd stood up beside Polly at her wedding, and while Frank had beamed at his bride like he was the luckiest man in the world, he hadn't shed a tear.

One slid down his cheek now.

"No. Please no."

"Vivian," his voice cracked over her name.

She shook her head, panic filling her. "No. You're not going to tell me what you want to tell me. You're not going to deliver news to me in that tone, not with that look in your eyes. Do you think I don't know what's coming next? I know what you're going to tell me. *No. No.*"

The last word came out with a shout, and she felt Polly's arms wrapping around her, holding her up.

"Why aren't you out looking for him? Why aren't you doing something to bring him back?" she shouted.

The sound of wailing filled her ears, and then she realized the sound was coming from her, and Polly held on to her tightly, whispering words in her ear that Vivian couldn't begin to decipher through the grief that threatened to destroy her.

"He's gone, Vivian." Regret threaded through Frank's voice. "I'm sorry. There's nothing we can do. We've lost the spacecraft. We've lost all of them. It's over."

POLLY WALKED HER TO THE BEDROOM DOOR, AND FOR A moment, Vivian stood in front of it, unable to recall how she'd gotten from Polly's house to hers, pockets of time that had slipped through her fingers.

"Do you want to be alone?" Polly whispered.

Alone.

She was going to be alone. For the rest of her life. It was the thing she'd feared most after she met and fell in love with Joe—the understanding that she'd found the person she was meant to spend her life with, the person who fit her like the missing piece of a puzzle, and the inescapable fear that one day his job would take him away and she would be left alone.

Once—before Joe, at the beginning when they were just getting to know each other, when he wasn't a part of her—she'd been comfortable, content on her own. But now she knew the loss of what it felt like to be seen by another person, and that was another beast indeed.

Vivian nodded.

Polly gave Vivian a hug that barely registered, and then she closed the door, leaving Vivian by herself in the bedroom she and Joe had shared.

Vivian walked over to the dresser, the squawk box gone completely silent, and even though she knew what Frank had told her, knew that the scientists had decided that something unknown but catastrophic had happened to the spacecraft, that there was no hope of recovery, desperation filled her as she stared at the radio speaker, willing her husband's voice to come out of it, begging Joe to give her some sign that he was still out there, that he wasn't dead.

Silence greeted her instead.

Vivian opened the top drawer, pulling out the sheet of paper resting on top of her nightgowns.

She stared at the words she'd written there, the eulogy she'd composed the night before Joe's launch.

She would deliver the words at his funeral at Arlington.

In the city where they'd met and fallen in love.

In the city where he'd be laid to rest among the men and women who had served the country. Where he would be honored as an American hero.

Vivian glanced to the closet, belatedly realizing that she had no black dress to wear to her husband's funeral. She'd gone to plenty with Joe, but each time she'd gotten rid of the outfit afterward. Even though dresses were dear, the sight of that black dress hanging in her closet had always felt like a talisman, a harbinger of things to come, as though death stalked them.

The eulogy fell from her hands.

From her vantage point near the dresser, she could just make out the corner between the side of the bed that had been Joe's and their closet. She'd bought him a chair from a good second-hand store after she moved to Cocoa Beach, and each morning before work he'd sat in it wearing his uniform as he put his boots on. He'd had a terrible habit of leaving the boots there even when he wasn't working, and Vivian had tripped over them a time or two or twenty considering the spot was right in front of the closet door.

Joe's boots were in the middle of the walkway near the closet.

They hadn't been there when she'd gotten dressed to go see Frank.

In fact, they hadn't been there since the day Joe had left to go stay in his astronaut quarters to prepare for the launch. She knew because she'd organized that very closet in a fit of pique three days before launch when she hadn't been able to take all the nervous energy coursing through her body. She'd placed those very boots—his spare pair—in the back of the closet.

What were they doing here now?

For a moment, Vivian considered the possibility that she'd gone mad in her grief, that she was hallucinating the boots in her desperation to feel a tangible connection to Joe.

She walked over to the closet on shaky legs, and sank down to the ground, her fingers brushing against the leather, the boots unmistakably real in her hands.

Was her husband haunting her now?

How had his boots gotten there?

It made no sense for someone to have come in and put them in front of the closet, and much like Joe hadn't shared their marital woes with Frank, she hadn't shared hers with Polly, didn't think she'd mentioned their playful arguments about the boots to anyone.

"Joe," she whispered, feeling a little bit silly for even entertaining the possibility that her husband was a ghost. "If you're here, please let me know."

Vivian waited for a sign, something to let her know that he was here, that he hadn't left her—a book knocked off his bookshelf, perhaps, or a chill in the air, or some kind of indicator that there was another presence in the room with her.

But she didn't feel like there was someone else with her, didn't feel Joe at all.

Tears spilled down Vivian's cheeks as she gathered the boots up in her arms, clutching them close to her as sobs racked her body.

THIRTEEN

1962

Vivian deplaned her flight to Venice's Marco Polo Airport, looking for—

Joe strode toward her, a bouquet of flowers clutched in his hand, a smile on his face.

By the look of things, he'd come straight from work, and he was still dressed in his flight suit. She never in a million years thought she would feel this way, but he made the green uniform look good.

"Viv."

Joe swept her up in his arms, kissing her so enthusiastically that a few good-natured cheers erupted around them.

"It's been too long," Joe said when he finally set her down, seemingly unconcerned by the attention they drew.

"It's been a month," Vivian teased, although it *had* felt much longer. Maybe because they were still in the early stages of their relationship, in that honeymoon phase where they couldn't get enough of each other. The twenty-four hours they'd had together in Houston hardly felt like it was long enough, and the letters and occasional phone call they'd exchanged had only left her wanting more.

"It felt longer," Joe complained. "I can't believe I have you all to myself for a week."

She couldn't believe she was here. With him. In Italy.

"I missed you," he murmured, pulling her in a half hug against his body.

"I missed you, too."

Joe drove her from the airport to the Air Force base with their hands linked, as he called out sights of interest, places he wanted to take her during her weeklong stay.

Joe lived on base, and as he drove her onto the installation, she glanced around, wondering if she would feel any familiarity from living on a military base in Arizona when she was a little girl. What would her father think of her life now? Would he be proud to see her with a fighter pilot like he'd been, or would he be filled with paternal worry knowing the challenges that lay ahead?

A wave of grief covered her, the knowledge that she would never know, would never be able to share this part of herself with him. He had forever known the little girl, would never get the chance to see the woman she'd become, to be proud of the choices she'd made.

There were so many moments—her graduation from college, when she got hired at the TV station—that she imagined sharing with him, missing him all over again.

They drove by the flight line, and a memory came to her—so vivid that she knew it had to be true—of listening to the roar of thunder in the air and looking to see if she could spot her father up there in his airplane. She had a sudden vision of her childhood bedroom in base housing; of how she used to perch herself at the window each afternoon and look to the sky to see when he was coming home.

She couldn't have possibly known which one he was, but she remembered the sense of connection she'd had when she looked up and knew he was out there. Strange how she'd forgotten it for all these years.

"Are you alright?" Joe asked her.

Vivian nodded, belatedly realizing her cheeks beneath her sunglasses were wet. She wiped away the tears.

"I—I don't have many memories of my childhood, or of my father, but being here, on base—I remembered something. We lived on base at Luke Field in Phoenix when I was a kid, right before he died. I used to watch for him to come home."

"SORRY, I KNOW IT ISN'T MUCH TO LOOK AT," JOE SAID, walking her into his apartment on base. "Kind of spartan, but I'll be honest, I've never really bothered to accumulate too much stuff. It's a pain having to move it around; easier to travel light, I guess."

"It's fine," Vivian replied, looking around the quarters. She grinned. "Very clean."

Joe laughed. "I'm glad you noticed. It wasn't about twelve hours ago, but I got to work. I wanted it to be perfect for you."

He set Vivian's bags down near the couch in the little living area. She'd never shared a space with a man for so long—never mind such a small one so far away from home. That they were staying in his apartment so early in their relationship felt like a big leap. What if they discovered that they didn't enjoy each other's company? What if he had little habits that annoyed her? What if her idiosyncrasies annoyed him?

Suddenly, Vivian felt a need to move, to release some of the nervous energy inside her.

A bookshelf sat next to the couch, and despite Joe's pronouncement that he liked to travel light, he'd amassed quite the collection of paperbacks in his travels. Curious to know more about him, his interests, Vivian walked over to the bookshelf and glanced at the titles there.

Her lips curved.

Even in his reading, he gravitated toward space.

She picked up one title with a picture of a man in an elaborate space suit on the cover.

"That's a good one," Joe offered, his gaze on her rather than the book. "You wouldn't like it."

Vivian laughed. "That's hardly a ringing endorsement."

"Don't get me wrong. It's a great book. And you're, well—"

"'Wonderful'?" she teased, referring to the way she'd described Polly when she was trying to push them together the night they met.

"I believe 'wonderful' was the word you used to describe my romantic prospects at the bar on the night we met."

"I did."

"I'm not sure I've ever been so interested in a woman who was so clearly trying to vector me in another direction."

Vivian flushed. "I wasn't trying to 'vector' you in another direction. Not entirely, at least."

"That's what it felt like. It was a crushing blow to my ego."

"I don't believe your ego gets dented very often."

"Touché. It did that night, though. Or maybe it was my heart."

Her heart sped up rather rapidly at that pronouncement, even if he did deliver the words in a light, teasing voice. Vivian was beginning to realize that when he used that tone, it was his way of testing things out, offering his feelings up in a casual manner to gauge her response. It felt a bit like he was easing her into this relationship that was developing between them.

"You thought I was 'wonderful'?" Vivian asked, glancing back down at the bookshelf as she set the book with the man in the space suit aside, no longer able to meet Joe's gaze.

"Something more than that," he replied, his voice soft.

Suddenly, those titles felt like the most interesting thing in the world.

Why was she giddy like this with him and only him?

With Graham there had been an early bit of hero worship for sure, considering how much she admired his career, but that had quickly subsided, and she'd settled into a comfortable rhythm in their relationship. But this—Vivian couldn't make sense of it. There were times that she felt more herself than she had with anyone when she was with Joe. There were also plenty of moments—far too many for her to be comfortable—when she felt like she was jumping off a cliff with no assurance that the fall wouldn't break her. It was more than a little terrifying for someone whose approach to the adage of "look before you leap" was to keep two feet firmly planted on the ground for as long as possible.

"What is it about these books that speaks to you?" Vivian asked, selecting one of the titles and flipping through the pages. "Beyond the obvious fact that they're all about space."

"Picked up on that, did you?" Joe grinned. "I've always wondered what's out there. The universe feels infinite, like it could contain wonders we've never seen, possibilities we've never imagined. Sometimes we feel like a very small piece of something far larger than us. I want my chance to explore it. To know if the things that exist in the pages of these books are possible—extraterrestrial life, time travel, undiscovered planets, all sorts of wonders."

"Time travel?"

He laughed. "You should see your face. What's so hard to believe about time travel? It's just a matter of physics, if you think about it."

"I try not to think about physics as much as absolutely possible."

He laughed again. "Fair enough. Maybe one day I'll convince you otherwise."

"Do you really think there's life out there?" Vivian asked. "Other people or beings besides us?"

Vivian picked up another book that had an alien figure with five heads and tentacles staring back at her. She set that one aside, too.

Joe's brow furrowed, and she got the sense that he took his response more seriously than the gravity she'd put in the question she asked.

"I don't know," he replied after a beat. "Maybe. Or maybe there's something else, something we haven't even imagined. I know some people think that the scenarios in these books are ludicrous, but not so long ago the idea of sending someone to space was unbelievable. I like to think we still have a long way to go before we reach the limits of our known universe. And maybe I'll get a chance to be there when we do."

It was a daring ambition, but she supposed that when you were used to pushing the envelope, life seemed limitless.

"Why do you say I wouldn't like these?" Vivian asked, her gaze drifting over an H. G. Wells title before she glanced at him.

"Because you're practical, not given much to the fantastical."

She wrinkled her nose and pulled a face even though she knew the description was spot-on. "That sounds awfully boring."

"I don't think it's boring at all. It's one of the things I like most about you."

"That I'm practical?"

Hardly a romantic sentiment.

"You keep me grounded. Remind me of what's important. I don't know—this lifestyle can be all-consuming. It's not just my job, it's my life, my identity. It's nice to see the world from a different perspective, to have that tether to hold on to."

Now, that was romantic.

What did it say about her that despite her propensity toward the mundane, one of the things she liked about him was that he was given to the fantastical, as he so aptly put it? That he was so romantic and passionate about the things he dedicated himself to. Maybe part of what made him so irresistible was that he inspired a romanticism in her that she rarely indulged.

"Now this one," Joe said, reaching to a shelf above her and pulling a book down. "This one is my absolute favorite."

He placed the title in her hands with something akin to reverence.

Vivian glanced down at the cover and title.

Infinity. By Michel Robert.

"It was my favorite when I was a kid," Joe told her. "It's still my favorite, to be honest. My dad gave it to me when I was a boy. I've probably read it a hundred times. It's pretty incredible that you can pick up a book at so many different points in your life and still love it every single time. If that's not the sign of a great book, I don't know what is.

"The first time I read it was in the hospital after the accident—well, my uncle and I read it together. He helped me with the hard words. I was so scared, felt so alone without my parents. It gave me hope, I guess. A man goes to space, and he comes back as a different version of himself. It's probably the first book that made me want to be an astronaut."

"Have you heard anything else about your application?"

"Not yet, but—"

A ringing sound interrupted his answer.

He glanced at the phone, an uneasy look on his face. "Excuse me for a minute. I should answer it."

Vivian flipped through his copy of *Infinity* while Joe went to answer the phone.

When he finished the call, he walked back over to her, his expression serious.

"I'm sorry, Viv. So sorry. But I have to go. My squadron just received orders."

"'Go'?"

"I'm sorry. It's an emergency. I'm sorry I can't tell you more. I don't know how long I'll be gone."

Vivian watched as he moved through his apartment methodically, packing up a military-issued duffel bag with the rhythmic precision of someone who had done it many times before. She couldn't help but contrast it with the haphazard way she had packed her own bag to come here, how she had agonized over and ultimately discarded choices.

"You can stay however long you want. Stay forever if you want to." He said it like it was a joke, but everything felt as though it was taking on a hysterical air, the world around her tilting madly. She had flown halfway around the world to see a man she had met in person four times, only to spend a few hours with him, and now he was leaving. She had no idea where he was going or how long he would be gone, if she should wait for him or not, or how the hell she was going to navigate the next week in Italy by herself.

She wanted to ask him why he had to leave, wanted to ask him where he was headed, so many questions that she sensed she shouldn't ask, so she settled on the one that felt the most pressing for now.

"Will you be safe?" Vivian whispered against his lips as he kissed her goodbye.

He rested his forehead against hers. "I hope so."

An hour later, when she was by herself listening to the radio, she realized what had called him away with such urgency, and even though she didn't know exactly where he was headed, she had a fairly good idea:

The Soviets had sent nuclear weapons to Cuba.

FOURTEEN

In the end, ten days after the Saturn V rocket launched Joe and his crew into space, they celebrated his life, commemorated his death in Arlington in a funeral with military honors that paid homage to his career, to the impact he'd had on the world, a ceremony that was so widely attended that when Vivian glanced out at the sea of faces during her eulogy, she wondered what Joe would think of it all, if he would have been a little embarrassed by the attention. Vivian imagined him going over and shaking hands with the distinguished guests in that very Joe way of his, when he would captivate a room with the force and charisma of his presence. She stood in his stead, channeling that quiet dignity she had seen the First Lady adopt following the president's assassination.

Vivian had written Joe's eulogy before the launch, and it had been a different exercise when it was a theoretical one. Delivering it in person in front of hundreds of people was another thing altogether. That her husband's body was somewhere in space and not interred in the ground made it even more difficult for Vivian to process what was happening. And at the same time, it was a situation she'd envisioned before—albeit in the context of Joe's career as a military pilot rather than his time as an astronaut. They had friends, colleagues of Joe's who had gone missing in Vietnam, who were presumed dead and whose families were faced with the horrifying prospect of never having a body to bury.

Physically, Vivian was there, present, but her mind was elsewhere—imagining Joe's last moments, puzzling over the strange things that had happened since they lost contact with him—the note in her dress pocket, her name over the squawk box, the blank postcard, the boots between his side of the bed and the closet. She hadn't told anyone else about them besides what she'd mentioned to Polly, was too afraid that if she did, they would think she'd gone mad in her grief. But they plagued her, the same way the memorandum the man handed her plagued her.

So here she was.

Vivian saw him as soon as she walked into the bar in Arlington.

For a moment, she felt like she'd gone back in time, as though someone had wound back the clock seven years, and all the intervening events that happened had simply disappeared.

Graham Carlson sat at a table in the back, hunched over his

usual—a gin and tonic—his suit a little rumpled, a notebook in front of him as he jotted down notes.

Her gaze only rested on him for a beat before it darted over to the bar, to the space where she had once stood—

What's more romantic than space, than flight? I've never felt more at peace, more in awe of the world around me, of life, than when I'm in the air. There's a poetry about it, a simplicity and beauty to how very small you feel when confronted with the vastness of the universe and your place inside it. It humbles you, I suppose. Or makes you feel like anything is possible. Maybe that's the humbling part. I can never decide.

She heard the words Joe had spoken that night so clearly that she felt like he was standing with her, and she closed her eyes, indulging in the memory, one moment in a string of them when she had fallen in love with him. It was a cruel irony that the thing he had loved had killed him, that the vastness of the universe that he had once spoken of with such possibility had consumed him.

For an instant, she time traveled seven years into their past.

When she opened her eyes, the bar was nearly empty save for a few gentlemen who seemed like regulars propped up at the bar, not looking at or bothering anyone. No doubt that was the reason Graham liked coming here so much. He'd never been a man who sought the limelight, even if the limelight loved him.

In its heyday, the bar had been the sort of place young professionals had gone to let off steam after work. Clearly, things had changed since 1961.

Now that she was here, now that she felt Joe all around her, she was grateful for the choice she'd made, for the ghosts of her husband that lurked throughout the room.

Wait for me.

She swore she heard the words whispered in her ear, in Joe's achingly familiar voice, and she'd never been one to believe in the idea of ghosts, but if she was being haunted by her husband, then she was at least grateful that she wasn't alone.

Graham looked up from his notebook and their gazes collided.

Vivian hadn't seen him in six years, since she'd ended things between them, and she'd been so consumed with the questions she wanted to ask him about the spacecraft that she hadn't thought about the pang of guilt she would feel over the way she had left him.

Graham rose from his seat as she walked toward him. He hesitated for a moment, and then he wrapped her in a half hug, and everything inside her froze. Polly was the only person who had embraced her since Joe disappeared.

Everyone else had treated Vivian like there was an invisible barrier erected around her that they couldn't breach, and she liked it that way, didn't want anyone to touch her right now, didn't want to be close to anyone. She existed on an island as she'd always preferred—except for with Joe, of course.

Vivian took a step back, extricating herself from the exchange, and she slid into the seat across from the one Graham had occupied.

His notebook rested inches away from her, his familiar scrawl taking up the page. She couldn't help but scan the words there, trying to untangle his messy penmanship.

Was that word "telemetry"? Or "transportation"? It was hard to tell. Graham tended to write parts of letters without finishing them, so they were half-formed thoughts that only Graham could decipher. She wasn't sure if it was an intentional exercise or not, but she'd always thought it was a genius move to keep his thoughts to himself in an industry where everyone was often jockeying for a scoop on the next big story.

If anyone in journalism was well-connected enough to have information surrounding the spacecraft, it was Graham.

"How are you?" Graham asked once he'd taken his seat again.

He reached out between them, pulling the notebook toward him in one smooth swoop.

The expression on her face must have said it all, because he frowned.

"Right. It's a ridiculous question to ask. I'm sorry, Vivian. So sorry. When I heard what happened to Joe's spacecraft—I wanted to reach out to you. Wanted you to know that I was thinking of you, of him."

"I got the flowers you sent. Thank you. That was very kind."

"It was the least I could do."

He might have felt that way, but the gesture had struck Vivian as incredibly generous given all they had been through together. Graham would have been forgiven if he hadn't sent anything at all.

The door swung open, the sound of footsteps filling the bar, and Vivian turned instinctively.

A man walked over to the bar.

Not Joe.

Of course it wasn't Joe.

It would never again be Joe.

Would she forever be looking over her shoulder, scanning rooms when she entered them, searching for him?

Wait for me.

The words were there, in her mind, in her ears, in her heart, and she wasn't sure if it was sheer stubbornness or a testament to the connection they had that she felt like Joe was still out there waiting to be found, waiting for her, asking her to wait for him.

"He was a great man," Graham added when Vivian pivoted to face him.

"He was."

It felt wrong speaking of Joe in the past tense. When her father had died, Vivian had accepted that he wasn't coming back. But now—

"I keep thinking he's going to walk in the door," she admitted. "Being back here, without him, feels strange. Not in a bad way, necessarily. It's just hard to reconcile the fact that he's gone, particularly without any evidence of the spacecraft or what happened to them."

Graham whitened. "I'm sorry—I'll admit when I suggested we meet here after you called, I was feeling a bit nostalgic. After all, this is where we met. You were standing over there . . ." His voice trailed off, and she saw the moment when he belatedly realized and remembered *who* she was standing with. That was the thing about a man like Graham Carlson. He was a star. His world naturally revolved around everything he did, the people in his life orienting themselves around him and his needs. He wasn't a bad man—in fact, she would argue that he was certainly a good man. He wasn't unkind, and he cared about people—he'd cared about *her* once upon a time—but he was so used to thinking of himself that sometimes he forgot to think of others. "Was that—was that the night that you met him?"

Vivian nodded.

"I'm sorry. I didn't know. I should have realized. We never talked about it."

No, they hadn't. In the beginning, there hadn't been a reason to, and then later, as she was falling in love with Joe despite being in a relationship with Graham, he had been a secret she had clutched to herself.

Vivian took a sip of her drink, struggling to keep from falling apart.

"The eulogy you gave was very moving," Graham said.

His was one of the few faces she'd clocked in the crowd while she was speaking. He hadn't been there in his capacity as a newsman, but he had sat in the audience honoring Joe.

"Thank you. He would have appreciated that you came. He had a great deal of respect for you." Vivian hesitated. "He always felt bad about the way things ended between us."

Graham chuckled. "I'm sorry, but I don't believe that for a second. Not that I blame him. I don't think he had any regrets. The Joe Mitchell I knew wasn't afraid to go after what he wanted and didn't apologize to anyone for the way he lived his life."

He wasn't entirely wrong. Joe had felt bad, but she also knew he wouldn't have changed a damned thing.

"I asked to see you because someone gave me this—" Vivian

reached into her purse and pulled out the folded piece of paper and handed it to Graham.

She waited while he read over it, and then he glanced up at her, concern on his face. "Who gave this to you?"

"I don't know. A man handed it to me at the press conference I gave right after Joe and the crew disappeared, but it was so crowded that I didn't get a chance to see who it was. He was wearing a hat, I think. A suit, I suppose. I saw him from behind, but it was only a glimpse. I didn't know the significance of what he handed me until later. I regret I didn't pay more attention in the moment."

Graham glanced around the nearly empty bar before leaning in more closely to her. He lowered his voice. "There are some rumors that there were problems with the telemetry system on the capsule. Up until now, that's all I've heard—rumors. This is the first concrete piece of evidence I've seen."

"I didn't know if you were working the story," Vivian murmured, even though that wasn't exactly true. She had certainly suspected. And most importantly, she had noticed that none of his reporting ever suggested that the crew might have been responsible for a mishap affecting the spacecraft, as others' had.

"It's the biggest story right now. Everyone is working it." Graham picked up his pencil, opening his notebook once more. "Did Joe ever talk to you about concerns with the capsule?"

"No, he didn't. That sort of thing—Joe wouldn't have wanted me to worry. He knew how I felt about his job, and—"

Vivian's voice broke off. For a moment, she'd committed the cardinal sin of forgetting who she was talking to. Yes, they had history, and yes, once they had been lovers—friends, even—but at the end of the day, Graham was still a reporter and a shrewd one at that. The last thing she needed right now was the press dissecting her marriage or writing off the entire business as an accident because Joe had been distracted.

"He didn't want me to worry," Vivian repeated. "I read the memo, but I'll admit, I didn't understand all the scientific information contained there.

"You said that you'd heard rumors—from who?" Vivian asked.

Graham shook his head. "Come on. You know I can't give up a source."

"I gave you the memo."

"You gave me the memo because you want me to do something with it. You forget that I know you, too."

"Perhaps."

Vivian wasn't entirely sure why she decided to give him the memo; these days it was hard to tell what was rational and what was a product of her grief. But if there had been a problem with the spacecraft and they'd sent the men up anyway, she needed to know. Maybe it would give her the closure she needed to finally feel like she could accept that Joe was gone, and at the very least, hopefully increased scrutiny and attention to the safety practices would keep similar accidents from happening again. Certainly, it would go a long way to clearing her husband's and the other astronauts' names. It felt like the least she could do.

"Why bring it to me?" Graham asked. "Why not take the story yourself?"

She shook her head. "My husband isn't a story. Not to me. I'm not—I'm not ready yet. I'm bringing it to you because you have the biggest reach of anyone I know. And because I trust you to do the right thing. You always have."

"Thank you." Graham cleared his throat. "Have you shared it with anyone at NASA?"

"I showed it to someone I trust, asked them if they'd heard anything about it."

She felt a loyalty to Frank, to Joe's friendship with him, to Polly's family. She didn't want to drag him into this if he didn't have anything to do with it.

"Had they?"

Vivian shook her head.

"And you believe them?"

"I do. Have you learned anything else?"

"No. I've been trying to talk to someone within the agency, to get an astronaut to speak to me on background, but no such luck even without me using their name."

"I have a feeling it's going to be hard to get anyone who wants to speak out even if they do know something," Vivian replied, recalling her conversations with Frank. "It's the Moon—"

"I know. Everyone wants to protect the possibility of trying to achieve lunar orbit, of eventually putting a man on the Moon."

So many aspired to go to the Moon, looked up at it with a sense of wonder and a zeal in their eyes. The sight of it haunted her now.

Would she ever look up at the night sky in the same way? Would she ever again be able to appreciate the beauty now that she knew the cost?

"This memo—you think that this is what went wrong? The reason they lost contact with the spacecraft?" Graham asked.

Had there been a problem with the telemetry system like the memo suggested? Had Joe worried about the mission? He'd been different in the days leading up to the launch—she'd chalked it up to nerves and the fact that he knew she didn't want him to go, that she was angry, but now Vivian couldn't help but wonder if there had been something else bothering him. They were supposed to be partners, and it hurt to know that he hadn't confided in her. But that was the trouble with his job. Given the sensitive nature of the space program, so much of his work had been off-limits to her, and they'd fought so much about it that it had become such a sore subject between them.

"I think it could be. What is your plan? What are you going to do next?" Vivian asked.

"Keep digging. See if I can convince someone to talk to me."

Vivian remembered those days, the thrill of chasing down a lead, watching a story unfold before her. A part of her craved that feeling again, how it had made her feel powerful, particularly now when she felt anything but; however, she had been honest when she told Graham that she wasn't ready, that the idea of covering what happened to Joe hit too close to home.

"Is the network behind this?" she asked Graham.

"They are," Graham replied. "Look, there have been enough problems with the space program that people are starting to have concerns. It's not as popular as it was when President Kennedy first proposed that we go to the Moon. The American public wants answers." He met her gaze. "I suppose I wanted to talk to you first to make sure you were alright with me pursuing this line. I want you to know that it's not just a story to me—it's a matter of national interest, yes, but I don't want you to get hurt in the process. You've been through so much, and I care about you, Vivian. Always."

"Thank you." As a journalist, Vivian understood how much it would cost Graham to walk away from a story like this, and considering she'd ended their relationship, she was grateful for the kindness he was showing her now.

"If there was a problem with the spacecraft, I don't want it to get buried. I want you to track down every lead you can. I know how often operator error is blamed, saw the beginnings of it with the questions the reporters asked me at the press conference, have been following the negative press coverage that has cropped up since then. I don't want Joe to be unfairly blamed, don't want the three of them to be forgotten."

"They won't be. I promise you that. I'll do some digging, make some calls. I promise that as soon as I know something, I'll let you know."

"What are you hearing from official channels?" she asked him.

"Probably the same thing you are."

"I very much doubt that. I'm being managed. Likely even more so because I'm not just Joe's wife, but a former journalist."

"There's been some talk about Joe's state of mind," Graham said, refusing to meet her gaze. "About everything he'd—your family—had been through." He swallowed. "I'm sorry, Vivian. It isn't fair."

"No, it isn't. Then again, life rarely is fair. We only have to open a newspaper or turn on one of your broadcasts to be reminded of that. It could always be worse. I'm sure somewhere it *is* worse."

Graham appeared as though he was at a loss for words, and she couldn't help but feel a little bit sorry for him. She imagined he had been expecting to see the girl he once knew, the girl he once loved, the girl she once was, but she'd lived a lot of life since then, and she was certain she was now a sanded-down, barely recognizable version of herself.

"I'm here for whatever you need," Graham finally replied.

He reached out to take her hand, and then he froze mid-motion as though he remembered the way she'd reacted when he'd embraced her, his fingers inches away from the wedding ring on her finger.

Vivian placed her hands in her lap, glancing down at her linked fingers.

"Thank you."

Graham was silent for a moment, and she knew him well enough to know that he was searching for the right thing to say, and nerves filled her as she waited for whatever he had to tell her.

"Have you thought about telling your story?" Graham finally asked.

"My story?"

Graham nodded. "People want to hear from you. Want to know what you're going through, how you feel about everything. If you have concerns about the program, if you think something went wrong, that the crew was sent on a mission that was flawed to begin with, then you would be the perfect person to bring the issue to the American public. What do you think?"

"I don't know. Let me have some time. It's—it's complicated. I need more time."

Vivian didn't know how to explain to him what this felt like, didn't know how to explain it to herself. She felt—suspended in limbo. She'd just come from a memorial service for her husband, and intellectually she knew what everyone was telling her, knew that he was gone, that he wasn't coming back. She just couldn't quite make herself believe it.

"I understand," Graham replied.

Did he?

Vivian bit back a response because it was a perfectly reasonable, perfectly polite thing for him to say, but she very much doubted that he did understand. Not to mention, *she* was going through it and she barely understood herself.

Wait for me.

She swore she heard it again, Joe's voice in her ear, or maybe he was a figment of her imagination, and she belatedly wondered why, if he was a ghost haunting her, she couldn't see him, even if he was a hazy, ephemeral presence. She was greedy enough to want more than the small pieces of him she was receiving.

She'd never believed in ghosts before, never held much credence for the intangible, but now she questioned everything.

Maybe she was unraveling completely.

"Are you alright?" Graham asked, his brows knitted together, worry on his expression.

"I'm sorry. I'm just distracted."

What was happening to her? How had she gotten to this place?

If Graham knew the direction her thoughts had taken, knew she was even contemplating the possibility that her husband was a *ghost*, he'd probably be very worried about her.

That was the thing about Graham—on paper, they'd made complete sense. They were both practical and grounded to a fault. When Graham took risks, they were entirely related to the stories he chased. Otherwise, he was an extremely cautious man, a quality they had both shared—until now.

Graham held her gaze. "Can I ask you something?"

Graham paused as though he was choosing his words with great care, and she knew before he spoke what he was going to ask her. It was the same question she'd asked herself after she and Joe had a big fight over his career, when her anger made her question her life choices, the aggravation of military life and the space program getting the best of her. And each time she had come to the same inescapable conclusion:

For reasons she never quite understood except to say that they were as constant as the stars, she loved Joe.

Vivian nodded, because she felt like she owed Graham this—owed him the closure of their relationship that he'd never received. That night of Polly and Frank's engagement party, when she called Graham to break up with him, she hadn't mentioned anything about Joe, hadn't focused on anything other than her feelings. But he must have wondered when he heard they were together.

Perhaps because she now knew what it was like to exist in this strange limbo, her husband officially declared dead, but no body to bury, no sense of finality to his death, she had sympathy for the questions that likely lingered inside Graham.

"If you hadn't met Joe, if things had been different, would we have had a chance? What we had—would it have been enough?"

Vivian knew the futility of such an exercise, of playing the "what if" game until you litigated your choices to death. In another life, if Joe had never existed, would she have been happy with Graham?

Perhaps. Probably. Yes.

They'd been good together. And she had been happy with him. It was also undeniable that in running toward him, she'd been running from the inevitability of Joe and the inevitability of this moment, of losing everything. Vivian wasn't sure if telling him the truth was a kindness or not.

And in that moment, she knew without a shred of uncertainty that she would never move on from Joe. That there would never be another man she loved. After her father's death, Vivian had watched her mother jump from relationship to relationship, searching for something she had presumably never found, and the idea of a never-ending string of failed relationships was too depressing to bear. Better to be on her own, and to make peace with that, than to keep trying to make a relationship fit that never would.

"I'm sorry," Vivian said instead, because at her core, she was sorry. She had hurt Graham, and he had deserved better than the way she had ended things. "You deserve someone who will love you the way you should be loved. I'm sorry that wasn't me."

"No, I'm sorry." Graham shook his head. "I shouldn't have asked. Shouldn't have put you in this position. Not with everything you have going on. I still care about you. I'm here for you as a friend, for whatever you need."

"Just find out whatever you can about what happened to the spacecraft. Please."

FIFTEEN

1962

When was the last time you slept?" Kerry asked as she slid a carton of takeout Chinese food to Vivian.

"I caught an hour or two on a cot last night," Vivian replied, gratefully picking up the food Kerry had brought her.

"Well, it's almost three o'clock in the afternoon now, so it sounds like you're due for another rest. It does no one any good if you're collapsing on your feet."

"Is anyone sleeping?" Vivian asked her.

How could you sleep when the world was on the brink of nuclear war?

The newsroom was brimming with people, the news that the Soviets had nuclear weapons in Cuba setting off a global panic that had children hiding under their desks at school and politicians scrambling for an end to the crisis.

"I went back to my apartment," Kerry replied. "Took a shower. Picked up the food. Trust me, you have to be careful about burning out in this business. It's smart to take care of yourself."

Kerry slid into the chair next to Vivian, her gaze pointed as it zeroed in on Brian Forrester, the network's star reporter who had filled the void after Graham left.

Vivian liked Brian well enough, had enjoyed working on the story of Kennedy's speech at Rice with him, but it hadn't gone unnoticed that Kerry had him beat in seniority. Ultimately, it hadn't mattered, and Graham's time slot had gone to Brian.

"The men in this business have more support than we'll ever get," Kerry added. "They have secretaries, and assistants, and the network gives them the tools to be successful. For the women— well, if you're successful, then they'll be happy with you, of course, but you aren't treated as though you have the same level of star power. Nobody makes it any easier for you. You have to work ten times harder to do the same job. Because I promise you, Brian's lovely wife Jan will be in here with fresh shirts for him and dinner in Tupperware dishes in a few hours. No one is bringing us freshly laundered clothes and dinners. It's why we have to make a point to take care of ourselves when we can."

Kerry didn't say it with an air of complaint, but matter-of-factly, as though it was something she'd learned and accepted a long time ago.

Vivian had never asked, had never felt comfortable with their relationship venturing into personal territory when it was strictly professional, but she didn't think Kerry was married, that she had anyone she was interested in romantically in her life. Kerry seemed to have decided early in her career that she was going to devote herself to it with everything she had, and now, hearing her speak about it, Vivian realized that Kerry's point was how much more difficult it was to have it all when you had to *be* it all, when you didn't have the advantage of someone at home to help you out, to take care of you so you could wholly focus on your job.

"I'm going on air later," Kerry said. "Do you want to help work on some of the copy? What these guys gave me to go off is pretty terrible. I'd clean it up myself, but I'm in the middle of trying to chase down a few sources at the White House." She leaned in closer to Vivian, her voice lowering. "An ExComm meeting just ended," Kerry added, referring to the Executive Committee President Kennedy had formed to address the missile crisis in Cuba. "I'm trying to see if I can get an update on whether the president's thinking has changed. On what the plan is."

The rumor was that military assets were standing by, jets ready to launch and act against the Soviet presence in Cuba.

Vivian hadn't heard anything from Joe since he left her in Italy, didn't know where he was or if he was one of those pilots sitting alert, waiting for the order to go to war. She'd heard through one of the reporters that they were using F-100s, which was the plane Joe had told her he flew, so she figured that was why they'd chosen to deploy his squadron from Italy, although she didn't know for sure where they'd been sent. There were rumors that planes were lining the runway at Homestead Air

Force Base near Miami, and Vivian wondered if Joe was among them.

As soon as she'd realized why he'd been called away, she'd changed her ticket and jumped on the first flight back to Washington D.C.

This was the kind of story careers were made on, the kind of moment when the world looked to the newsroom to inform, to inspire, to comfort.

This was the kind of moment that made her want to be a journalist in the first place.

And still, now that the world was faced with the possibility of nuclear war, the greatest regret that Vivian faced wasn't a professional one, but rather that she hadn't spent more time with Joe when she had the chance.

VIVIAN STUMBLED INTO THE HALLWAY OF HER APARTment building at nearly midnight, feeling like she'd worked for thirteen days straight. The Soviets had finally removed the nuclear weapons from Cuba, and the world was no longer on the brink of nuclear war. It was terrifying to realize how close they'd come.

Vivian headed down the hallway, walking toward her apartment—

A dark shadow filled the doorway.

Vivian took a step back, unease filling her.

It was a safe building, but ever since Polly had moved out when she married Frank, Vivian had to admit that at times she felt a little—not scared, just aware of the fact that she was a single woman living alone in the city. After Polly left, Vivian was finally making enough money at the station that she didn't necessarily need a roommate to pay the rent, and the idea of another woman moving into the apartment felt wrong considering the bond she'd shared with Polly.

The shadow moved.

"Viv."

Joe emerged into the dimly lit hallway.

Vivian rushed toward him, throwing her arms around him.

"What are you doing here?" she asked, pulling him more tightly toward her.

"I took leave. I wanted to see you. Needed to see you. It's been a hell of a two weeks."

Joe leaned back slightly, cupping her face with his hands, his thumbs brushing at the tears falling from her cheeks. "Are you alright?"

Vivian nodded. "I'm sorry—it's silly, I don't even know why I'm crying; everything is catching up with me at once."

"I know. I feel the same way. I haven't been scared all that much doing what I do, but this week—I was scared for all of us. We came so close to everything ending—to the world as we know it being annihilated."

He took a deep, shaky breath. "I was scared I'd never see you again, never get to tell you this." His expression turned serious. "I love you, Viv."

The words landed with a force that she felt in her bones.

And even though the urge to panic was there, the fear that if she said it back to him, she would cross some imaginary line there would be no going back from, she did love him. She couldn't hear the man she loved put himself out there and not return his truth with her own.

Not after the two weeks she'd just lived through.

Joe was right—anticipating the end of the world had changed Vivian's perspective on things, made her realize that she didn't want to live her remaining days with regret for the opportunities she'd missed, for not following her heart.

"I love you, too."

For a moment, they just stood there in the hall, their bodies intertwined, and she could see and feel the exhaustion overtaking him, the toll that the last two weeks had on him.

"Viv?" Joe murmured finally. "Can we go to sleep?"

VIVIAN WOKE UP TWELVE HOURS LATER IN BED, HER arms wrapped around Joe's bare chest.

"You're awake," she said, feeling more relaxed than she had in a long time—maybe ever. He'd held her the entire time they slept, and there was something intensely comforting about waking up in his arms. The intensity of the bond that had sprung up between them still surprised her.

Joe, for his part, didn't look relaxed at all. His brow knitted as he looked at her.

"What's wrong? Do you have to leave again?" Vivian asked him.

To be fair, he'd never said how long his leave was for or when he was expected back in Italy. She'd hoped they would have a bit more time together, but—

"No. Nothing like that. I just—can we talk?"

"Can we talk" always had a particularly ominous ring. Vivian was pretty sure she'd used those same words with Graham right before she ended things with him.

"Alright."

"Do you want coffee first?" Joe asked. "This might be a coffee conversation."

"What's going on? No, I don't need coffee."

"I wanted to talk to you about us when you came to Italy. The phone calls and letters are great, but this felt like a conversation we should have in person. But then, of course, all hell broke loose, and I had to leave, but when I was in Florida—"

So he had been sent to Homestead during the missile crisis, had been sitting in one of those F-100s waiting to launch.

The thought terrified her.

"How do you do it?" Vivian asked.

"What do you mean? It's a job like any other one. There are risks to any job."

"I doubt dentists face death as much as you do."

Joe pulled a face. "I'm not sure I can envision anything as boring as being a dentist. I can't be afraid of death every single time I go up. It wouldn't do me any good; in fact it would only make things worse. If I don't believe I'm invincible up there, then I'll spend too much time worrying I'll make a mistake."

"I still wish I'd fallen in love with a dentist."

"You're killing me, Viv." Joe took a deep breath. "When I was in Florida, I thought more about how badly I wanted to have this conversation." He hesitated. "I guess I want to know where you see this going between us."

"I don't know. It feels like a whirlwind. Things have been happening so quickly, and—"

"Have they, though? We've known each other for a year and a half. Our best friends are married to each other. We've written each other how many letters?"

"We've only seen each other a handful of times."

"We've corresponded a great deal more than that."

"We have," she acknowledged.

"I guess in my line of work it isn't unusual to not see each other in person very often. You make a relationship happen however you can, whether it's phone calls, or letters, or the occasional visit. I suppose in my circles, none of this feels particularly fast at all. When you live like we do, with the uncertainty that constantly hangs over our heads, time moves a little differently. Sometimes you move quickly because you don't know if that's all you'll have."

Nothing about his lifestyle sounded appealing. In fact, it sounded downright awful and left her with a sinking feeling in her stomach.

"That's not you," Joe observed.

"No, it's not."

"What are you looking for?"

"I'm still figuring that out," Vivian admitted. "I'm only twenty-four. I know plenty of women my age are already married and having kids, but it feels so young to me. I didn't have much stability growing up. After my dad died—even before—there wasn't a place where I felt like I could be at peace. I didn't have a home. I had four walls that changed constantly depending on which bills my mother couldn't pay or the new man who swept her off her feet and promised to take all her troubles away until he just became another one of them.

"And I told myself I wouldn't be like that. That I wouldn't be like her. That I wouldn't let myself be twisted up in knots for some man, that I wouldn't lose myself like I watched her do time and time again, that I wouldn't lose sight of what was important. My job is important to me. Being independent is important to me. It makes me feel—" How could she explain it? "Knowing that I can take care of myself makes me feel safe."

Joe was quiet, and she could tell he was giving what she said a great deal of thought.

"My lifestyle won't make you feel safe."

"No, it won't."

And yet, she was still here.

"It's going to be rough, being with me. My job is dangerous, and unpredictable, and the Air Force doesn't care about my family, doesn't care about much else besides the mission. I get paid pennies to do what I do, and our life is never going to be fancy. We're going to move every couple of years, and I won't get much of a say in where I go, or when I go, or how long I'm there. There will be years where I'll be gone more than I'm home. It's a hell of a life."

"You're really selling it to me," Vivian joked, even though her voice was shaking, because she had a feeling he was building up to something, something she wasn't ready for.

"I just want to be honest with you. There are a lot of guys out there who are richer, and smarter, and could offer you the stability you're looking for. I know that. I feel selfish for even asking you to choose me when I know how hard it's going to be, but I learned a long time ago to go after what I want, to take my shot when it comes.

"I love you, Viv. For as long as you want me, as long as you'll have me, I'm yours." Joe took a deep, shaky breath. "If it's alright with you, I'd like to spend the rest of my life with you."

Vivian stilled for a moment, and then suddenly, she had to move, the nervous energy coursing through her. When she was a kid and life became overwhelming for her, the urge to flee could be all-consuming, and now it had her getting up from the bed, needing to put space between them, needing to *think*.

"Spend the rest of my life with you" sounded a lot like a promise, a commitment with all kinds of strings attached.

Vivian sank down on the chair in the corner of her room, hugging her knees to her chest, studying him.

It was easier to think when Joe wasn't right next to her, when she couldn't feel the heat from his body, when he wasn't so close that she could reach out and touch him and forget all the reasons that this was a spectacularly bad idea.

"You should see your face," Joe whispered, raking his hand through his hair.

He looked a little stunned himself.

"Shit." Joe crouched down next to her until they were eye level. "Too soon?"

Vivian laughed, gazing at him through watery eyes.

"I've been trying to hold it back—the forever part," he added. "I know this is a lot for you, that it takes some time for you to warm up to this stuff. I figured I'd save an impending marriage proposal for a better time, not right after the world escaped a nuclear war. Sorry about that."

There were a million things she wanted to say, a million questions and protestations running through her mind. He was right—this was big. Flying terrified her, but knowing on top of it that he wanted to go to space? It was a whole unknown, an uncharted path that few had gone down. She'd seen the astronauts and their families on television, observed the way the whole country looked at them like they were celebrities, heroes, and gods all rolled into one. How did you prepare for a thing like that? How did you welcome a thing like that into your life?

But when a man like Joe got down onto his knees in front of you and offered you forever, how did you walk away? How could she turn her back on this feeling inside her?

"Is this a proposal?" Vivian asked.

Joe was silent for a moment that stretched on between them, and she thought of his earlier warning of what it would be like to be with someone like him, and while Vivian couldn't say she completely understood what she was getting herself into—how could anyone when the future stretched before you as a vast unknown—something in his eyes, in the way he looked at her told her everything she needed to know.

"Do you want it to be one?" Joe asked, his voice steady.

For a heartbeat, she hesitated.

In this moment, if someone asked her how she saw things working out between them, she would have told them the absolute truth.

She had no idea.

It seemed impossible.

Their careers took them in different directions.

Their lifestyles could not have been more distinct.

He lived in Italy. She lived in D.C.

But she thought about what the last two weeks had been like, the threat of nuclear war looming before them, how much she'd worried about him, and at the end of the day, the little things just didn't seem to matter as much.

Vivian nodded, the emotion of the moment overwhelming.

Joe took a deep breath, his chest heaving slightly with the effort, and for the first time since they'd met, it occurred to her that he looked unsure of himself, of the risk he was taking and his odds of success.

"Will you marry me?" he asked her.

She leapt.

"Yes."

SIXTEEN

Vivian flew home from Arlington to Florida, Polly beside her on the plane. When they landed, Polly drove them from the airport to the little beach house she and Joe had rented months ago, and it occurred to Vivian that now that the memorial service was over, she was going to have to make some tough decisions.

The fact of the matter was that she was only in Cocoa Beach because of Joe's work at the Cape. As much as she'd been able to find the positives in living here, just as she had in the other cities they had called home, the reality was that Cocoa Beach largely existed around the space program. There weren't a lot of job opportunities here for her, and while she was sure someone would hire her solely based on the fact that she was Joe Mitchell's wife—widow, now—this was a town that revolved around some tourism, but mainly the industry that the space program brought.

She didn't really have friends here—Polly was in Houston, and that was one place Vivian never saw herself returning. She would get a little money after Joe's death, but it wouldn't be enough to live on indefinitely, especially at her relatively young age. She needed to formulate a plan, build a future for herself, and she didn't miss the irony that after years of complaining that her life revolved around Joe's career, now that she had a chance to live on her terms, she had absolutely no idea where she wanted to be or what she wanted to do.

And even though she didn't have a life here anymore, the idea of moving out of the last home where she'd lived with her husband felt immensely painful, yet another thing she wouldn't, couldn't face.

Vivian rolled down the window to Frank's car that he kept at the Cape, which Polly had commandeered for airport transportation. The fresh air felt good on her face after hours of being cooped up on the flight. They'd offered to fly her to and from Arlington on a NASA Gulfstream, but Vivian had declined the ride on the way back, wanting the flexibility to stay in the city a bit longer, needing the opportunity to meet with Graham to give him the memo she'd received.

She hadn't heard anything from him, but she knew how long it took him to work a story, knew how secretive he could be when he was putting it all together.

She figured she'd give him a day before she'd reach out again.

Polly cursed when she turned onto Vivian's street, staring at the line of cars parked there—six, seven.

"I told Frank to send everyone away, let him know that the last thing you needed was to be surrounded by people. I'm sorry, Vivian. I know this doesn't help things."

"It's fine," she lied, even though she had big plans to lock herself in the bedroom as soon as she got into the house.

When they got up to the front door, the noise hit her, the familiar sound of spouses trying to fill the vacuum of grief with their own unique brand of comfort. It was a routine they'd all been through—first as military spouses and then later as astro wives.

Vivian pushed open the door, dread filling her at the outpouring of sympathy that likely awaited her. Her body went numb at the thought of being on the receiving end of their proffered sentiments. She knew they meant well, understood that they were doing their best to offer their condolences, but invariably Vivian found herself offering comfort, assuring them that she was coping, even though she felt like a liar each time she said it. The whole thing was exhausting.

Her gaze drifted around the room at the assembled crowd, Polly whispering apologies beside her.

Polly navigated the path from the front door to the bedroom Vivian and Joe had shared, running interference if anyone came too close. Polly gave Vivian a quick hug before turning back to handle the crowd in the living room, leaving Vivian alone once more.

Vivian rounded the edge of the bed—

A book sat on Joe's nightstand.

A book that hadn't been there when she left for Arlington six days ago.

Vivian glanced over at the little bookshelf in the corner of their bedroom. It was a mix of titles—some classics that had been favorites of hers since high school, her much-loved copy of *The Feminine Mystique*, some beloved romances, and Joe's collection of science fiction novels that he had moved from assignment to assignment. All the books were where they were supposed to be, no empty gaps on the bookshelf, nothing appearing obviously out of place.

Had the book been in Joe's effects at his astronaut quarters?

Frank had brought his stuff over before she left for Arlington, but there hadn't been a book in there. She would have remembered.

Perhaps this one had been left behind?

The nausea receded a bit as she sank down on the edge of the bed, her breathing a bit ragged, the air coming into her lungs calming her.

Vivian picked up the book, imagining that it was still warm from Joe's touch, and she wondered when he'd last read it, when he'd last held it, and how it had suddenly appeared on her nightstand.

The Mystery of Time.

A smile played at her lips, a wave of grief coming over her. It had been like this ever since they'd told her they were officially declaring Joe dead, that they didn't believe any of the crew could have survived in space. Her emotions were all over the place, and she found the nostalgia that hit her at various moments to be a source of both comfort and pain.

How Joe had liked his science fiction books. He'd always been better than she had at suspending disbelief and opening his mind to a vast number of possibilities. She'd never outgrown the stark practicality that had dominated her life for so long, even if now she was considering the very *impractical* possibility that her husband was haunting her.

She opened the book—

A paper rested there, the handwriting familiar.

Joe's.

Her heart thundered as she read over the message written there.

Wait for me.

Her hand shook as she reached into her pocket and pulled out the paper that she had carried with her since she first found it.

Wait for me.

She put the two pieces of paper side by side on top of the book, studying them.

They were both undeniably done in Joe's handwriting. Same color black ink.

Same phrasing.

Vivian flipped them both over, sliding them together like two puzzle pieces.

The math equation that she hadn't understood before, the calculations that Frank said were his, was now complete.

She still didn't understand what it was trying to solve for, or the mathematical gymnastics that had gone into it.

She tried to puzzle it out—so Joe had written this message, one he considered to be so important that he wrote it not once, but twice. He'd torn it into two halves and left one for her in the pocket of her dress and one for her in the book he'd been reading?

How? When? Why?

A book about—

She scanned the book description on the jacket, surprise filling her.

It wasn't a work of science fiction like she'd thought it was. Instead, it was an academic treatise published by a university press she'd never heard of.

Instantly, she was transported back to that day she and Joe were in his apartment. When they talked about the books he liked to read and what inspired him about them.

The universe feels infinite, like it could contain wonders we've never seen, possibilities we've never imagined.

The very words Joe had said to her were the first lines of the book.

Vivian flipped through the pages, phrases jumping out at her—

Wormholes.

. . . shortcut between space and time . . .

. . . space and time bending . . .

. . . communication between time and space . . . objects moving . . .

Vivian's heart pounded as she began to read.

An hour passed by.

Then two hours.

Three.

A couple of times Polly knocked on her door, only for silence to greet her as Vivian pretended to be sleeping, unable to set the book down. A lot of it she didn't understand—the writing was unbelievably dry and technical, and despite Joe's passion for the subject matter and his engineering degree, she was surprised this was a favorite of his. It lacked the romanticism of space travel that he had espoused to her so many times. And yet, the more she read, the more convinced she became that she had solved the mystery of these little signs cropping up everywhere.

What if it wasn't a ghost haunting her? What if Joe had been right all along and time travel was possible? What if her husband was stuck in a different time, or a different place, trying to communicate with her?

"Time travel?"

He laughed. "You should see your face. What's so hard to believe about time travel? It's just a matter of physics, if you think about it."

"I try not to think about physics as much as absolutely possible."

He laughed again. "Fair enough. Maybe one day I'll convince you otherwise."

She didn't understand all the nuances of how something like this would work, wasn't even sure she wholly believed it was possible, but she knew with certainty that this was the closest thing to hope she had felt in a long time.

Vivian flipped to the back of the book. There was no picture of the author, a Dr. Calvin G. Robbins, just a short biography that said he had studied at the Massachusetts Institute of Technology and was currently working at NASA's Langley Research Center in Hampton, Virginia.

Vivian glanced at the suitcase sitting at the foot of her bed, waiting to be unpacked from her trip to Arlington, the decision already made.

She was going back to Virginia.

SEVENTEEN

1963

I just heard a rumor that can't possibly be true. Please tell me you aren't seriously quitting your job and moving to Italy."

Vivian hovered over the threshold of Kerry Krieger's office. Of all the conversations she knew she was going to need to have after accepting Joe's proposal, she'd dreaded this one the most. In the two years since she began working at the television station, Kerry had become someone Vivian looked up to, tried to impress, one day hoped to emulate. It was hard to not feel like she was letting her down.

Vivian stepped into Kerry's office, closing the door behind her. It was somewhat pointless—the news that she was leaving the television station had clearly spread like wildfire for it to have reached Kerry, who was fastidious about not engaging in something as banal as office gossip.

Kerry stared at her expectantly, and it was the worry in

her gaze that flooded Vivian with guilt. She wasn't sure how she could explain something that she was just working out herself.

Two empty chairs sat in front of Kerry's desk, practically begging for Vivian to sit down and reevaluate her life choices, but instead she stayed where she was, a bit fearful that if she sat down in one of those chairs, she'd be talked out of the decisions she'd just made.

Vivian took a deep breath. "I am moving to Italy."

"To get married?"

Kerry said the word "married" like it was an infection you caught.

Vivian nodded.

Kerry sighed. "And he's in the Air Force? A fighter pilot?"

Vivian nodded again.

"I suppose if I told you that you're too talented to throw your life away for some man it wouldn't do anything to change your mind, would it?"

As Vivian was growing up, her mother hadn't been the most engaged of parents. She'd been so occupied with her own life that she hadn't had much time or energy left over to pay atten-tion to Vivian's. It wasn't lost on Vivian that the compliments Kerry gave her, the way she'd taken Vivian under her wing, had meant more because of that absence in her life. And so, it was harder to know that she was letting her mentor down.

"Your opinion means a great deal," Vivian answered hon-estly. "And I know how this sounds—believe me, I sometimes still can't believe I've made this decision myself."

"But you're in love?" Kerry interjected, not unkindly, even if the way she said "love" made it sound like it, too, was an infection you could catch.

"I am."

"And that's enough?"

"I don't know. I hope so."

Before Joe, Vivian had never imagined it could be enough, never wanted to fall in love, to get married, to live the life that society seemed to expect of young women her age. Maybe it was seeing how poorly marriage played out in her own mother's life that soured her on such a commitment. Or perhaps it was her own personality and her need for independence that made the notion of tying herself to one man unappealing.

But now there was Joe.

And he changed everything.

"I saw myself in you," Kerry replied. "I thought you had the same fire for this business that I have. I know you said that you never wanted to be on air, that you were comfortable behind the scenes, but you're a pretty girl, and most importantly a smart one, and I always thought you had a shot. You just had to believe in yourself."

For a moment, Vivian considered calling off the whole thing—Italy, marriage, Joe. She saw the future Kerry laid out before her, saw the potential in what Kerry suggested she could be. And once upon a time, Vivian would have thrown everything away for the chance Kerry described even if she *still* didn't envision herself as on-air talent. But Joe offered her a future, too, a home, albeit one that she would have to pick up and move every few years based on the military's whims, one where she was happy, one where she felt as though she'd found the one person who made her feel like no one ever had before, and that was a pretty difficult possibility to walk away from.

Kerry sighed. "Go. Get married. I hope he's worth it. I hope you find what you're looking for."

The words would have stung if Vivian hadn't seen the sadness in Kerry's gaze, the caring in her eyes.

"He is," Vivian vowed.

Kerry made a noise somewhere between dismissal and disbelief, and then she returned her attention to the papers at her desk, the conversation over.

Vivian lingered for a beat, knowing that the moment had already passed her by, that Kerry was on to the next story, one Vivian would never get to work on.

"ARE YOU NERVOUS?" POLLY WHISPERED TO VIVIAN AS she handed her a bouquet of flowers.

Vivian glanced around, feeling like she was in a fever dream. A truly putrid color of pink stared back at her, the walls, the flowers, the elaborate decor over-the-top.

"I'm in a wedding chapel in Vegas about to marry a man who I've thrown my career away to be with, who I'm planning to move to Italy with in two days. I don't speak Italian. I don't know anyone in Italy. I don't have a job lined up or any idea how I will fill my days. And to say our romance has been a whirlwind is an understatement. I'd be worried if I wasn't nervous."

Polly laughed. "Don't tell Frank—ever—but I was so nervous that I threw up on our wedding day."

"I had no idea."

Polly grinned. "I hid it well. Which is to say, I don't know any woman who isn't a little nervous on her wedding day considering what a risk marriage is and all that. 'Till death do us part'? How isn't that a little terrifying?"

"Even for you and Frank?"

Polly laughed. "Especially for me and Frank. There's nothing wrong with being nervous, Vivian."

"I love him. I know that. And I know what a good man he is, too. It's just so big, you know? It's a giant leap."

Polly reached out and squeezed her hand, and then she stepped back as Vivian left the side alcove to head down the aisle to where Joe waited for her.

Vivian clutched the bouquet of flowers in her hand, the bright pink blending in perfectly with the aesthetic of the little wedding chapel.

She took a deep breath just as the first strands of music began to play.

She'd never thought much about her wedding, never envisioned the song she would walk down the aisle to, had just assumed it would be the traditional "Bridal Chorus."

The strands of Elvis Presley crooning "Can't Help Falling in Love" greeted her instead.

Vivian walked down the aisle with a smile on her face and laughter in her heart, at the song she realized Joe had chosen, at the future that waited for her.

And as soon as she took her first step, as Elvis sang of the unpredictable, unavoidable inevitability of love, all of Vivian's fears receded into the background.

She knew.

If given the same decision to make time and time again, she would choose Joe every single time.

EIGHTEEN

1968

Eighteen Days Gone

Vivian came to the end of the hallway and stopped opposite a door that looked like it had once doubled as a broom closet. Someone had handwritten a sign with the name "Dr. Robbins."

The sign was crooked.

The sign's author had originally included only one "b" in Robbins, so the other had been hastily added with the universal editorial sign for an insertion followed by a second letter "b."

Hardly an auspicious beginning.

Polly had tried to convince Vivian to let her accompany her to Virginia, but Vivian could see the strain that being away from her girls was having on Polly, especially given everything the Abbotts were going through. It felt like too much of an imposition to ask her friend to follow this lead with her, and she was more than a little embarrassed by the fact that she was even considering the possibility of something as far-fetched as Joe having time traveled. Well, perhaps time traveled was the wrong word. When she thought of time travel, she thought of H. G. Wells and his time machine. What Dr. Robbins had proposed in his book seemed more nuanced than that.

The more she considered it—the more she turned it over in her mind—there was something about the possibility that felt right. The finality of death didn't ring true to her, not as it had when she'd lost loved ones before; this seemed more like a temporary absence, like when Joe had been called away on a mission for work—unreachable, but not permanently gone.

Although now that she was here, using her military spouse identification card to finagle her way onto the base and to the office where Dr. Robbins worked, the first strong stirrings of doubt emerged. If Dr. Robbins was an expert in his field, then wouldn't his office be in a more prestigious location, not this annexed building with no security that had been easily accessible to her with her military ID? And she could appreciate an academic who didn't stand on ceremony, but a handwritten sign hardly inspired confidence.

Vivian raised her hand to knock on the door, just as it swung open and a man appeared.

She'd envisioned the author who'd written a treatise on time travel with the dry recitation of a university professor lecturing before an auditorium of bored undergraduate students to be someone who'd been entrenched in his discipline for decades, but the man who exited Dr. Robbins's office was young. He honestly didn't look that much older than her—a decade or so, perhaps.

He was tall and lean, a pair of wire-rimmed glasses atop his angular face, a mop of light brown hair flopping over his brow.

He froze, only inches away from colliding with her. "I'm sorry—I didn't expect that someone would be there."

"Are you Dr. Robbins?" Vivian asked.

"I am."

She looked him over for a moment, taking in the rumpled trousers, the shirt that suggested no one was at home providing him freshly pressed clothes. He looked harried, and she wondered if that was his perpetual state of being or if there was something particularly pressing going on in the world of space-time studies.

"I'd like to talk to you if you have a moment. Is this a convenient time?" Vivian glanced over his shoulder at the open office behind him. Her original estimation that the exterior of the place looked like a converted broom closet wasn't far from the reality. It was a dimly lit room, the entirety of which was nearly dominated by an enormous desk covered in a mess of papers that had her itching to organize them. The walls were a bleak white. No pictures hung from the walls, their appearance as stark as the rest of the space, save for a chalkboard that was covered in what looked to be mathematical calculations. If she were making a movie, this would have been the perfect eccentric scientist's lair.

Time travel? What was she thinking?

What if this had all been a mistake? What if her grief was causing her to act in erratic ways?

Vivian hesitated for a moment, hovering over the threshold, ready to pivot on her heels and board a plane back to Florida.

Vivian reached into her purse, pulling the book out. "I read your book. I have some questions about it."

His eyes widened slightly as his gaze settled on the cover. "You read *The Mystery of Time*?"

The incredulous note in his tone raised her hackles. How novel, another man who was going to imply that a woman wasn't smart enough to understand complicated problems. She hadn't understood it, true, but that was entirely a result of the utterly dense way it had been written and not her gender.

Vivian straightened, lifting her chin so she could meet his gaze head-on. "I did."

"You must be one of five people who did, then," he replied, his voice dry. "My editor read it, but he complained the whole time that it was a sludge to get through, so hardly an auspicious start to my career as a published author. Apparently, I'm not good at synthesizing my thoughts for a general audience."

Vivian had to bite back a laugh at how succinctly he diagnosed his own writing. That was exactly what she had struggled with while reading it.

"My mom and dad said they read it, although I suspect they lied to spare my feelings, as parents do. And my grandmother was more honest and said that she read the first page before she was bored to tears, so while I'm not sure she counts, I must give her points for honesty, and four people reading my book seems much less sad than three, especially considering one was paid to do so. Since you're the first nonfamilial relative or reader who wasn't actually paid to do so, I'd say you're entitled to more than a few minutes of my time. You have my eternal gratitude as well." Dr. Robbins took a step back, into the inner sanctum that was his office. "What do you want to ask me?"

He left the door open as Vivian followed him inside. Dr. Robbins sat behind his desk, gesturing for Vivian to take the empty seat opposite him.

"Are you a student?" he asked her.

"No. I— The book was my husband's." Vivian waited before offering more information, wondering if he would recognize her now, considering her face had been splashed all over newspapers and television screens for the past couple of weeks.

He frowned as she said the word "was."

"At least—I found it in his personal effects," Vivian corrected.

"I'm sorry for your loss."

"Thank you."

Dr. Robbins might not have been good at synthesizing his thoughts for a general audience, but there was something in his manner that was distinctly reassuring, as though he were almost overly solicitous. It could have been off-putting, but instead it came across as earnest, and it made Vivian want to put him at ease.

The part of her that had always been intensely private wanted to get through this discussion without revealing who she was, but she couldn't figure out how to inject enough details into the conversation to get the answers she sought. She could pretend that she was a reporter working on a story— impersonating a fellow scientist was out of the question given the complexity of the subject they were discussing—but she didn't want abstract answers to theoretical possibilities. She wanted, needed, to know how this could possibly apply to her husband's exact situation.

"My name is Vivian Mitchell. My husband is Joe Mitchell, the astronaut—"

She didn't have to go any further. She saw the moment it connected for him. He may not have recognized her, but he was a scientist, interested in space exploration. He knew who her husband was.

"Mrs. Mitchell, I am so truly sorry for your loss. What happened to your husband and the rest of the crew is a great tragedy."

"Thank you." Vivian struggled with the right phrasing for a moment before realizing that there simply was no right phrasing. She might as well dive in headfirst. "As I said, I read your book. I found it among my husband's things. And since you had written on the subject matter, I was wondering what your thoughts are. Is there a way that someone in space could communicate with someone on Earth? Not with a squawk box, or something—I mean they could use a squawk box—but I suppose through nontraditional technological means.

"I know how this sounds—" Vivian added before he could say more. "But it's not my grief talking. At first, I thought it was; at first, I thought that the shock and pain of losing Joe was driving me mad, but that's not it." She took a deep breath. "There are things happening. Messages. Objects that were Joe's appearing in unusual places. It feels like he's trying to communicate with me. Is there a way that my husband could be trapped in time as you've described in your book?"

Dr. Robbins paled. "Mrs. Mitchell—"

"No. Please. Before you speak—don't dismiss me. Everyone has dismissed me. Everyone believes that I'm just an over-wrought widow, that these things are too complicated for me to understand. Maybe they're wrong. Maybe this is too difficult for *them* to understand. When I read your book, I thought that perhaps you would be open-minded enough to look at things from a different perspective. My husband believed that there was still so much we don't know about space, about the possibility there. When I read *The Mystery of Time*, I got the impression that you believe that, too. In fact, some of the words you wrote in the first chapter are nearly identical to the ones my husband used when describing his views to me. Did you know Joe? Did the two of you ever meet in person?"

If she had to guess Dr. Robbins's age, she would place him near Joe's age. He had the look about him of a man who spent a great deal of time indoors, whereas Joe had been Joe, but it wasn't improbable to think that their paths might have crossed at NASA or some other place.

Dr. Robbins glanced wildly at the door for a moment as though longing to escape.

"No, I never had the pleasure of meeting your husband, I'm afraid. I did follow the launch, though. I'm not—I'm not a reli-gious man, Mrs. Mitchell. Perhaps if you talked to a priest, or a counselor, or a friend—"

"No. I'm not looking for a meditation on life after death. I want to talk to you about space, about the possibility of time travel. Something happened to my husband and the rest of the crew. Did you know that they haven't even recovered the spacecraft? There's no sign of it. No debris. Nothing. How can that be?"

A gleam entered his eyes as she spoke of the spacecraft.

"I don't need a theological explanation," Vivian continued. "I'm looking for a scientific one. I read your book. The things you wrote about there—I've never heard people talk about any of this. These wormholes you mention—could something like that have sucked up Joe's spacecraft?"

Internally, she cringed a bit even as she asked the question, because it *did* sound like something out of one of the science fiction books Joe loved to read. Besides, no matter how many times she'd read over the section on wormholes in his book, she didn't entirely understand what one was.

Dr. Robbins shot her another wary look. "They buried me back here because they don't think very much of the things I'm studying. You should understand, things like wormholes, time travel, they exist very much on the fringes of the kind of science that sent your husband to space." He glanced back at the book in her hands. "Sometimes I regret writing the damned thing. Maybe I wouldn't have if I'd realized how much of a negative impact it would have on my career. People laugh when I enter a room now. I exaggerated earlier about the fact that only five people read my book. It was more than five when you include the reviewers from scientific magazines who read it and wrote the whole thing off as a load of balderdash. I had a promising career before I blew it up with that book. It has made me a laughingstock of the scientific community. I wouldn't put much consideration in it. No one else has."

"Then they think we're both mad. Fine. I don't care what

other people think. I want to know what could have happened in space. How a spacecraft could simply disappear like that. What do you think happened to it? You can't tell me that you haven't considered the possibilities. I saw the look in your eyes as soon as I mentioned the fact that there isn't a shred of evidence that the spacecraft was even where it was supposed to be."

"Mrs. Mitchell, I don't want to—"

"What, give me false hope? Confuse me? Let's make a deal, Dr. Robbins. Whatever you tell me, however outlandish it may seem, I won't discount it. And I won't entirely rely upon it, either. But please stop treating me as though I somehow need to be protected from all of this. I can't stand by while I feel like Joe is trying to reach out to me for something, like he needs me, and I'm not doing anything. I keep wondering if he's still out there. In space. Or time. I keep wondering if he needs me."

It was the pity in his eyes that made her want to cry—the way he looked at her as though he could see how much all of this had messed her up and how desperately she was trying to keep it all together.

"What has NASA told you?" he asked, finally.

"Not much. Just that there was no trace of them. That they were unable to communicate with them, unable to locate them, and they didn't know why. A friend suggested that there may have been a problem with the navigation system on the spacecraft. That it may have malfunctioned somehow."

"It's certainly possible. As much as it irks us to admit it, computers are only as good as the people putting in the data. Mistakes can be made."

"They finally declared the crew dead because they said that

they'd been missing for too long, that without any trace of the spacecraft it was likely something catastrophic had happened. And if something catastrophic happened to the spacecraft, it wouldn't have been survivable."

"I'm far from an expert on spaceflight, but as a scientist, I would concur with their assumption. It's unlikely, yes."

"Unlikely, but not impossible?"

He hesitated. "I don't think anything in science is necessarily impossible. I would say rather that it is unknown. But I understand how they concluded what they did, particularly in such a sensitive circumstance. There is no easy explanation for what happened to your husband and the rest of the crew."

She could tell he was dismissing her before he rose from the seat behind his desk, but once he did, well—

"I'm sorry for your loss, Mrs. Mitchell. But I don't have the answers you're looking for."

NINETEEN

1963

Six months after their wedding, Joe was officially selected for astronaut training and they moved to Houston, Texas. On the plus side, Frank had been selected for astronaut training as well, and Vivian took comfort in the fact that Polly would be by her side as she acclimated to yet another transformation in her life.

As soon as they arrived in Texas, the full weight of what she'd signed up for began to hit Vivian. Life in Italy had been relatively quiet, but astronaut training was another beast entirely.

Her relaxed, happy, confident husband became stressed-out and singularly focused as if overnight. Competition for the astronaut spots was exceedingly tough, and the competition spilled over from the astronauts themselves to their spouses.

Project Mercury—which comprised the first seven astronauts—was finished, and while the space program was turning its sights to the next phase, Gemini, there was a growing contingent of public opinion that was strongly questioning whether the cost of manned spaceflight was worth the reward. To that end, it felt like the astronauts were called to do more, be better, in order to justify their existence.

In addition to how difficult the training was, Vivian saw how much Joe worried about whether he'd get his chance to go up at all before the manned space program was scrapped entirely. It was ironic that for so long Joe had been focused on getting selected for astronaut training, and now that he was there, it seemed like the dream was growing even more out of reach.

She barely saw him, spent most of her time in Houston either looking for jobs or helping Polly set up the nursery in her house now that she and Frank were expecting their second child. Whenever Vivian felt frustrated with the turn her life had taken and how difficult it was to maintain a relationship that most certainly came second to the space program, she only had to look at what Polly was going through to feel like she had little to complain about. At this point, she hoped Polly had the good fortune to go into labor during one of the few breaks she and Frank had, because otherwise Vivian had a sneaking suspicion she was going to be the one by her friend's side while she gave birth.

Each day, Joe came home from training more discouraged than the day before.

"How was your day?" Vivian asked him one evening, staring up at the ceiling as she lay beside him in bed.

He sighed. "Not great."

Surprise filled her. She asked him the same question every evening, and every evening he said the same thing, that training was "fine," even though "fine" sounded like a synonym for something, well . . . "not great."

"Do you want to talk about it?" she asked.

Vivian had realized early on in their marriage that Joe wasn't used to sharing his concerns with someone else. Most of his problem-solving seemed to happen internally, and only when she pushed a bit did he let her in and share what was bothering him. Little by little, he was talking to her more, but she also understood that he had built a career on his own, one that he was proud and fiercely protective of, and sometimes when confronted with professional struggles, he was reluctant to let her in.

"Some of the guys don't respect me," he told her after a beat, and knowing Joe as she did, knowing how proud he was, she understood how much it cost him to admit that.

"Why wouldn't they respect you?"

She was learning things about herself in this marriage, too, and Vivian realized that she was incredibly protective of her husband, and when Joe was slighted at work, she became irrationally angry.

Besides, this was Joe. Everyone loved Joe. Everyone looked up to Joe.

"Because of the test pilot thing. I'm just a fighter pilot and everyone knows it."

One of the challenges with Joe going through astronaut training was how much Vivian didn't know—or understand—about the subtle nuances of his career. As newlyweds, Vivian felt like she was playing catch-up on the things that the other spouses who had been married far longer than she had learned long ago. And the other wives judged her for it.

"You're not 'just a fighter pilot,'" Vivian protested. "You're a great fighter pilot. I seem to remember someone telling me that," she joked, trying to lighten the mood.

Joe groaned. "I was an ass for saying that."

"No, you were just confident. You should be confident now. You're great at everything you do."

He arched an eyebrow at her, making an exaggerated face. "Everything?"

She rolled her eyes, but she didn't lie. "Everything."

He kissed the top of her head. "I'm sorry you're having to see me like this. I think it's starting over that feels so hard. I've been flying for so long that it's as natural to me as breathing. But this is all new, and I'm starting to think I'm too old to learn something new.

"This is the hardest thing I've ever done. It's exhausting. The doctors poke at you; you're constantly a lab rat. They're hunting to find something they can use against you, some ailment that's disqualifying.

"I keep watching pilots around me—good pilots, *great* pilots—wash out in the program. We all know that some of us are going to be cut, and I keep thinking that it's only a matter of time until I'm next."

"That's not going to happen," Vivian replied. "You're going to be an astronaut. And you're going to go to the Moon, just like President Kennedy promised. I have no doubt of that."

Joe pressed his lips into the curve of her neck, a line of goose bumps pebbling on her skin.

"You know it doesn't matter to me whether you're an astronaut or not," Vivian murmured. "I just want you to be happy. Just want you to be yourself, whatever version of that I get. I don't understand the whole astronaut thing. I didn't get the fighter pilot thing, either," Vivian confessed, her hand stroking Joe's chest.

He snorted. "That's not exactly news. You've made that point abundantly clear a time or two or one thousand. Be honest—you wish you'd married someone utterly boring and not nearly as dashing?"

Vivian laughed. "You are entirely too handsome. I've always thought that, too."

"Too handsome? And to think of all the years I spent when I was young worrying girls would never find me attractive."

"You were cute when you were young," she protested, remembering the photographs she'd seen of the skinny boy with the serious expression on his face.

"I was all limbs and no sign of growing into them. The names they called me—"

"I would have loved you then. Just like I love you now."

"I know." Joe said the words solemnly, like a vow just between them. "I think that was what attracted me to you most in the first place. The fact that you weren't interested in me because I was a fighter pilot."

"Because I was attracted to your hidden depths?"

Joe had the good sense to look abashed. "Well, no. Actually, it was because you were a challenge at first. I'd gotten used to not having to work hard, you see, and—"

She shoved him lightly. "Pig."

"I'm being honest," he protested. "But then there you were, making eyes for Graham Carlson"—he made a face as he said the newsman's name—"and all I could think was that I would tie myself up in knots doing whatever it took to have you look at me like that."

"That's all it was—that I was a challenge?"

It wasn't the first time they'd had this conversation, hopefully wouldn't be the last time they lingered over the details of how they met, as though they needed to say it aloud to remember the marvel of it—the way he wasn't supposed to be in town at all, but he'd broken his arm, and Vivian never would have agreed to go on a double date with him and Frank if Polly had told her they were fighter pilots before she'd walked into the bar that night, the tenuous manner in which their paths had crossed, in which it felt like fate had a plan for them despite their best intentions, as if the stars themselves had aligned to bring them together.

"Of course not," Joe replied smoothly, shifting in the bed so that he tucked her against him. "You were everything."

She laughed. "Good line."

"Great line," he corrected. "Also, completely the truth."

"And to think, we never would have had this if Frank hadn't stolen Polly away from you."

Joe laughed. "You think Frank stole Polly away?"

"Well, didn't he? After all, you set the date with her and then she ended up with Frank."

This part, they'd never discussed.

It was strange looking back on how it unfolded, knowing what she did now. At the time, Joe had been singularly unruffled by the entire experience, which now knowing him like she did, knowing the way he looked at her, the way he felt about her, it was difficult to imagine him being so nonchalant about something he cared about slipping through his fingers.

"First off—Frank didn't steal Polly away, and he never would have. Neither would I if the roles were reversed. We're brothers. We wouldn't do that to each other.

"I was interested in Polly when I met her, yes. She's pretty, and smart, and funny. But that was all it was. When I got there, I saw you."

"And let me guess, you were swept off your feet by how dazzling I was?" Vivian joked.

"I thought you were extraordinary. And then you expressed your doubts about whether we should go to space, and I'll admit it gave me pause and I nearly revised that opinion." Joe grinned. "Are you really going to make fun of the single most important moment of my life?"

"I thought the first moment you ever sat in a fighter jet was the single most important moment of your life."

"Please don't ask me to choose between my two great loves."

"Because it isn't a competition? Flight has your heart every single time, doesn't it?"

Her tone was light, teasing, because she'd come into this marriage with her eyes open about who she married and what his priorities were.

"Maybe I'm afraid it's the other way around," Joe replied, matching her teasing tone with a more serious one. "Maybe I found something that means more to me now."

"I was just joking, Joe. I'm sorry, I shouldn't have given you the impression otherwise. I wouldn't ask you to choose—not between me and flying. Or me and space."

"You say that now, but this lifestyle isn't the easiest. I've seen what the other guys go through in their relationships, in their marriages. It's part of why I never wanted that for myself. We get the glory, and the family gets stuck with the hardships. It's a lot to ask anyone to bear and it's a lot of strain to put on any marriage."

"I know the risks. I know the weight families are forced to carry."

Maybe she had been too young at the time to remember what it was like when she lost her father, but she was all too familiar with the risks and the aftermath of tragedy.

"I worry that you'll regret it."

"I worry about that, too," she admitted.

"Why me?" Vivian asked after a beat. "Why did you want to be with me?"

"I don't know. I've asked myself that a thousand times, and I still couldn't tell you. I hope you don't take this the wrong way, but I've often thought that you have the absolute worst personality for this lifestyle."

Vivian laughed despite what he said. "I don't disagree with you at all. I truly cannot imagine a worse role for me. I worry constantly. And after a childhood spent moving, all I want is to stay in one place, to have some measure of certainty in my life, to have a home and a career, and the comfort of stability. To build a life for myself somewhere where I feel as though I am part of a community, and I have a routine. I want a boring, quiet life."

It wasn't until she got to the end of her speech that she realized how true the words she spoke were; it wasn't until tears had begun to fall on her cheeks that she realized how much she mourned the loss of her dream, how lonely she'd been since he started training.

She'd seen how stressed-out he was, how worried he was, and she hadn't wanted to add to his plate, but she also wasn't sure how much longer she could hold it inside.

"I know," Joe whispered. "I'm sorry."

Perhaps if he had dismissed her words, Vivian would have been able to shrug the whole thing off, to tell herself that really she should be tougher about the entire business, that she should learn to deal with the difficult parts of his job, but it was the emotion in his voice that unraveled her instead, because despite everything, it seemed like he understood.

"I don't know how to do this," Vivian added.

"Do what?"

"All of it. I don't—" Vivian struggled to find the words, to tell him how she felt without saying the sorts of things she didn't think you were supposed to say in a marriage. "I love you. I don't know how not to love you. But sometimes—sometimes it feels like I'm losing part of myself here. This version of me that I feel like everyone wants me to be—I miss working. I miss the life we had before when everything was simpler. I don't want to be on magazine covers. I don't want to give interviews, and knowing that's what the future holds if you're selected as an astronaut—

"It feels"—Vivian took a deep breath—"it feels like all the other wives have this playbook that they follow, and I never got my copy. They're always so poised and they are so dedicated to the mission. I don't—"

How did she explain it to him? That this was his dream, and so of course she wanted it for him, wanted to make him proud, wanted to be an asset to him like the other wives seemed to be for their husbands, but she didn't care about the mission, didn't care if the United States went to the Moon beyond the fact that he wanted it.

"You don't have to do any of that, then, Viv. I didn't marry you because I wanted you to be my cheerleader. I married you because you're the most interesting person I know. Because you're loyal and you feel things deeply. I married you because I couldn't imagine spending my life with anyone else, because what we have is special. I don't want a day to go by when you're not by my side. In this unpredictable, chaotic world, you remind me of what matters."

A strangled sound escaped from her lips somewhere between a laugh and a sob. "That's the problem, you see. Every time you fly, every time we talk about the reality of you going to space, I worry that you're not going to come back. And the thing is—I never wanted to get married. I've been on my own for so long, I envisioned myself being on my own. Paying the bills and managing the household feel easy to me, and I know that if I was by myself again, I would manage just fine. Or at least, I would endure. But I can't imagine what it would feel like to have what we have, to know what it's like to feel this way, and then to lose it all."

"Viv. I know."

"I hate that I feel like this. Hate that I'm scared all the time. I wish I could push the thoughts out, but even when I try my hardest, even when I think I've succeeded, they always creep back."

"Nothing is going to happen to me."

"You can't promise me that."

"I can," he shot back. "I'm a good pilot; no, I'm a great pilot."

She laughed despite the tears spilling down her cheeks, his confidence apparently returned once more. "Tell me what you really think."

What would it be like to go through life with such brash confidence? She couldn't fathom it, wasn't entirely used to it despite their time together. She worried about every move she made, doubted every decision, and sat back and watched as he launched himself at life with wild abandon. And as surprising as his loss of confidence had been moments ago, there was something peaceful knowing that he was back to believing in himself, because it was that belief that kept him safe, that would eventually take him to the Moon.

"You know it's true."

She did.

He *was* a great pilot, had worked for years to get to this point in his career, to achieve a milestone many had dreamed of but very, very few would ever reach.

"Fine, let's take the issue of whether or not I'm a great pilot and try it this way—have I ever broken a promise to you?"

"No."

She'd learned that early on in their relationship—that when Joe gave his word about something, he meant it, wholly, completely. It was one of the things she admired most about him.

"Then I'll make you a promise now. I'll always come back to you. Always."

"You can't make a promise like that. No one can."

"I can and I will."

Vivian looked into his eyes, and she saw the conviction

there, the confidence that had been missing earlier. And that was when she realized what had happened—that when he felt scared, when he had doubts, she became someone he could lean on, someone who could help him find his way back to himself when he was lost. And when she felt the same way, he in turn offered his strength to her.

"How are we going to make this work?" she asked him.

"I don't know," Joe replied. "But we will."

VIVIAN WAS WIPING DOWN THE COUNTERTOPS IN THE kitchen in their rental home in Houston when Joe came home, beaming from ear to ear.

"We need to talk," he said, scooping her up in his arms and twirling her around, her feet just off the ground.

"Not exactly words a girl likes to hear," she joked, the look on his face making her stomach lurch.

She knew that look. Recognized that gleam in his eyes.

He set her down on her feet.

"How do you feel about being married to an astronaut?" he asked her.

"Depends on the astronaut." Tears filled her eyes. "You made it?"

He nodded, his own eyes filled with a wet sheen.

She'd never been so happy and so terrified in all her life.

TWENTY

1968

Eighteen Days Gone

Ｈow is it going there?" Polly asked her over the phone line.
"Not as well as I'd hoped." Vivian leaned back against
the headboard in the motel room, staring up at the ceiling, her
gaze fixated on a faded water mark.

Joe's military pay hadn't left much room for savings, and the
healthy *Life* contract that the original Mercury Seven had received for sharing exclusive interviews and stories with the
magazine had since been subdivided between so many astronauts as more and more joined the space program that it
wasn't much to go on. Vivian would get some money now that
Joe was gone, but it was hardly going to be enough to support
her for the rest of her life, and having come all the way to Virginia only to be turned away, she was beginning to regret the
money she'd spent on the plane ticket and motel room. She

didn't have the luxury of going off on a wild-goose chase like she'd done.

"I'm sorry," Polly replied. "Are you coming back soon?"

"In the morning."

"I'll pick you up from the airport."

"I can get a taxi," Vivian protested, guilt filling her at how much Polly had already done for her. They hadn't discussed it yet, but Vivian figured Polly needed to get back to Houston soon.

"I'll pick you up at the airport," Polly repeated. "Get some rest, Vivian."

As Vivian hung up the phone, someone knocked on the motel door.

She walked over and glanced through the peephole, surprised to see Dr. Robbins standing on the other side. She opened the door a crack.

"I'm sorry to bother you," he said. "I tried calling first from the front desk, but they said the line was busy. I wanted to apologize to you. When you came to see me, I was caught off guard and I didn't know what to say. You were clearly—understandably—upset, and I was worried that whatever I said would only make things worse." He hesitated. "Do you have a moment to talk?"

Vivian glanced around the motel room, feeling a little strange about the idea of sharing such an intimate space with a stranger.

"It's a nice night," he said, seemingly noticing her discomfort. "There's a picnic table out front. Do you want to sit there?"

"That would be perfect. Thank you."

Vivian locked up her motel room, and Dr. Robbins followed her through the motel yard until they both sat down on the old wooden picnic table near the parking lot. There were three other cars parked besides the one she rented, and she got the impression this wasn't high tourist season in this part of Virginia.

"How did you find me?" she asked him.

"There are only three hotels in town. This was my second choice. I figured you'd want to stay as close to the research center as possible. Or the airport. Seemed practical. You gave me the impression that you were the sort of person who took such things into consideration."

Vivian laughed. "I showed up at your office saying that I think my husband is communicating with me from space because he's somehow caught in a space-time loop or something and you got the impression that I'm a practical person?"

"Fair point. On the surface, it does sound impossible. Outlandish. But I suppose at one time space travel seemed impossible, too. I don't like to deal in impossibilities. Maybe there are no impossibilities; it's merely that our understanding of such things hasn't caught up yet. I figured perhaps you saw it the same way, too."

For the first time since he'd dismissed her earlier in the day, Vivian felt a stirring of hope, and she clung to it like a lifeline.

"How would that work?"

Dr. Robbins hesitated once more. She got the impression that he was a cautious man, one who thought a great deal about what he said before he said it.

"You have to understand," he finally answered. "My earlier reservations when you came to see me—they're still here. When we study and discuss these things, it's always done in the abstract. These are theories. Applying them to real life, to your husband's life, well, I don't want to give you false hope. I don't know what's possible. No one does. I know what I think *could* be possible, but—"

"Then tell me that."

Dr. Robbins glanced off into the distance for longer than seemed natural given the conversation.

"Are you trying to break it to me gently?" Vivian asked.

"No, I'm trying to synthesize my thoughts for a general audience," he replied, his tone dry.

She laughed again.

"You said you read my book."

"'Read' might be a bit of an exaggeration. I'll admit I was one of those general audience members that needed a bit more synthesizing—or I suppose a PhD—to understand it. I got the gist—just not the particulars. The science you described was nothing like any of the science classes I ever took in high school or college."

Dr. Robbins nodded. "The foundation of it comes from Einstein. But where it's going, well—we're still figuring it out."

"You mentioned wormholes in your book. I'd never heard of them before."

"I'm not surprised. They're theoretical. A way of understanding space and time. A shortcut, if you will, between space and time."

"A shortcut between space and time? Like time travel?"

"The idea is that you could enter a wormhole at one moment in space and time and exit it in another. Like a bridge. But you must understand—there's no evidence that wormholes even exist."

"Then why do scientists think that they might?"

"Because Einstein's theories include wormholes, and when we test his theories, they hold up. So it may be that there are wormholes out there, we just haven't found them. I mean, look, black holes have only been accepted within the last few decades. In comparison, wormholes are a much newer science. And considering our space exploration is still in its nascent phase, it's very possible that they're out there."

Once again, it sounded like an idea from one of those science fiction novels Joe loved to read. Vivian had tried one once and she hadn't been able to suspend disbelief enough to follow the plot, had found the scenarios that played out on the page to be too implausible for her to get out of her own head as she questioned the decisions the characters made and the environment they traversed.

And yet—

"If Joe's spacecraft went into one of these wormholes—"

He hesitated. "*Theoretically*, then it could exist in another space or time. But we don't even know if a spacecraft would fit through a wormhole or if the wormhole would collapse. And to be honest, the idea that there is a wormhole somewhere between Earth and the Moon is highly unlikely."

"Unlikely, but not impossible?"

"Like I said, Mrs. Mitchell, nothing is impossible."

"You can call me Vivian, if you'd like. Lately, I feel like whenever anyone calls me Mrs. Mitchell, it's because they're delivering bad news."

Not to mention how old it made her feel. How much life did she have left in her? Another fifty, sixty years without Joe? It seemed like an eternity.

"Alright, Vivian. You can call me Cal." He hesitated. "Dr. Robbins always makes me feel like I should wear a tweed blazer and give lectures first-year undergrads fall asleep in."

She laughed. "Do you happen to teach at the university near town?"

He grinned. "Alright, I do. And only seven have fallen asleep."

"You keep a running count?"

He reached into the pocket of his tweed blazer and pulled out a folded white sheet of paper with hash marks on it.

Seven.

He showed it to her for a moment before he placed it back in his pocket with the solemnity of someone who valued the document a great deal. For a man who wrote a book as dry as the one he'd published, he had a surprising sense of humor.

It gave her hope that a man who didn't take himself too seriously had the good sense to acknowledge his own limitations and be open to the possibility of things he didn't yet understand.

"I realize this requires some suspension of disbelief and accounting for scientific theories that exist but have not been proven; however, let me get this straight," Vivian said. "What you're telling me is that if the spacecraft encountered a wormhole, Joe could exist in another space or time. Could he be using this 'bridge' to somehow communicate with me?"

"Theoretically," he corrected.

"Theoretically," she echoed.

"Yes. There has been some conjecture that there can be alternate realities."

"An alternate version of Joe could be trying to communicate with me?"

"Perhaps."

"How would that work?"

"Well, *theoretically*, of course—"

She grinned despite the bizarreness of the entire conversation.

"—if the spacecraft had gone through a wormhole, then space and time might have warped. He could have seen an opportunity to travel through time to a different moment in his life, not the moment when the spacecraft entered the wormhole, not the point when everything went wrong, but maybe a different point. An earlier one or a later one. It would be chaotic. It would be unpredictable. It could be a distortion of the original timeline of his life."

"And the objects? How could he move them? I don't understand."

Dr. Robbins—Cal—was silent for a moment, and Vivian could see it all playing out in his mind, could envision him conceptualizing how such a thing was possible.

"I—I don't know exactly. If I had to guess, I would say that someone could try to time travel in a wormhole, but due to the instability it wouldn't be entirely possible to slip back into our time. Maybe the best he could do was to interact with objects in our time, but there wasn't enough of an opportunity to fully return, to completely time travel. It's like a tunnel that's collapsing. Maybe you can stick your hand through an opening, throw something through it to the other side, yell through an opening, grab something, but that doesn't necessarily mean your body can move through the rock. There are limitations. Or maybe there aren't. No one knows because there is no known case of someone going through a wormhole, or even a guarantee that they exist. I wish I could tell you with more certainty, but no one can."

It was clear that the scientist in him was fascinated by the possibility, that he wanted to explore it further. It was also evident that he was terrified of giving her false hope and likely wished to be excused from the entire business.

"I'm sorry."

He blinked behind his glasses. "Why are you apologizing?"

"I feel like I'm making you uncomfortable putting you in this position. I apologize. I promise I won't hold any of this against you if we're wrong about the entire business and Joe didn't go through a wormhole somewhere, and isn't trying to communicate with me, and all of this is just a product of my grief."

"These objects you've discovered. The ones you think your husband is trying to use to communicate with you. What are they?"

She told him about the squawk box, and the boots, and the postcard, and reached into her pocket and handed him the two notes from Joe that resided together in the pocket of her dress.

She watched him study them with scientific precision, looking at the equations, the handwriting, placing the notes side by side before giving them back to her.

"And there's no way that your husband could have slipped this in your pocket before he boarded the spacecraft?"

"I don't see how. His friend said that he gave Joe the paper with the equations on it right before Joe boarded the spacecraft. I didn't even interact with him the morning of the launch. We saw each other briefly the night before, but I was wearing a different outfit, and he didn't put anything in my pocket. Besides, the other note I found inside your book in our home."

Vivian looked at the notes again. "Why 'wait for me'? Why would he write that to me repeatedly? If he needed to get a message to me, why would he choose that one? Why not 'I'm stuck in space, and I need help, this is how to find me' or something obvious like that?"

Cal hesitated. "Do you want me to answer that as a man or as a scientist?"

"Both, I think."

"Well, as a man, I would say that he wrote 'wait for me' because he wanted you to wait for him."

"I figured that much out," Vivian answered, not unkindly.

"Because he loved you so much that he was determined to do everything in his power to come back to you, and that he was so certain in his ability to do so, that he asked you to wait because he knew that what you had, the love you shared, was the kind that a man would risk everything to get back to."

Cal removed his glasses at the end of his speech, reaching into the breast pocket of his cream linen shirt and pulling out a handkerchief folded into a meticulous square, the corners so precise that someone had clearly ironed it for him into neat, incisive points. Or had he done it himself? For some reason she didn't envision him with a wife or significant other waiting for him at home. Although, perhaps her assessment of him was incorrect. Maybe he had a whole family waiting for him at home.

Vivian blinked, reordering her impression of him, wondering if she'd misjudged him as he cleaned the lenses in a habit that spoke to years of muscle memory. His wrists peeked out from beneath the cuffs of his shirt, a fine sprinkling of hair there, and she glanced away, flushing a bit. She hadn't realized it, but somewhere in the interim between the inception of their conversation and now, they'd moved quite close to each other, his shoulder nearly touching hers, and at that realization, the warmth of his body closer than made her comfortable, she slid over on the bench, putting distance between them.

If he registered the movement, she didn't realize it, so total was his absorption in the cleaning of his glasses, his hair a bit longer than was fashionable, looking as though a trip to the barber was in order.

"And your answer as a scientist?" she asked him.

Cal glanced up, sliding the glasses back into place, his eyes meeting hers. "You said that your husband used to read a lot of science fiction books, right? That he was interested in the science of space and time travel, that he believed in the possibility of such things?"

Vivian nodded.

"Well, there's a theory about time travel. A concern that if you make a change in the timeline, it can have a ripple effect that reverberates in potentially catastrophic ways. Your husband would have known that to be a consideration, a possibility. So maybe he was afraid that if he told you too much, if he made too many changes, it could alter the timeline in a way that he would no longer be able to get back to you.

"Maybe 'wait for me' was the best he felt he could do to try to send you a message without disrupting the timeline. It's an elegant solution to an unwieldy problem. For what it's worth, I'd have done the same in his shoes."

It made sense in a way if you suspended disbelief and believed that anything was possible, which wasn't so hard considering the alternative was that she was being haunted.

She didn't realize she'd voiced the thought aloud until he frowned at her.

"Ghosts aren't real," Cal announced.

He looked so insulted by the idea, so affronted by the very fact that she would have considered the possibility that she couldn't help but laugh again. It reminded her of the expression Joe had given her the night they met when she'd suggested that perhaps the United States shouldn't participate in the Space Race.

"Ghosts aren't real, but time travel is?"

"Time travel is an extension of physics, a mathematical equation to be solved. Ghosts are—I don't know, something wholly unscientific."

He said "unscientific" like it was a very bad thing indeed.

"If Joe has gone through a wormhole, and he's in some weird space-time loop or living in an alternate timeline, do you think he's aware of it? Would he know and be panicked, actively trying to find me? Or could he just be out there, living his life, with no idea that the life he's living isn't the real one?"

"Who's to say it isn't the real one? That all those alternate realities aren't just as valid?"

"If that's true, if he's just out there, aware or not—how do I find him, how do I save him? How do I reach him?"

"You don't."

"What do you mean, 'I don't'?"

"Mrs.—Vivian—you can't follow him through a wormhole if that's even what happened. When his spacecraft encountered the wormhole, his fate was sealed. Now if he was able to find a way to slip time, to interact with objects in his present timeline without being physically present, then I'd look at the clues he's already given you—the strongest ones being those notes in your pocket. If it were me, I'd wait."

"Wait for what?"

"I don't know. I'm sorry. I know you're looking for certainty, but this isn't an established science and I'm afraid there are no certainties."

She wanted to scream. If she were being honest with herself, she would admit that ever since she picked up *The Mystery of Time*, ever since she came across Cal's writing, she'd been driven by the hope that she still had a shot at a happy ending, however improbable, however hard-won. She'd been ready to beg and cajole until he would help her, to do whatever it took. But to hear the man extinguish that hope—to understand how fragile time and space could be—

"What you're saying is that you don't think there's a possibility that Joe could survive a wormhole and come back to me in this timeline as he was?"

The sympathy in his expression made her want to cry.

"I'm sorry, but no. Wormholes—if they even exist—are thought to be unstable. They're a rupture in space and time. They're not navigable in the way that they would have to be navigable in order to bring your husband back to Earth in this timeline. It just isn't possible. And for you to somehow travel to him in his timeline—"

Cal shook his head. "Impossible."

VIVIAN CLOSED THE MOTEL ROOM DOOR BEHIND HER, her mind racing. Even as she considered going to the nearest library and checking out every single book she could find about space and time travel, she recognized the futility in it.

This was the end of the line.

It was time to accept that Joe wasn't coming back.

She would probably never know for sure what had happened to her husband. There would be investigations, and maybe they would yield some answers, but she realized that she would have to content herself with some measure of unknowing, that she could spend her life searching for some justification for what happened to Joe and never be satisfied.

She was stuck, had been stuck for longer than she wanted to admit, considering she'd been feeling this way even before she lost Joe, and now she needed to start moving forward, to navigate how she would survive the unthinkable.

There was at least one thing she could do—for herself and for Joe.

Vivian picked up the phone and called Graham Carlson.

TWENTY-ONE

1967

"Viv."

"What's wrong?"

After four years of Joe training to be an astronaut, she knew by the way he said her name, by the sound of his voice—rough and low—that something had happened.

Something bad.

It wasn't the first time he'd called her bringing news of a tragedy in the space program, and she doubted it would be the last.

"Listen, I wanted you to hear it from me first. There's been a fire during a routine test."

It was the way he said "fire," the word a portent of loss. It sank into her bones, that word, that feeling of dread that constantly lived in the pit of her stomach swelling.

"I'm so sorry. Are they—"

"Dead. All three of them. The fire was in the command module. They couldn't open the hatch to get them out."

Joe bit out each word with military precision, the same way one might recite facts or figures, the way someone might do math problems, but beneath his tone she could tell that he was fighting to keep it together, that whatever he had experienced today had been very bad indeed.

"I'm sorry. I'm so sorry, Joe."

Vivian struggled to keep her voice steady, to match his unemotional tone. It wouldn't do if she lost her composure. He didn't say it, but they'd been together long enough that she knew what he needed, could tell that despite the bravado he'd showed her, he was grieving, and she wished she weren't so far away in their house in the Houston suburbs, that she could be by his side at the Cape when he needed her most.

These days, Joe was gone more than he was home. He spent the workweek living at the Cape, and then he came home for Friday and Saturday nights and then left again. Vivian was alone most of the time, and while being alone had never bothered her before, maybe it was the fact that she didn't feel like she was alone by choice. As beautiful as Clear Lake was, it didn't feel like home, didn't feel like a place she would have chosen to live. And while it was nice having Polly nearby, Vivian had struggled to find a role for herself in the Astronaut Wives Club—or A.W.C., as they called themselves. She was lonely, and as much as she loved her husband, she was beginning to wonder how she fit into his life.

"I'll need to be here a bit longer," Joe added. "I don't know if I'll make it home this weekend."

"Of course, whatever you need. I love you, Joe."

"I love you, too, Viv."

She swallowed past the unshed tears. "Be safe."

"I will. I'm coming home to you, Viv. I always will."

Vivian hung up the phone, and she stood there for a moment, her hand on her stomach, feeling the baby kick, and she offered a prayer to the heavens that everything would be alright.

VIVIAN HELD ON TO JOE A LITTLE MORE TIGHTLY WHEN she saw him again after the fire, the realities of the dangers of his job—even in training—hitting home.

Up until this moment, they had lost astronauts to flying accidents, but there had been none in training. NASA was standing the mission down, trying to understand what went wrong.

Vivian lay beside her husband in bed, her head resting on his heart. His hand cupped her stomach as he liked to do when they were together now. Each week he saw her, she grew bigger, and she could tell he was dazzled by their child, marveling at the kicks and rolls that happened in her stomach with stunning regularity.

Tonight, though, he was quieter than normal, and she sensed he was working through something in his mind, something he wasn't quite ready to share with her yet.

And then he sighed, like he was releasing a great tension that had been building inside himself. "I love you, Viv."

"I love you, too," she whispered, holding him more tightly.

"You and the baby, you're everything. All of this—you're the thing that gives it meaning. I love what I do, and until I met you, I didn't think I would ever find anything I loved as much. But this life—I don't know—I see the toll it takes on families. Frank and Polly—" He sighed.

"Frank and Polly—what? Is something going on with them?"

"No—I just—it's a hard life. Hardest on the wives. On the kids. On the families. I know what you've given up being with me, the sacrifices you've had to make. I don't want you to have to keep making them."

Vivian rose from her position on his chest, bracing herself on her elbow, staring down at him, not quite believing what she was hearing.

Usually, when Joe started conversations like this, she was dreaming.

"What are you saying?" she asked him, her heart thundering.

"I guess I'm saying that maybe it's time to hang things up. All of this—going to the Moon—maybe it's too much."

Hope filled her, swelling inside her until it built with a crescendo. It would be a chance at something that felt like a normal life. A chance to be happy, to not worry every time he went to work that he wasn't going to come home like so many of his coworkers. A chance for their child to grow up with a father who they saw on a regular basis. For their child to not have to live with the kind of anxiety and fear Vivian experienced on a daily basis. Their child wouldn't lose its father like she had.

"I'm getting to be an old man," Joe continued. "Maybe it's good to go out on top and not be forced out like some of the others. To end things on our terms."

"How long have you been considering this?"

"Since the fire."

Ah.

"Hell, maybe since before that, too. Maybe since I realized that it constantly feels like I'm being torn in two different directions. Things aren't going well at work. The tests—there have been lots of failures. Too many. Too many things going wrong. To be honest, the Moon feels farther than ever."

Surprise filled her. Joe rarely spoke about the intricacies of his job given the sensitive and secretive nature of what he did. She rarely asked because the science of it was somewhat beyond her, and if she was being honest, it felt like speaking about his dreams of space only heightened the differences between them. The chasm between them felt great when he was constantly looking to a journey that took him so far away and she was left behind, trying to make a home for them, a corner of the world that she could call hers, where she could feel safe.

"When President Kennedy gave his speech at Rice saying that we would go to the Moon, it seemed inevitable. After all, he had a way of making you feel like anything was possible, like you could be something greater than yourself," Joe continued.

"He did."

That day in Houston felt like a lifetime ago, like it belonged to someone else's memories.

"Now it seems like we still have so long and so far to go," he added. "Maybe we overestimated our own abilities, our own potential. Maybe we reached too high."

The instinct to offer Joe comfort was there, the desire to tell him that he was capable of anything, that she believed in him and his dreams. But try as she did, the words wouldn't come. Because the alternative existed—the potential that he would give all of this up. She wouldn't have to keep worrying about the possibility that he would go to work one morning to run a test, and he wouldn't come home. Or that the next time he jumped into his T-38 to fly to Houston it would be his last.

The prospect of peace was too compelling to ignore.

Instead, she said what felt like entirely the wrong thing.

"I'll support you in whatever you decide."

Something that looked like disappointment flashed across his face, and Vivian instantly wished she'd never said it, wished she'd told him that he shouldn't give up, that she'd watched him fight his way to being an astronaut and now that he was so close to the Moon, he should see the realization of his dream through.

"Maybe I should just go back to the Air Force. Go back to flying," Joe suggested as her heart sank.

She knew what going back to the Air Force meant, what would happen if he was flying fighters again.

Vietnam.

Not only did she oppose the war in principle, but the idea of him being over there, possibly shot down or worse—

It felt like no matter what he chose, she would lose.

TWENTY-TWO

1967

There was a child.

A baby boy.

With his father's hair and her eyes.

A little boy who gave them nine months and twenty-one hours of joy, their lives orbiting around his existence.

And then he was gone.

A problem with his heart, the doctors said in the hospital after she'd given birth, which was the strangest thing for her to wrap her mind around considering she would have given him hers if she could.

And as she grieved in the hospital alone, recovering from the cesarean section, her husband was called away on a mission because the mission always came first.

TWENTY-THREE

1967

Vivian stabbed the seal on the box, slicing through the packing tape the moving company had placed there.

What would greet her when she opened it up?

The contents of half the boxes had been filled with broken items, mementos from the early days of their marriage in Italy, heirlooms that had been passed on to Joe after his aunt and uncle died. She should have done a better job of overseeing the move from Houston to Cocoa Beach, but even as she was annoyed with herself for not managing things better, for not making sure everything was carefully wrapped, she had to acknowledge that she had been in no state to do so.

They'd had to leave Togethersville. The house that they'd gotten for a song from a builder who offered deals to the astronaut families no longer felt like the dream they'd been promised. The room at the end of the hall, the one Vivian had lovingly painted every square inch of while Joe was away at the Cape, the walls stenciled with airplanes and rockets despite her reservations about encouraging such pursuits, was a constant reminder of all that they'd lost.

The doctors told her that she was young, and healthy, and there was absolutely no reason why they couldn't try for another child, that what happened was so rare, they were just unlucky, and Vivian wanted to scream.

Finally, she couldn't take it anymore and asked Joe to please put the house on the market so they could move on with their lives. He'd balked at first before they'd finally come to the compromise of renting it out for a year to one of Joe's NASA colleagues and his family.

At least in Cocoa Beach there were fewer memories to haunt her.

The boxes that contained all the items from the baby's room had been carefully packed away by Joe and immediately taken to a storage unit after they arrived here. She'd wanted to go after him and ask him to bring them all back, and at the same time she needed them to disappear, needed to forget everything that had happened, needed to disappear herself.

Vivian pulled items out of the box, setting them on the Formica countertop with a thud. How many more times would she do this? The other spouses talked about careers that had them moving every two or three years. One of the perks of being an astronaut was that it kept the families in Houston, at least, but Vivian couldn't forget her earlier conversation with Joe and the mention he'd made of going back to flying, the guilt she knew he felt that so many of his friends were being sent to Vietnam while he stayed in the space program, treading water. Selfishly, she didn't want her husband going to space, but she didn't want her husband going to war, either, and she didn't think she could face one more loss, not on the heels of the staggering one she'd just suffered.

"Viv!"

Joe called to her from the bedroom.

She hadn't even realized that he was home; he'd taken a day off to help her with the movers and to assist with the unpacking, but something urgent had come up at the space agency, leaving her to tackle it on her own.

When had he come back from work?

He must have come in through the garage.

Vivian headed through the little house they'd rented, walking toward the back room they'd chosen as their bedroom.

Vivian stopped in her tracks, her gaze drifting from the open suitcase sitting on the bed next to Joe, a shirt in hand.

At first, she thought he'd come home and decided to unpack after all, but then she realized that Joe was neatly folding the shirt and putting it *in* the suitcase, not taking it out.

"What are you doing?" she asked him.

Joe looked up from the suitcase. "I'm sorry. I got a call from Frank. I need to go to Houston."

Houston.

Vivian glanced around the room at all the boxes surrounding them, the lack of furniture, the mattress still on the floor.

After her C-section, her body still pained her, and she was be-yond ready for the rest of their furniture to be delivered, sleep-ing on the mattress on the floor more uncomfortable than she'd imagined when she first agreed to it.

"We just moved into the house," she protested.

As soon as the words left her mouth, she regretted them, hated the way in which they snipped at each other now. She felt like she was holding herself together with tattered threads, and even though Joe said he understood, even though Joe promised he was there for her for whatever she needed, she didn't know how to convey to him what she needed, how she felt like she had fundamentally changed and she wasn't sure she would ever go back to the version of herself she'd been.

Joe frowned. "I know. And I'm sorry. I promise I'll help you get set up when I get back from Houston."

She knew him well enough to tell that he was distracted, his mind not on her but looking firmly ahead to whatever reason Frank wanted to see him.

Vivian didn't say the rest of it, couldn't voice the words that were stuck in her throat, the pain that ate away at her until she couldn't look at him the same way that she once had.

You went to work when I needed you most.

"I'm sorry, Viv. I'll make it up to you. I promise."

She doubted that. He would try, yes. And she really did be-lieve he was sorry. But there were some moments you couldn't get back, some memories you couldn't replace, and she wasn't sure she would ever forget that she'd been forced to grieve their son while he had gone back to work.

"Why does he want you to go to Houston?"

Joe glanced away, his gaze focused on some spot she couldn't see. "I don't know."

He was lying. He'd never been any good at it, and he certainly wasn't now.

"Why does he want you to go to Houston?" Vivian repeated, dread filling her because she knew the answer even before he gave it, could see it in his eyes.

They were filled with zeal.

There were two reasons why Frank would ask Joe to drop everything and come to Houston. One—that Joe had finally told him about his intent to retire and Frank was determined to talk him out of it. The other—the other terrified her.

"I don't know. Honestly. He didn't tell me."

"But you have your suspicions."

"Viv."

She used to love the way he would say her name and inject so many different emotions in it. How he could convey so much with the tone of his voice. Now she heard apology and resignation, and she hated the way the sound of it filled her with dread.

"You're getting the next mission."

She said it flatly, as though they were talking about him working late rather than going to the Moon, but this lifestyle had leeched the romanticism of space—if she'd ever believed in it at all—right out of her.

Joe didn't confirm it, but then again, he didn't have to. That gleam said it all.

It was surprising that they would give it to him considering the loss they'd just experienced, but Joe must have impressed the doctors with how well he was handling everything. They never would have sent an astronaut up on a mission if he was too filled with grief to do the job at hand. The fact that he was doing so well felt like another betrayal.

"He couldn't tell me the reason he wanted to see me over the phone."

Because it was a sensitive topic. Like the next mission.

"What happened to you walking away?" Vivian asked. "To looking for a job in the private sector? To going back to flying?"

Not that flying was necessarily a better alternative.

What happened to the future he'd sold her, that day he'd told her he was thinking of giving it all up? What happened to the healing she desperately needed? She needed time, needed some peace and quiet. Without it, she felt like she would break, already felt as though she was breaking.

"I want you to stop."

Five words had never sounded louder. They filled the bedroom, bouncing off the walls, too much to be ignored.

Joe stilled; his head bowed.

He didn't speak, gave no indication that he had heard her, save for the fact that he looked like a man who had just been dealt a felling blow.

She said it again, louder now, the confidence that those five words gave her filling her with purpose. In their years together, she'd shouted it in her mind time and time again, but she'd never voiced it aloud to him. Not once.

All this time, she'd told herself it was because she was a good wife, a loving wife, a supportive wife.

It was a lie.

Now that the words hovered in the air between them, now that she couldn't take them back, she couldn't deny that she'd never said them because she'd been afraid of what would happen once she did, that she would be carrying them both to the point of no return, that when faced with a choice between her and flying, between her and space, she would lose every single time.

"Viv."

"What happens when the luck runs out?" she asked him.

He looked at her, instinctively widening his stance in a move she had seen him adopt countless times when facing off with an adversary, but never with her.

Joe had given an interview once, not long after he'd been accepted into the space program, and they'd asked him what made him such a good pilot, what would make him a good astronaut.

Without hesitation, he'd replied in that charming, smooth way of his—"I suppose I'm too stubborn to accept otherwise. I don't know how to quit. And I refuse to give up."

The interviewer had laughed right alongside Joe as he ended the quote with a good-natured chuckle and a self-deprecating shrug, but if he had known Joe like Vivian did, if he'd watched him choose a career that would knock him down time and time again, only for him to claw and fight his way to the top, then he would have known that if there was anything Joe was deadly serious about it was his job. He hadn't been joking at all. It was simultaneously the thing she loved most about him and her greatest fear. Because that was what had drawn her to him in the first place—his drive.

"It won't run out," he vowed.

"You can't promise me that. You can't say that to me." Her voice shook. "Not after everything."

"I loved him, too."

He said it so quietly that it sounded like he shouted it at her.

"And I'm grieving, too," he added.

"I wouldn't know. You won't talk about it with me. All you do is work."

"Because when I'm at work it distracts me." This time he did shout. "Because when I'm at work, I don't feel helpless all the time. I can't save you and I couldn't save him. And I don't know what to do anymore, Viv. I don't know how to fix this. I can't fix it. At least at work I feel like I'm doing something, like I'm not letting you down."

She wanted to tell him that she understood. She wanted to tell him that she loved him, that she forgave him. She wanted to tell him that she was sorry.

"When will you go to the Moon?" she asked instead, her voice stiff, her anger and hurt too far of a chasm to cross.

"In a few months, I'd imagine. You can't tell anyone, though. What we're trying to do—orbiting the Moon—it's audacious. They'll want to keep it under wraps as long as possible in case something goes wrong and they have to call off the mission, to keep the Soviets from finding out. NASA can't afford any public failures right now." He hesitated. "Will you be there when I come back? Will you wait for me?"

This time she didn't answer him.

TWENTY-FOUR

1968

They gave Joe the lunar orbit mission, just as he'd predicted they would, just as she'd dreaded. For the next four months, from the end of 1967 to the beginning of 1968, her husband threw himself into training with a gusto she hadn't seen him apply to anything else. She wasn't sure if he was running toward something or away from it, but either way, it felt like going to the Moon stretched their marriage even thinner than it already was.

Joe was gone most of the day training for the mission alongside the two other astronauts who would be joining him. Vivian occupied her time by setting up their new home and volunteering with some of the local organizations in town. It wasn't nearly enough to keep her busy, and she'd begun thinking about going back to school or applying for jobs in some of the larger cities farther away. It already felt like she and Joe were living separate lives; maybe it would be easier if they had a commuting marriage—they certainly wouldn't be the first or only couple in their circle to do so.

Eleven days before the launch, the astronauts were sequestered into the flight crew apartment at the Cape. Access was limited to contain any possibility of them becoming ill. They tried to sneak away when they could to spend a few minutes with their families, but considering where they were going and the possibility that they weren't going to come back, it hardly seemed like enough time.

Vivian felt especially bad for Michael's children, who at one, three, and five years old were clearly too young to understand the implications of what was happening, to comprehend much beyond the fact that their daddy wouldn't be around for ten days, that he was going to space. Considering what an amorphous concept it seemed to her, the challenges Vivian faced conceptualizing the mission, she couldn't imagine what it was like for them at such a young age. How their mother, Bridget, managed to keep it all together with a constant smile on her face, Vivian would never know. The press ate them up, and Vivian was grateful for the way Bridget gravitated toward the limelight, leaving her mostly to her own devices, which she vastly preferred.

Polly and her daughters arrived at the Cape before the launch, and Vivian spent her free time visiting with them, she and Polly sitting beside each other on the beach while the girls played in the sand.

"How are you doing?" Polly asked Vivian.

"Honestly? Barely holding it together."

Polly reached out and patted her hand. "Can't say that I blame you. From where I'm sitting, you're doing great. You have a very stoic look about you."

Vivian snorted because she was pretty sure Polly was full of it. Yesterday she'd hidden in the back seat of her car for an hour to avoid a group of reporters who had somehow followed her to the grocery store.

"Are you going to sit in the VIP section tomorrow?" Polly asked, referring to the sectioned-off seats where the family of the crew usually sat, although lately the crowd had been growing larger and larger until you were packed in like sardines and the view wasn't all that great anyway.

Vivian shook her head. "I don't think so. I'm not sure I'm in the right headspace to have all that attention on me. I asked Rick to find me a good spot to watch it somewhere a little more private, away from the crowds."

She wanted to be somewhere where she could be invisible, where she could process her worry in private rather than feeling as though all eyes were on her. It was strange to reconcile the fact that every single television network would be covering her husband's ascent to space, that this was the broadcast the world would be watching while she was going through her own personal hell. She remembered that day years ago when they'd viewed Alan Shepard's launch and Vivian had thought about what it must have been like for his wife, Louise, to watch that Redstone rocket carry her husband to space. Now Vivian was joining the small club of women who had been in a similar position.

"Do you want some company?" Polly asked her.

"I'll be fine on my own, but thank you. You should sit in VIP with the girls. It's as much Frank's launch as it is anybody else's, since he's the mission commander on the ground."

Suddenly, Polly glanced over Vivian's shoulder. A smile spread across her lips. "Look who it is."

Vivian whirled around.

Joe strode toward them, dressed casually in a pair of jeans he'd rolled at the ankles and a faded blue T-shirt he'd had as long as she'd known him.

Vivian rose on unsteady legs as he walked toward her on the sand, his shoes in hand.

Joe stopped a few feet away from them and offered a quick hello to Polly before drawing Vivian to the side.

"How did you sneak away?" she asked, drinking in the sight of him, the surprise of seeing him when she'd mentally prepared for the fact that they wouldn't have a moment together until after the launch.

Joe shrugged, spreading the sand around with his feet, looking down at the ground, anywhere but at her.

"Told them I needed some fresh air. Michael did the same earlier and said bye to the kids and Bridget. Paul called his parents. I tried calling you, but the phone at the house just rang and the operator said no one was answering. Frank mentioned Polly was taking the girls to the beach, and I had a feeling you would be with them."

"Sorry—if I'd known you were going to call, I would have been there."

"I understand. I didn't tell you ahead of time. Besides, I wanted to see you. Didn't want to say goodbye to you over the phone." His voice lowered. "Especially after the last few months."

Vivian glanced over her shoulder, wondering how much Polly could hear of their conversation, her gaze drifting to the other beachgoers. She wished they were doing this in private, wished she'd had a chance to say goodbye to her husband without an audience around them, wished for the space to say all the things that she wanted to say, to apologize for their last fight, to assure him that she loved him, to somehow make this right.

She shouldn't have waited so long to have this conversation with him, should have tried to repair things earlier, but the timing had never felt right with Joe so focused on the Moon, and even as she balked at it, even as she knew how hard it was to bottle her feelings up, she'd lived with the refrain for long enough that she was loath to do anything that might jeopardize his safety while he was undergoing a dangerous mission like the one before him.

"We'll talk about it when you get back," Vivian whispered, and something that looked a lot like hope flared in his eyes.

"Will you wait for me?" Joe asked, moving closer to her, matching her tone with his.

She nodded, because what other answer could she give? Of course she would. She loved him.

"I'm sorry, Viv. For everything."

"I know. I'm sorry, too."

Neither one of them moved, neither one of them seeming to know how to navigate this situation they'd found themselves in.

"I love you," Joe vowed.

She felt like crying. "I love you, too."

And she did love him. That was the part that made this so hard. She loved him even as she wondered how she could possibly continue in this lifestyle, loved him despite all the sacrifices she'd been forced to make, loved him in spite of the hurt that lingered. Maybe she loved him so much because it was hard. Because it was a choice she consciously had to make day after day, because she saw the weight and measure of that love, the sacrifice of it. It had value because she paid it time and time again.

Joe walked away from her—

"Wait—I—" Vivian called after him.

Joe stopped in his tracks, his back to her, and for a moment, he seemed very much unlike a man who was going off into space, who was joining the great unknown where anything was possible. Instead, he looked like a man who was carrying far too much on his shoulders, who had been broken down by the weight of life just as she had been, a man buckling under the responsibilities of it all.

He turned—

She saw the doubt, the nerves, the worry.

The parts of him that he never shared with anyone but her.

And in that moment her fears, and her anger, and her pain disappeared, and Vivian went to him like she always did, because despite a million little slights, despite the frustrations and seeming impossibilities of it all, he was her husband and she could see that he needed her, needed something to ground him.

Vivian wrapped her arms around his waist, laying her cheek against his chest, and she felt the tension leave his body as he embraced her, as he held on to her.

"You're going to be great tomorrow," she whispered. "I love you."

They stayed like that on the beach until Joe had to go back to the astronaut quarters to get the required crew rest before they woke up in the middle of the night to prepare for the launch, until the sun began to set in the sky.

He kissed her once for goodbye, the kind of kiss that still dazzled her years later, and then he was gone.

THE NIGHT BEFORE THE LAUNCH, VIVIAN BARELY SLEPT more than an hour or two at a time. Each time she woke with a jolt, convinced it was morning, that the event she had been waiting for—and dreading—was finally here, only to realize it was one a.m., or two a.m., or four a.m.

Finally, when it was six in the morning, Vivian rose from the bed and began getting ready, the dress she and Polly had picked out on a shopping trip earlier in the week hanging at the front of her closet.

The other dress they'd picked—the somber color in case something went wrong and she had to appear before the press—had been shoved in the back of her closet in the hopes that she would never actually have to wear it.

Vivian glanced at herself in the mirror, not quite recognizing her reflection. It was her—yes—the same face she had stared at for nearly thirty years, time having changed it a bit, but she couldn't help but think—*you're married to a man who is going to the Moon today*—and shake her head in disbelief that her life had come to such a moment, that such things were even possible.

Once she was dressed, Vivian grabbed a scarf and a pair of sunglasses Jackie Kennedy would have approved of and headed out the door.

Even though it was not quite seven in the morning, the roads to the Cape were lined with cars that had pulled over on the shoulder, eager to watch the launch. Children sat on the hoods next to their parents, dogs running around and barking, picnic baskets laid out for families who had decided to make an outing of a group of American men orbiting the Moon.

Thankfully, the weather was good today, something she knew the astronauts and their wives always worried about before a launch. There was a lot of frustration when launches were scrapped due to weather conditions, and as nervous as Vivian was about today, the only thing she could imagine that would be worse than having to go through this anticipation once was having to go through it twice because of a redo.

The excitement in the air was palpable, and the entire thing had taken on the air of a day at the beach or a giant party as a group tossed a football around, another playing with a Frisbee.

The decision made, Vivian navigated Joe's sporty convertible into an open spot on the shoulder of the road and killed the engine, climbing out of the car and sliding her heels off before perching on the hood, hoping she hadn't scratched the paint. She could see the launch site off in the distance, the mighty Saturn V rocket that was going to carry her husband to space.

Around her, someone had tuned the car radio to the launch broadcast, the announcer's voice calling out the countdown.

"T-minus thirty minutes and counting."

Joe and the other astronauts would be standing by on the

launchpad waiting for all the systems checks, talking to Mission Control to make sure that everything was operating as it should.

Vivian could envision the scene playing out as clearly as if she were standing there herself. The sentimentality that Joe had displayed last night when they'd embraced on the beach, the vulnerability he'd shared with her, would be gone, and the man standing on that launchpad would be a different iteration of her husband. Joe would be wholly focused on the mission at hand, his concentration and attention on making sure that the spacecraft was safe, checking out the systems as he had done before, when he flew a jet.

The radio announcer walked them through what was happening on the launchpad, Vivian's ears perking up every single time they said Joe's name. By the sound of it, everything was operating as it should, no problems or concerns with any of the systems.

Maybe she had worried for nothing. Maybe everything was going to be fine.

"T-minus ten minutes and counting."

All around her, the excitement became even more noticeable, cameras pointed at the rocket as people shot pictures, smiling faces on the other side of the lens. Some of the sheen might have worn off the space program, but you wouldn't know it by the crowd who had assembled today to watch this momentous trip to lunar orbit.

Today her husband was making history.

She thought of President Kennedy, of his audacious promise that Americans would go to the Moon, of that same sense of shared purpose she had felt despite her reservations in the crowd at Rice that day. His legacy was being played out in the Apollo program, and while there were still more missions to go before they could accomplish the goal of putting a man on the Moon, this was one important step in a long line of them.

"Four minutes and counting."

She knew Joe was busy in the spacecraft preparing for the launch, but she wished he could see the enthusiasm on this stretch of road, thought of the little boy who had once dreamed of flight, remembered the man who spoke to her of his passion for flying and space that fateful night at the bar, the same man who had watched Alan Shepard's spaceflight with longing. How far he had come, likely further than his wildest imaginings. Or maybe not. Maybe he'd foreseen this moment from the beginning, when he was playing with toy rockets and dreaming up ways to launch himself into space.

"Three minutes and counting."

Vivian glanced around her as the excitement surrounding her reached a fever pitch, and she was at once back in her apartment in Arlington watching the first launch, and at Rice University listening to President Kennedy speak, and in what had been a truly horrible year for the country at large and herself personally, she saw what Joe had spoken of, what the president had alluded to, how space could perhaps bring the world together and provide hope where it was desperately needed.

"Two minutes and counting. T-minus two minutes and counting."

Her heart beat in time with the countdown, time slowing so that everyone else around her disappeared, falling into the ether, and it was just her breath, her heartbeat, and the count-down of the rocket that would take her husband to space.

The announcer continued to run through the systems checks, and some of them she recognized, others she didn't, but she took comfort in the knowledge that Joe had his training to guide him, that he'd run through these same simulations time after time until they had become rote. And as hard as the last four months had been, as difficult as it had been to see so little of her husband considering what they faced, now that they were here at this moment, she was grateful for the training that he'd had, the preparation that would bring him home.

"T-minus fifty seconds and counting."

There was no turning back now.

She heard President Kennedy's voice in her head, his speech that day at Rice, telling the American people that they would go to the Moon.

What would they find there?

What version of her husband would come back to her after an experience like that?

"Three. Two. One."

Liftoff.

Tears filled her eyes as she watched the Saturn V rocket soar into the sky.

The crowd cheered around her, and Vivian held her breath, her gaze pinned on its ascent, waiting, watching, feeling as though her heart had left her body as she stayed rooted to the ground, her husband headed to space, on his way to the Moon.

TWENTY-FIVE

1968 ·
Twenty-One Days Gone

A re you nervous?" Graham asked her.

"Is it that obvious? I'm terrified," Vivian replied.

"There's no need to be nervous. You'll be great. You worked in television enough to know the drill."

"Yes, but that was behind the camera, not in front of it. I don't know how you do it every single day."

"I like the attention," he joked.

Vivian smiled, glancing around the newsroom, the energy infectious. "I miss this. Miss working in an environment where I feel valued. Important."

"Why did you stop?"

"When I married Joe and moved to Italy, well, I knew what I was giving up. I'll be honest that I thought it was temporary, that when he received a stateside assignment, I'd find a television station to work at. But when we moved to Houston, it was hard for me to find work. I'd been out of the industry for a couple years, and it wasn't exactly easy being a woman and a journalist before that, but when you add in the fact that I had a gap in my work experience, especially so early in my career, it became next to impossible.

"One man told me in the interview that there was no point in hiring a married woman like me when I was just going to get pregnant and quit a few months later."

Graham frowned. "That isn't right."

"No, but it's also not surprising. Those sorts of things happen all the time."

"What are you going to do now?" Graham asked her.

"Go back to work, I hope. Joe didn't have life insurance. No company would insure him. Not that I blame them given the risk. I'll get some money from the government and there's the money from the *Life* contract, but it's not much. Certainly not enough to support me for the rest of my life. Besides, I can't imagine not having something to do every day. I think I'd be very lonely waking up each day without him and not having anything to occupy my time."

When Joe was in the military, he hadn't been flying for the money. Their finances had always been tight. Vivian was used to living on a frugal budget after her childhood, and things had definitely improved after Joe left the military and became an astronaut, but she was never more grateful than now for the fact that she hadn't married straight out of college, that she had a career she could hopefully go back to even if she did have an embarrassingly long gap in her résumé.

"I can put out some feelers. Ask around for you to see if any stations are looking for someone," Graham said. "You're a terrific reporter. Are you looking for something here in Washington D.C.?"

"I think so. I thought I'd look for an apartment in Arlington, maybe."

Now that they'd had a conversation and settled things between them, it felt good to be able to consider him a friend once more. After all, it was how they had started out, and it felt like a more natural friendship between them than anything romantic ever had.

One of the producers walked over to them. "Are you both ready?"

Graham looked to Vivian for confirmation.

She nodded.

Vivian followed him out onto the interview set. She sat still while they checked the lighting and sound, Graham making chitchat with the various crew members he normally worked with.

She glanced down at her hands, folded in her lap, at the wedding ring she wore, and hoped she was doing the right thing.

And then it was time.

Graham pivoted away from her slightly, facing the camera, that warm, reassuring smile on his face that greeted millions of Americans each night filling her with a sense of calm.

"Tonight, I'm joined by a very special guest for a very special broadcast. As many of you know, three weeks ago we lost a spacecraft on a mission to complete a lunar orbit. Three astronauts were on board, and I am joined by Vivian Mitchell, the widow of Joe Mitchell, mission commander . . ."

She imagined this was the point when the powers that be at the space agency started getting very upset.

Press engagements were supposed to go through the press office at NASA. Usually, everything was coordinated for them, but Vivian was tired of being handled. She hadn't told anyone other than Graham that she was planning on giving this interview, hadn't even shared it with Polly out of fear of putting her friend in an awkward position with her husband. She felt a twinge of guilt for not giving Frank a heads-up considering he was probably getting an earful about it at work, but the last thing she wanted was to have them try to suppress or change what she needed to say.

There had been more articles published over the last week since she called Graham to set this interview up, articles suggesting that Joe and the rest of the crew were somehow at fault for what had happened, and she needed to do her part to clear the air and protect her husband's reputation. Graham was still researching what happened, and she hoped that doing this interview would inspire someone to come forward and share what they knew about the navigation system, that bringing things out into the open would force a broader conversation about the safety of spaceflight.

Graham opened the interview talking about how he had received a memorandum from an anonymous source who was employed by the contractor who worked on the spacecraft. He talked about how there were internal concerns that corners were being cut to advance the space program quickly.

"How does that make you feel, Mrs. Mitchell? Hearing that what happened to your husband and to the two other astronauts aboard the spacecraft with him might have been avoidable?"

"It concerns me greatly," Vivian replied. "Not just because of what happened to my husband and the crew, but because of future spaceflights. I don't want to see this happen to another astronaut because in our singular focus on beating the Soviets at the Space Race we're more concerned with winning than we are about loss of life."

"Is that why you're speaking to me today?"

"Partly, yes. But also, because I feel a responsibility to speak for Joe since he's no longer with us. I've seen the news reports, read what the papers are saying. 'Operator error,' they're calling it, which often feels like a catchall phrase for 'we don't know what happened.'"

"Do you think the agency wants you to speak out about this?"

"I'm certain they don't. It would surely be easier for the space program if I didn't say anything, if I kept my head down and continued on. But I'm not going to go away and I'm not going to be quiet. I'm not going to let them sweep this aside. Joe gave his life to serve his country. So did the rest of the men. I know they would all want to see the necessary changes made so that a tragedy like this doesn't happen again."

"There are some critics who would argue that this is what your husband signed up for, Mrs. Mitchell. That he knew the risk he was taking, both during his career as a fighter pilot and now as an astronaut. That he was dedicating his life to something greater than himself?"

They'd discussed some of the questions beforehand, and this was one of the ones Vivian had wanted Graham to ask her, this argument one that she heard time and time again, that made her blood boil.

"My husband agreed to take risks in his job, yes. And he understood those risks. But he also trusted that there were systems and mechanisms in place to protect him. He was not a foolish man, and he wasn't a careless one, either. He believed in what he was doing, but he also believed that things were being done the right way. That's all I'm asking—to make sure that the spacecraft is safe, that there aren't any material defects, before you send a person up in space in one of them."

"Are you saying that you think we should scale back the manned space program?"

They'd agreed before the interview that it would be better if the discussion between them appeared to be more of a conversation, and given their history and friendship it had seemed like an easy enough endeavor. They hadn't prepared this one, and it took her a moment to think of her answer, to separate how she felt as Joe's widow, filled with anger and regret, and how she felt as Joe's wife, knowing how much he'd dreamed of space.

"I apologize, Mrs. Mitchell," Graham added when she remained silent. "I realize that is a big question, although it is at the crux of what we're discussing here tonight. I suppose on a more personal level I'd ask you, if your husband Joe had known he wasn't going to come back, do you think he would have still gone into space?"

"I'm not sure."

Graham looked surprised by her answer, and she realized he'd intended it to be a softball question, expected the answer to be an obvious "no."

"I just wonder—" Graham tried again. "If he'd known how things would end up, would he have made different choices? If he'd known that the cost of the Moon was so high, would he have still gone up?"

It was the question she wrestled with in the late hours of the night. It was the question she would ask herself every day for the rest of her life.

They were surrounded by loss. When Joe was a pilot, and in the space program, there was an inevitability to the fact that one day he would go to work and would come home having lost men he considered to be brothers. It was the risk they all accepted to tackle something so audacious as flight and then the Moon. But did it have to be? Was it worth it in the end? Certainly not from her perspective. But would it have been from Joe's?

And then she remembered that man she had fallen in love with. The man she met at a bar who spoke of chasing the universe with a romanticism that had nearly taken her breath away. And she laughed, because sometimes the universe was cosmically funny, and she knew the truth, no longer had to wonder what her husband would have done.

She knew.

"He would have gone up."

Graham startled. "I'm sorry—are you saying that you believe your husband would have still made the same choices even if he knew he wasn't going to come home?"

"Yes."

For a moment, the facade slipped, and Graham stared at her not as the world-renowned newsman, but as a man who had loved her, and she could see the incredulity in his gaze, could read all the unspoken words there, saw the moment that he grappled with the knowledge that she had just admitted on national television that she, Vivian Mitchell, a woman who lived her life with the goal of avoiding as many risks as possible, who was as pragmatic and responsible as anyone could be, had fallen in love with a man who would have willingly gone to space with the knowledge that he likely wasn't coming back.

"I loved Joe," she said more by way of explanation to Graham than to the audience. "And he loved me. And he loved space. And if my husband was sitting here today, he would demand answers. He would want accountability; he would want better for the spaceflights to follow his. And he would want to know that America had put a man on the Moon by the end of the decade, just like President Kennedy vowed years ago."

Silence filled the air for a few more seconds than necessary, and then Graham recovered smoothly, ever the consummate newsman.

"Thank you so much for speaking with me today, Mrs. Mitchell. Before we go, is there anything else you have to say to the audience?"

Graham referred to the viewing audience, of course, but pure instinct had her looking out at the sea of cameramen and television crew watching the interview.

Vivian froze.

Kerry Krieger stood in the back by the door.

She hadn't changed much in five years, was exactly as Vivian envisioned her each time she thought about picking up the phone and asking Kerry for the chance she'd offered before.

The chance to make her voice matter once more.

There were so many things she wanted to say, so many emotions inside of her. She was angry, and she was sad, and she felt like Joe was sitting here beside her, and as much as she had told Polly that she wanted to burn it all down, as much as she wished the damned space program had never existed in the first place, that the Soviets had never launched Sputnik and started this whole Space Race, as much as she wished she'd fallen in love with a dentist, or an accountant, or the postman, she was here on as big of a stage as she ever would be, and she was Joe Mitchell's widow, and considering she had loved him with every breath inside her body, she couldn't be the one to bring down the dream he had loved so much. And at the same time, she thought of Bridget and Polly, the widows and wives who had been pushed aside so much, and she knew that she had to speak because she would regret it for the rest of her life if she did not.

She had spent so much of her life standing in the shadows of other people, often by choice. But she had changed. Life had changed her.

It was time to take a step into the spotlight no matter how much it terrified her.

It was time to be brave.

Vivian looked straight at the camera.

"It is an audacious thing to go to space. It is an awesome thing to see an astronaut be launched into the universe, to dream of putting an astronaut on the Moon one day. It is glamorous, and exciting, and heroic. What is far less glamorous, or exciting, is the wife who is waiting for her husband to come home at the end of the day. The child who wakes up Christmas morning without a parent.

"There is a cost to all of this. One that is often hidden behind the glossy magazine articles and press conferences. One that is hard to see when your gaze is focused on a Saturn V rocket heading to the Moon. This lifestyle—it's breaking us. It's breaking our families, our marriages. It doesn't have to be like this. It doesn't have to be so hard all the time. We deserve better."

In the back of the studio, Kerry smiled.

Vivian waited patiently in her seat as Graham signed off from their interview, as the cameras went down, as the crew removed her microphone.

She thanked everyone who had helped, and then she walked off the stage to where Kerry waited for her.

"I told you that you would be good on camera," Kerry said by way of greeting. "When I heard the news—I'm sorry for your loss, for what happened to your husband, to the other astronauts."

"Thank you. I'm surprised to see you here."

Kerry nodded toward the stage. "Did you know I got my start at this station? I heard a rumor that Graham was going to interview you and, well, I called in a few favors." Kerry cocked her head to the side, studying Vivian. "I was surprised you didn't call me for the interview, although I suppose with your history, it isn't wholly unexpected that you would reach out to Carlson. You could have made the story your own, you know."

"I wasn't ready," Vivian replied.

"And now? What's next for you?"

Vivian thought about Joe—the risks he'd taken chasing his dream. Of the way those people had cheered on his launch, of the sense she'd had when she was watching the Saturn V fly through the sky that she was part of something bigger than herself, something that was unifying them all, giving them hope when they desperately needed it.

She'd never go to the Moon, of course. But there were other ways to make a difference. It was time.

"I'd like to talk to you about a job. I'd like to try my hand at delivering the news—on camera."

TWENTY-SIX

1968

Forty-Five Days Gone

Vivian opened the door to her Cocoa Beach house, surprised to see Dr. Robbins—Cal—standing on her doorstep.

"I'm sorry to bother you—I tried calling first, but the operator said no one answered," he said. "I thought I'd drive over here and leave this on your doorstep, but, well, I saw the car in the driveway and figured I'd take my chance and knock on your door. We really should stop meeting like this," he joked.

Vivian laughed, surprised at how pleased she was to see him. "Come in. Sorry about the phone earlier. Ever since my television interview, people keep calling, and sometimes it's just easier to ignore it."

He followed her into the house, turning down her offer of lemonade.

They sat on the couches opposite each other in the living room.

"I saw your interview," Cal offered. "I thought you were wonderful."

"Thank you. I hope it will make a difference. I'm starting a reporting segment as well—I'll be on-air. One of the first stories I'm working on is interviewing some of the astronaut spouses about their experiences—maybe talk about the struggles military spouses are facing as well."

She was simultaneously nervous about being thrust in the limelight and excited about the possibility there, about this new direction her career was taking. It gave her a sense of purpose. It gave her hope.

"That sounds amazing. Congratulations."

"Thank you. The agency has asked to meet with me, to talk about quality-of-life issues for astronaut families, so I'm hopeful that they're really interested in making a change," Vivian added.

"They'd be foolish not to, considering you highlighted the struggles astronaut families are facing on national television."

"I hope I can do their struggles—our struggles—justice. I never really wanted Joe to go to space. I mean, I did, as his wife, because he wanted it and I wanted to love and support him, but it's never meant the same to me that it seems to mean to everyone else. I didn't understand why he wanted to go to space so badly. Didn't understand how he could risk so much."

Cal remained silent across from her while she spoke, and there was something about his presence—or perhaps how much she'd been speaking her mind lately after being silent for so long—that emboldened her.

"I worried. When he was a pilot—I worried constantly. The nights before he would fly, I would lie beside him in bed and I would just watch him sleep, and I didn't want to let him go. It seemed like we were tempting fate in a way.

"With as many horrible things going on in the world, I felt so lucky to have found him. It felt like an impossibility of sorts that we could love each other so much, that I could find someone with whom I felt so at peace. I suppose I was always waiting for the other shoe to drop, for him to not come home one day. I would watch it happen to families we knew, watch pilots he flew beside crash, hold their wives' hands while they grieved, and it felt like we were hurtling to this moment. To one day it being us." Vivian took a deep breath. "I'm angry. And it's not even that I'm angry with NASA—I mean, I am angry with NASA, angry with Joe, angry with the whole damned world and this country's bizarre obsession with going to space. My hope is that this television opportunity gives me a chance to turn that anger into something that could make a difference."

"I don't know you very well," Cal said. "And perhaps I'm speaking out of turn, but from where I'm sitting, I'd say you're doing the best you can to manage a very difficult situation. I don't think many people could imagine being in your shoes, and if they were, who knows how they would react."

"Thank you."

He reached into his jacket pocket and pulled out a small paperback novel. "I came here to give you this. I mean—not Cocoa Beach, here—I'm here for work at the Cape—but I wanted to bring this to you," he finished, his cheeks flushed.

Cal handed the book to her. "I know you said science fiction isn't your favorite genre to read, that it was more your husband's, but I thought you might like this book."

Vivian glanced down at the cover and title.

Infinity. By Michel Robert.

Something went very still inside her.

It had been a month since her interview, nearly six weeks since she traveled to Hampton, Virginia, and there hadn't been another sign from Joe, no more notes saying "wait for me," no objects out of place, nothing since she'd found his copy of *The Mystery of Time* and gone to see Cal.

"It was my favorite when I was a kid," Cal continued. "Sorry it's a little worn. It's the original copy my parents gave me when I was a boy. I've probably read it a hundred times." He looked a little embarrassed by that fact. "It's pretty incredible that you can pick up a book at so many different points in your life and still love it every single time. If that's not the sign of a great book, I don't know what is.

"Anyway, I know it seems like a strange thing to bring you, but what you were saying about your husband—it got me thinking. There's a similar storyline in this book. A man goes to space and basically comes back as a different version of himself, only he doesn't know it. It's fiction, of course, but—"

"It was Joe's favorite book," Vivian whispered. "He has a copy in the bedroom. He read it when he was a kid. It was one of the books that made him want to become an astronaut."

Cal smiled. "He had good taste, then. I confess when I read it, it made me want to be an astronaut, too." He pointed at the glasses on his face. "Didn't have the vision for it, though. I tried to join the military first—wanted to be a pilot—but I was disqualified on account of my eyesight."

"And yet, you found a way to work in the field you love even if it isn't exactly what you imagined."

He nodded. "I'm not going to lie, it's not as exciting as going to space, but I like what I do. There's a poetry to science, something romantic about using it to understand the world around you. It's like a secret language or a series of coded messages that unlocks the meaning behind our universe.

"I should go," Cal said, rising from his seat on the couch.

Vivian rose at the same time he did, and they stood there staring at each other, and Cal shook his head slightly as though he was confused, and for the first time, she wasn't.

After all, they lived in a universe filled with infinite possibilities.

"Would you like to get a coffee or something?" Cal asked her.

"'Or something,'" Vivian echoed. She smiled. "I'd like that very much."

TWENTY-SEVEN

1968

Vivian was packing up the last box in the kitchen, wrapping newspaper around Joe's favorite coffee mug, when someone knocked at the door.

She set the mug down gently on top of the box, a rush of déjà vu hitting her as she remembered standing in her kitchen in Houston, packing this very same mug to take to this house in Cocoa Beach. She'd been grieving then as she was grieving now, and she'd taken hold of the mug, a flash of anger filling her at how impotent she felt against the weight of the world. The mug had felt hefty in that moment, solid, and she'd imagined taking it and just chucking it at the wall with all her might, watching it smash into smithereens as she felt like her life was breaking all around her.

Now she glanced at it, grateful for the fact that she hadn't destroyed it, that it would be another memory of Joe that she would have to carry with her to the apartment she'd rented in Arlington.

When she opened the door, she was surprised to see Frank standing on the other side, looking like he'd just come from work, his briefcase still in hand.

"Sorry to bother you," Frank said. "I tried calling, but it says the phone's been disconnected."

"It has. Come on in." Vivian stepped back, allowing him room to move over the threshold as she closed the door behind him. She saw the moment it hit him—the impact of the nearly empty house a final reminder that Joe wasn't coming back.

Vivian put her hand on his shoulder, holding him steady.

"Damn, I miss him," Frank whispered, the grief in his voice making her knees wobble. He glanced at her. "He would have been so proud of your interview, what you said on television. He'd be so proud of this new television job you have. Would be telling everyone they have to watch you on the news."

"Thank you."

Letters had begun arriving after her interview with Graham. Many of them were supportive and encouraging, but others called her a traitor for even speaking out about the space program as little as she did, said she should be ashamed of herself for being un-American and not wholeheartedly supporting the astronaut program, for being critical of military life and the Space Race. It felt like no matter what she had said in her interview, someone was going to take issue with it, but the thing she worried about most was the notion that Joe might have taken issue with it, the nagging worry in her mind that she had perhaps broken some unspoken code.

Hearing otherwise from Frank, Joe's best friend, meant everything.

"I'd offer you a place to sit, but they've already taken the furniture. How are you doing, Frank? How are things at work?"

"They're alright. There will be investigations about what happened, I promise you that, Vivian. Everyone's already starting to ask the right questions. Your interview put the spotlight on this thing in a way that we won't be able to look away from it. We're facing a lot of scrutiny right now."

"I'm not trying to take down the space program."

"I know that. I'm sorry if I made you think I was anything but in your corner. In the aftermath of the launch, it felt like everything was falling apart. I lashed out because I was scared, and I was grieving. Because I felt responsible in a way because I was the one on the ground. I shouldn't have. You were right to ask the questions that you did. Right to push the way you did. Joe would have done the same for you if the roles were reversed."

Vivian hadn't realized until now how badly she needed to hear him say this, how badly she needed to know that their years of friendship would survive, that by continuing to have Frank in her life, it would be another link to her husband that she would have to hold on to.

It wasn't something she took for granted. She saw how it was for so many of the other widows, how they were excluded and pushed to the fringes, treated as though they were a constant negative reminder of all the things that could go wrong in spaceflight. Considering how much they supported their spouses—and how much the astronauts and, subsequently, the space program relied upon that support—it had always struck Vivian as shameful the way it seemed like they were left with so little after they had given so much.

"Thank you, Frank. That means a lot. Your friendship means a lot."

He cleared his throat. "I have you to thank, too. What you said in that interview . . . it really made me think about what it's been like for all of you for so long. What it's been like for Polly and my family. I want to do right by them. I want to do better than I have. If that means giving this all up, then so be it. I don't want to be looking down the end of my life, alone, separated from my girls, or on my second or third wife, regretting the choices I've made."

"You're a good man, Frank."

"I'm trying to be. I have a date with Polly on Friday. I'm taking her out to dinner and dancing. I figure it's a start."

Vivian smiled. "It sounds like a fine one."

She didn't tell him that she spent the last weekend dress shopping with Polly while she was out in Cocoa Beach visiting, figured she'd let him be surprised.

Frank's expression changed, the hope in his eyes becoming something more serious. "Vivian. The reason I came by to see you today is—" Frank was silent for a moment. "Before the mission, the astronauts decided they wanted to record messages for their families." He swallowed. "It's something we all started doing in case the worst happened. In case we didn't make it back." He reached into his briefcase and pulled out a videotape. "Joe asked me to give you this before he left in case—"

Vivian stared at that tape in his hands, torn between a greedy eagerness to yank it from him and play it as quickly as possible, and a heaviness that filled her at the thought of seeing Joe again and hearing his last words to her. Up until now she had this image of Joe in her mind, an image that she had carried with her that felt finite and complete. And now it was going to change again, evolve to encompass this new, unforeseen moment in their history, and she wasn't ready.

She didn't feel ready for any of this.

Vivian glanced around their little house, at the boxes there, and that familiar urge returned—the urge to scream, to break something, to rail against the futility of the world.

Sometimes grief, like love, played on an infinite loop.

"Thank you," she replied, taking it from Frank.

She stared at the tape in her hand, and then back at her husband's best friend. Frank looked worn down by the entire experience, and she realized this likely wasn't the first time he'd had to go through this process.

"Have you had to do the same with the other families?"

He nodded. "I gave Bridget an audio cassette tape that Michael left for her and the kids after the funeral. Paul did an audio recording for his parents as well."

Of course, of all the mediums he could have chosen, Joe went with a video. It almost felt like another message from him—a callback to that first night they met when she explained to him what television meant to her, the comfort it gave her when she was a little girl at home alone, trying to make sense of a confusing and ever-changing world where she never truly felt safe. It seemed like another way Joe was trying to give her comfort despite the immeasurable loss she was forced to navigate.

VIVIAN WAITED UNTIL THAT EVENING, UNTIL SHE WAS alone in the motel room she'd rented since their furniture had already been moved out of the house. Since they were hard to find, Frank had brought over a Sony CV-2000 videotape player he'd gotten from work and set it up so that she could watch Joe's video when she was ready.

If she was being honest, she took her time before watching it, slowing down the pace of the evening as one might prolong and savor a favorite meal. It was the finality that struck her the most, the sense that she would never again experience Joe walking into a room or taking her into his arms. There were so many moments in their relationship when the sight of him had set off a thrill inside her, and it was the absence of that pure, unadulterated joy that she felt so keenly. In a manner of speaking, this felt like the last one of those moments she would ever have before she had to say goodbye.

Her hand shook as she pressed "play."

There was a pause, the screen fuzzy, and then Joe stared back at her.

Alive.

Vivian took a deep breath, the sight of him a shock she hadn't prepared for. Seeing him like this—it almost felt like he was alive, still with her, existing in this tape he had made and the last words he wanted to share with her.

And then she recognized the outfit he was wearing—

It was the same shirt and pants he'd worn that day she asked him to leave the astronaut program, when they'd had that terrible fight, and he'd walked out the door.

Had he known while they were arguing that he was going to be recording this later, or had he gone into work and needed to release some steam and decided to leave this message for her?

She wished she knew.

Vivian reached out, her fingers touching the glass on the television screen, hovering near his face as though the surface between them would simply disappear and she could stroke his skin. She imagined the warmth of his breath on her lips, imagined the future they would have had if things had been different, if he'd never gone to space.

"Viv."

Her breath hitched at her name leaving his lips, the sound one she hadn't thought she would ever hear again.

The affection in his voice rang through, and with that one word she knew that their fight hadn't diminished how he felt about her, that the awful day hadn't defined their relationship, that he loved her as he always had, as she'd always loved him. They had always been able to communicate with each other without saying anything at all, and she knew that he had intentionally chosen to record the video on this specific day, had wanted her to know that their last memories together weren't defined by the struggles in their marriage, but most importantly, by the love they'd shared.

"If you're watching this, I want you to know that I'm sorry. More than you can ever know. This life—I never wanted to put you through all this. God knows you've had to weather more than anyone should. I know you always thought I loved flying and space more than you, but I want you to know, Viv, what I said to you that day, about you keeping me grounded, being the thing that tethers me to what's important. I meant it. Every word. I couldn't do any of this if I didn't know that I had you to come home to.

"You've given me that—a home. The family I always wanted. This life we've made together, difficult as it can be, has meant more to me than anything—flying and space included." He took a deep breath. "I know it's going to be hard for you now, Viv, and I'm so damned sorry that I'm leaving you alone. I wouldn't blame you if you moved on. Just promise me you won't do it with a Navy man," Joe joked, and despite the tears running down her cheeks, Vivian laughed.

The jovial rivalry between Air Force and Navy pilots was something Vivian had gotten used to over the years, even more so because the astronaut corps was comprised of a mix of military flying backgrounds, offering countless opportunities for banter and good-natured ribbing between them.

"Seriously, though, Viv. I just want you to know that I love you. More than anything. Always. I promise I'll find you again. In this life or the next."

Joe said it with such conviction, such certainty, that she felt it in her bones, knew that despite the impossibilities of such a promise, she could count on it.

His gaze was unwavering as he said it, and for a moment, she thought he'd finished; all things considered, he'd ended things on a pretty perfect note.

But then he smiled.

A quintessentially Joe smile that sent a thrill through her body and gave her that Coney Island roller coaster feeling all over again, like in the beginning when she was falling in love and in all the moments in between.

"And who knows? Maybe all that science fiction reading will come in handy." Joe's smile deepened, and by the faraway look in his eyes she knew he was remembering that day in his apartment in Italy and the conversation they'd had. "Maybe there's something out there. Maybe there's some chance to find my way back to you. Maybe I can come back as someone with a boring job," he joked, referencing her frequent quips that she desperately wished he had a different job, any job. Something like a postman, or an accountant, or a dentist—

Her heart thudded, and she knew what he was going to say before he said it, thought of the rivalry Frank had alluded to, the way the astronauts liked to give them a hard time—and the story Cal had told her of his favorite book as a boy and how it had made him want to be an astronaut, the same book that had been Joe's favorite, and how Cal had pointed at his glasses and explained that his eyesight kept him in a lab somewhere rather than in space.

She whispered the words at the same time her husband said them on the screen.

"Maybe I'll come back as a scientist."

EPILOGUE

Earth is below him, and the sight of it fills him with awe, bringing him nearly to tears.

It's everything he ever dreamed of; it's everything he trained for.

He remembers the first time he ever went up in an airplane, when he was just a little boy grieving his parents, desperately searching for something to ground him, something to hold on to in this terrifying and chaotic world. He remembers the first time he ever went up in an airplane, and then he looks back at Earth once more, and even that moment of first taking flight doesn't compare to the awesomeness before him.

Around him, Paul and Michael seem to be having similar reactions.

They'd all heard from the astronauts who had gone before them, had thought they were prepared for what they were about to experience—something between an awakening, a deeper understanding of their place in the vast universe, and, simply, the coolest thing any of them has ever done.

It doesn't disappoint.

He can't wait to tell Viv about it. Can't wait to share this moment with his wife. Because even up here, even when they've been fighting for weeks, months, even as they're grieving a loss he's not sure he'll ever recover from, there's an invisible string connecting them, and he's filled with peace as he looks at Earth knowing that she's down there waiting for him to come home.

And in that moment, a certainty fills him.

They will be alright.

Everything will be alright.

Until it isn't.

It starts as a tingle at the base of his spine. Then he sees it playing out in the navigation systems of the spacecraft going haywire, space around him shifting, changing.

They never ran tests for this, never practiced the scenario before him. And then the tingle explodes into a full-body panic, except he *doesn't* panic. He shuts down the fear and the worry the way he'd shut down a failing engine when he was a pilot, and the training takes over, the routine he's done in the simulators thousands of times coming back to him, muscle memory guiding his actions, his mind calm as the three men work in tandem to deal with the situation unfolding before them, to recover the spacecraft, the Moon no longer the goal, survival superseding all else.

They must get home.

Time slips through his fingers, as they race against what

feels like an invisible clock to make things right, as they try to understand what has gone wrong, as the darkness sucks them in.

His life flashes before him.

Moments in time.

Moments he remembers.

Moments that haven't happened yet.

He is young.

He is old.

He is a cocky pilot with the world at his fingertips.

He is sitting on a couch, a pair of glasses perched on his face, his hair gone gray, his grandchildren opening Christmas presents at his feet.

And there she is.

Viv.

His wife. His love.

He is falling, and the universe feels infinite in all its possibilities, in all the paths that lie before him. He reaches out, grasping through space, through the timeline of his life, through what was and what could be, and he grabs hold of the only thing that is solid, the only thread that feels tangible and real in his hands.

The tether that grounds him.

Viv.

Relief fills him.

Peace.

He yanks on it, tugging it toward him until he pulls it closer, holding on to the thread as though his life depends on it, this slip of magic between time and space that takes him back to her.

AUTHOR'S NOTE

I still vividly remember the first C I ever received in school. It was in my fifth-grade science class. It was followed by my second C, which came courtesy of ninth-grade geometry. I offer this bit of personal history first and foremost to say that I am not a scientist. Or a mathematician. In fact, when we were discussing this book idea, my publisher suggested that I should make the heroine a scientist or mathematician so that she could help get my hero home. While I normally try to be an agreeable author, after I finished laughing at the suggestion and realized they were serious, I told them there was no possibility where I could write a mathematician or scientist and have it be believable.

So here we are.

You might have gotten to this point in the author's note and asked yourself why someone who clearly is not a math or science person would choose to write about the Space Race and time travel. And here, as with so many of my novels, it was my personal connection to the topic that hooked me. The first American astronauts who were introduced to the country in 1959—the Mercury Seven—came from different backgrounds and military services, but they all had one thing in common: They were former fighter pilots.

Years ago, my husband suggested we watch *The Right Stuff*, a favorite of his. I hadn't seen it before, and prior to watching the movie, I had only a basic familiarity with the space program— most of it geared toward an international relations perspective, given my academic background. I knew very little about the astronauts themselves and their families, but I was moved by how much I identified with the stories of those early astronaut wives. After spending nearly two decades married to a fighter pilot, to say that their struggles resonated with me would be an understatement.

Many of the challenges and frustrations they faced are similar to ones military spouses face today. And still, these women did so on the world's stage, as global celebrities, the pressures and stakes immensely high, distinguishing their experience as something rather singular and extraordinary. I was in awe of their ability to navigate all that they did in the face of the additional pressures they faced. As with my previous books, I was drawn to the stories of these incredible women whose courage moved me, and it was that strength that inspired me.

While this novel is a work of fiction, and the characters are fictional, as is the mission, I wanted to capture the spirit of the Space Race in the 1960s and to set the novel in that environment. In doing so, I read *The Right Stuff* by Tom Wolfe, *A Man on the Moon* by Andrew Chaikin, *Apollo 8* by Jeffrey Kluger, and *Rocket Men* by Robert Kurson.

As most of my emphasis was on the spouses' perspectives, I found *The Astronaut Wives Club* by Lily Koppel to be a wonderful book that offered fascinating insights on the wives' lives. To learn more about the spouses' perspectives from the wives who lived it, I also read *Starfall* by Betty Grissom and Henry Still, and *The Moon Is Not Enough* by Mary Irwin with Madalene Harris.

In my research, I also visited Kennedy Space Center, the Smithsonian Air and Space Museum, the Smithsonian Air and Space Museum Chantilly Annex, and the Frost Science Museum.

This novel is a bit of a shift from my earlier novels in that there is a speculative element to Vivian and Joe's love story. The concept of time and space still contains many unknowns even though much of the research around these topics is rooted in longstanding scientific theories. In the 1960s, this was especially true. Ultimately, this is a work of fiction, and I can neither confirm nor deny the existence of wormholes or time travel. What I can say, though, with absolute certainty as a hopeless romantic, is that I believe some people are meant to find each other, over and over again.

ACKNOWLEDGMENTS

Thank you so much to the incredible readers, booksellers, librarians, and reviewers who have championed my work throughout the years. Thank you for your support and for joining me on this publishing adventure! I couldn't do it without you.

Thank you to my agent, Kevan Lyon, for all your hard work on my behalf. I'm so fortunate to have such a wonderful advocate in my corner. Thank you to my editor, Kate Seaver, for an epic brainstorming session that brought this novel to life and for all your insights and support!

Thanks to the wonderful team at Penguin Random House and Berkley: Ivan Held, Christine Ball, Claire Zion, Craig Burke, Jeanne-Marie Hudson, Erin Galloway, Amanda Maurer, sales, art, production, and subrights departments. I am so grateful to the fabulous publicity and marketing representatives who work so hard on my behalf: Tara O'Connor, Ariana Abad,

Stephanie Felty, Katie Ferraro, Jessica Mangicaro, and Hillary Tacuri.

Thank you to Taryn Fagerness, the team at the Taryn Fagerness Agency, and to the publishers and translators who are sharing *An Infinite Love Story* with readers around the world.

I am so grateful to my colleagues—especially The Lyonesses and the Reese's Book Club community—for your encouragement, advice, and friendship. It's an honor to be part of such a special community.

To my friends and family—thank you. I am so fortunate to have you in my life.

AN
INFINITE
LOVE
STORY

——∞——

CHANEL CLEETON

———

READERS GUIDE

———

QUESTIONS FOR DISCUSSION

1. Were you familiar with the Space Race before you read *An Infinite Love Story*? What was your impression of it? Did you learn anything new that surprised you?

2. Have you ever watched a space launch either live or on television? What did you think of it?

3. Do you support space exploration? Why or why not? If given the opportunity, do you think you would want to go to space?

4. Vivian believes that her career in television provides an opportunity to connect the public through the shared experience of major televised events. Joe similarly believes that going to the Moon will provide hope and inspiration. Are there world events that you remember in

your lifetime that created the sense of connection Vivian and Joe aspire to? What memories do you have of these events?

5. Vivian struggles to be taken seriously as a woman working in television. Did you identify with some of the challenges Vivian faced? Why or why not?

6. When Vivian initially meets Joe, she doesn't really think he is her type. Little by little, she starts to realize that they have more in common than she thought and her attraction to him deepens. What interests or traits do you think they share? How are they different?

7. Despite the love that they have for each other, Vivian and Joe struggle with navigating their marriage amid the demands of his career in the military and later as an astronaut. Did you identify with some of the challenges they faced? Were you surprised to learn that the divorce rate was so high for members of the Mercury, Gemini, and Apollo space programs?

8. Vivian talks about her struggles with feeling as though she is somewhat of a celebrity due to the interest in her husband's job. What did you think about the way she was expected to share her grief with the world? Did you understand her point of view? How would you feel if you were put in such a situation?

9. Throughout the novel, Polly and Vivian's friendship is a source of strength for both women as they navigate triumphs and tragedies. What examples of their friendship did you see in the novel? Do you have a friend like that in your life?

10. Joe views space travel as an opportunity to explore the universe around us and to gain a deeper understanding of the relationship between space and time. Do you believe time travel is possible? What do you think exists in space?

11. What similarities do you see between Cal's and Joe's characters? What differences? Do you think one is better suited for Vivian's personality?

CHANEL CLEETON is the *New York Times* and *USA Today* bestselling author of *The Lost Story of Eva Fuentes*, *The House on Biscayne Bay*, *The Cuban Heiress*, *Our Last Days in Barcelona*, *The Most Beautiful Girl in Cuba*, *The Last Train to Key West*, *When We Left Cuba*, and Reese's Book Club pick *Next Year in Havana*. Originally from Florida, she grew up on stories of her family's exodus from Cuba following the events of the Cuban Revolution. Her passion for politics and history continued during her years spent studying in England, where she earned a bachelor's degree in international relations from Richmond, the American International University in London, and a master's degree in global politics from the London School of Economics and Political Science. Cleeton also received her Juris Doctor from the University of South Carolina School of Law.